*Swell*

ALSO BY JILL EISENSTADT

*From Rockaway*

*Kiss Out*

# *Swell*

# JILL EISENSTADT

A LEE BOUDREAUX BOOK

LITTLE, BROWN AND COMPANY

NEW YORK BOSTON LONDON

Lee Boudreaux Books/Little, Brown and Company
Hachette Book Group
1290 Avenue of the Americas, New York NY 10104
leeboudreauxbooks.com

First edition: June 2017

Lee Boudreaux Books is an imprint of Little, Brown and Company, a division of Hachette Book Group, Inc. The Lee Boudreaux Books name and logo are trademarks of Hachette Book Group, Inc.

The publisher is not responsible for websites (or their content) that are not owned by the publisher.

The Hachette Speakers Bureau provides a wide range of authors for speaking events. To find out more, go to hachettespeakersbureau.com or call (866) 376-6591.

Library of Congress Cataloging-in-Publication Data
Names: Eisenstadt, Jill, 1963- author.
Title: Swell / Jill Eisenstadt.
Description: First edition. | New York ; Boston : Lee Boudreaux Books/Little, Brown and Company, 2017.
Identifiers: LCCN 2017009952 | ISBN 9780316316903 (hardback)
Subjects: LCSH: Domestic fiction. | BISAC: FICTION / Contemporary Women. | FICTION / Family Life. | FICTION / Literary.
Classification: LCC PS3555.I844 S94 2017 | DDC 813/.54--dc23
LC record available at https://lccn.loc.gov/2017009952

10 9 8 7 6 5 4 3 2 1

LSC-C

Book designed by Marie Mundaca

Printed in the United States of America

*For Mike*

# GOLDEN VENTURE

*Sunday, June 6, 1993*

HE'S WAITING FOR her to die, Rose knows. She's no dummy. Every June her son, Gary, itches to inherit her big house on Rockaway Beach. "You're getting up there" is this year's catchphrase, as if turning eighty-one begins the ascent. Up and up, she'll levitate a little higher each birthday, while Gary, Maureen, and the kids fan out on the sand below her waving bye-bye. Gary's latest brainstorm is he moves in now—this weekend. "We'll take care of you," he insists, oblivious to the way this sounds. "Maureen's a doctor." (Close! A veterinarian.) "You'll get to play Grandma. *All the time!*"

"Oh, he'd love the free child care," Rose is griping to her new friend Li, a real (if ill) Chinaman, right here under her dining-room table. "But I know those grandkids think I'm boring and smell weird. And I am. And I do. I'm no dummy."

This strikes Rose as so hysterically funny that soon she has to steady herself on the marble sideboard. Harboring an illegal alien is one of her first-ever crimes (give or take a little parking on her late husband, Vincent's handicapped permit). She feels Sambuca giddy, puffy with pride. If only Vin could see his favorite shirt (the ivory with black piping) draped big as a dress on this true outlaw. Wouldn't *he* be impressed! Donning their cowboy best, Vin and his buddies from the social club used to spend Sunday mornings riding around Belle Harbor on their mopeds. "The Good Guys," they called themselves, and went out looking for good deeds to do. But Vin had never risen to *this* Robin Hood level: a good deed and a crime too!

"It was mostly his excuse to get out of church," Rose explains to her guest and crosses herself, a reflex.

"Yesu *Jidu!*" Li moans from under the table, where he'd crawled like a sick crab. To hide? So weak; it seemed miraculous that he'd even made it into the house. "Yesu *Jidu?*"

Is he dreaming with his eyes open? He's so spacey and emaciated, it's like taking care of a child again. Like Vin at the end, even wrapped in the same orange crocheted blanket. But this fellow can't be over thirty. A large bruised head on a skeletal frame and wet-looking hair even now that it's dried. With one hand he clutches a Ziploc bag containing a small roll of bills and a phone number written on a scrap of newsprint. With the other he points at the iron crucifix from Calabria hanging above the sideboard and Rose's head.

"Yesu *Jidu,*" he repeats. "Me."

At last Rose gets it. "You're Jesus Christ! No wonder we're hitting it off!"

And not an hour ago he was on his knees, in his undies, puking up Atlantic Ocean all over her shower house.

For no reason, this memory cracks Rose up all over again.

༄

When the helicopters whirred her awake, the phone was also ringing. Rose fumbled for it in the dark.

"Is the TV on?" Gary panted from his Hoboken apartment. Eighteen years he'd lived there and Rose had been invited twice. She retrieved her bifocals from the white pocketbook she'd begun to take with her to bed. The clock read... "Three a.m.? Gary. It's three—"

"Are all the doors locked, Ma? A whole boatload of Chinks—"

"Who taught you to talk like that?"

"What's that? I heard something."

"Helicopters?"

"Oh, Christ, Ma! Get up! Turn on the TV!"

It was easier to push aside the window curtain and confirm that she was right. Helicopters weren't at all unusual here on the shore, called in often for drownings, drug trafficking, and bigwig airport transport. And what with that 120,000-pound whale that just washed up in Arverne on Friday? The sky had been pocked with press aircraft all week. But this was a swarm—police, Coast Guard, *and* media. And this time the giant metal insects were buzzing above the opposite end of the beach, at Breezy Point.

"Get Dad's gun, in my closet, I'll feel better."

"Gary..."

"They'll be storming our house!"

"*My* house."

"Get the gun, Ma, or I'll come get it for you."

So what choice did Rose have but to slowly unload herself from the bed? She'd never get back to sleep anyhow. Instead of a robe, she preferred one of Gary's old, hooded surf-shop sweatshirts. Instead of slippers, flip-flops. Better to accommodate a hammertoe or two.

The pitted gray revolver, still loaded and ready to guard Vincent's Bootery, was hidden, fittingly, in one of Vin's old cowboy boots. But which? No sign of it inside either of the pointy black ones, which once kicked and broke Rose's elbow. Nor was the gun in the fringed white jobs from the '60s, nor in the scuffed beige-suede numbers Gary wore every day of Brooklyn College. One boot box was crammed with old photographs of Rose's father's medicinal-herb garden (the remnants of which still grew out back). Another hid—hmmm—Vin's Cuban cigars. Still a third had been turned into Gary's Box of Pain, artifacts from childhood no one normal would collect, like scabs and splints and bloody pulled teeth. It was agonizing, physically and every which way, for Rose to kneel there amid the pinewood-derby cars, shoehorns, and porno magazines. But once she found the correct boot, she lingered, running her hand along the soft, red leather and bumpy white stitching, letting herself miss the husband she'd mostly despised. The gun sagged heavily in her front sweatshirt pocket but the feeling was not altogether unpleasant, a little like a baby there. After Vin died, the bootery space became Rockaway Video, Clothesliner, Sean's Liquor, the Photo Hub, Pickles 'n' Pies.

⌒

The back door always stuck. To open it, you had to lean with your whole weight, shoulder first, *wham*. Each time Rose did this, she imagined falling onto the brick patio and lying there in crumpled agony until Gary came by to check whether she'd been drinking and forced her to wear that medical leash with the button to press in case of emergencies.

"*You* wouldn't treat me like that," Rose says now, lowering herself and a wicker tray down to Li. (Can he hear all her joints popping?) "*You'd* be nice. If you found me out there on the ground?"

Li just bows, or has a cramp. From his fetal position, he tries and fails to reach up for the tray. Never mind. Rose places it beside him on the scratched-up tile. All the while, Li's shiny black eyes both avoid and study her, as if she's a phantom or royalty.

"The queen of Queens, Rose Impoliteri, and Yesu Jidu will commence to dine. Choice of Fiberall, orange juice, Sambuca."

It's a far swim from the meals Rose used to make for her daddy, then her husband, then her son, for the endless stream of relatives from Italy and Bensonhurst, for Good Guys and Bad Guys, their loud wives, sandy children, pets! On a Sunday like this, she'd be expected to serve the antipasti *and* the pasta, two meats, a vegetable side, salad, dessert, espresso, a digestif, and mints. She'd prayed for a daughter to help her. When that failed, she'd prayed for an air conditioner. Finally: "I just prayed they'd leave me the fuck alone, excuse my Italian. And here I am. Until Gary puts me in a place. Or that dead whale saves me."

*A bacterial time bomb,* the papers are calling the washed-up finback. If the city doesn't get rid of her before the next high tide, she could infect the whole waterfront. The summer of '93 will be an environmental disaster, a PR nightmare. Ah, but a blessing for Rose. No one will bother coming near her house if the beach is closed. Rose can live happily ever after for one more summer. Rose and Li—

Sadly, no one's ever seen a Chinese person in Rockaway other than the delivery boy for Wok 'n' Roll. People would definitely notice. Li's oily dark hair and sparse eyebrows are actually a lot like young Vin's were, but that's about all for the resemblance. Li has those nearly lidless eyes, high cheekbones, a nose like some kind of exotic sliced mushroom. He sniffs with what might be disgust at the box of Fiberall.

"If Gary trusted me enough to leave my gas on, I'd make you my famous pasta with sardines," Rose says. "Or soup. I know your people like soup. The nerve of that kid, after forty-five years of scarfing my rigatoni. On a Sunday like this, I'd serve an antipasti *and* a pasta. Two meats—"

Eyes closed, Li hauls himself up onto his forearm and begins quickly eating the cereal with his hands, from the box, no milk. He's got a way of chewing with his whole head that Rose has never seen before. And Rose has seen *a lot* of people chewing.

"I'd go easy on that Fiberall," she warns.

༄

He ripped through the rhododendron hedge just as Rose made it out the back door. There he goes, she thought. There goes the neighbor's black Lab, Blacky, off his leash again, en route to pee on her shower house *again*. And though his bark did sound odd, like a croup, Rose was too busy fuming to dwell on it. No point protesting to his owner, Tim Ray, a man so deeply unoriginal that he'd name a black dog Blacky. A divorced alcoholic firefighter living with his mother, Tim had probably peed on Rose's property too—mark some more territory. Both houses sat on the same beachfront plot (once owned in full by Rose's father) but the Rays' side was half the size. Their wooden house a shack by comparison.

And it wasn't just Gary or the Rays who threatened Rose's seaside bliss. All the neighbors were jealous. The Mole-Kacys on her driveway side regularly sent their kids on trikes to spy. *Is that old bat still alive?* The Fitzwhatnots across the street brought Christmas *and* Easter cookies so as to get double peeks inside. Rose is no dummy. She can tell her house is watched, this brick house her father built, the house in which Rose was born and has lived—eighty-one years now. They're watching, waiting...to buy, steal, or tear it down. More room, more view, more parking. Owning things that others covet might make some feel powerful, but it consumes Rose with fear.

In the distance, Ambrose lighthouse pulsed on, off, on; its usual soothing rhythm jangled by searchlights. She heard sirens. Screams? The helicopter din confused the sound. Then that bruiser of a policeman appeared, coming around the side of the house.

Rose clutched at her sweatshirt, alert. She'd been hassled by the law once before, after starting a fire on the beach.

Had she actually fallen when opening the back door, this officer would have been the one to find her. Quite by accident, it would have been. His long flashlight roaming enviously over her climbing ivy, decorative inlaid tile, and large picture windows would have suddenly illuminated *her*, or what was left of her. Rose Camille Joan Russo Impoliteri. A bloodied and desiccated human carcass. An ugly nuisance requiring removal.

"We were ringing, but you were out here, I guess," said the thick policeman, bouncing in place. Only then did he remember to flash a badge. "Sloane. And you are—"

"Who needs to know?"

Something was moving in the background, down below, on the lawn, where a long wall protected garden from beach. Squinting, Rose made out a second, trimmer uniform, skinny head, loping walk, nightstick. "I know him!" An old classmate of Gary's, wasn't he—Kevin? Kieran? But then, they all looked alike, those fair-haired Rockaway boys, lifeguards and rangers, cops and firemen, Coast Guard and sanitation. Almost all of them could pass for larger versions of the St. Francis grammar-school bullies who tagged her son "Guido" and "greaseball," "zipper-head," "bait-eater."

So perhaps it wasn't the officer but his heartless nightstick that seemed familiar. It trailed down the length of Rose's plants, pausing now and then to take a random, vicious whack.

"Why's he doing that?" Rose's frail voice failed to rise.

"Just checking around," Sloane said. "You see anything unusual?"

"Yeah. Over there, your partner beating on my foliage. Hey! You! *Basta!*"

"Any Chinese, I meant. A boatload of illegals just ran aground off of Breezy. The *Golden Venture*—"

"That's my cherry!" Rose screamed, starting for the tree. Sloane caught her arthritic elbow. "Oh..."

By the time he released her, the other cop had moved on, the nightstick held up in two hands like an ugly erection. At his back, the ocean moaned along with Rose. Pain radiated the length of her manhandled arm.

Sloane had resumed his bouncing, up and down, off and on the balls of his feet. "Sorry, ma'am. But it's total mayhem out here. They're drowning, they're running. We gotta check around." Up and down, up and down. Was he trying to peer over her head into her house? Or—"Do you need the toilet?"

"What?" The question caught the cop on the upswing, where he froze and asked, "Anyone else home? Husband? Kids? Companion?"

"I take care of myself."

Which is when Blacky started up barking again, barking from inside the house next door, the same high-pitched bark Rose was used to. So Blacky wasn't actually out here, Rose realized. So it hadn't been a dog that ran past her just—

"Wait," she called uselessly. Both cops had already gone off down the side of the house to search the garage. "Wait! You can't do that!"

Rose's elbow throbbed, but still she followed. "You can't do that! Wait!" She kicked off her flip-flops, trying to move faster along the rhododendron hedge. "No, I think you're not allowed to do that. Without a warrant."

Was this true? She hadn't the vaguest idea. All she knew for sure was "this is *my* house!"

◦⌒

The back door sticks; the tile is scratched; the basement floods every time someone cries, Vin liked to joke. But according to that broker who called just this week, the massive brick cube and the lot it's on is now worth two million, easy. Five thousand was what her father paid in construction costs, back in the 1940s. "Germans came ashore then, did you know? U-boats in Rockaway! I doubt they were trying to immigrate."

Total strangers regularly hang over the beach wall and call, "Yoo-hoo," to make offers on the place. Once or twice, they've come right up to the house, even peeped into her picture windows. Just thinking about it usually frightens Rose. But here under the table with Li, it's good. She's safe.

"I have a mind to fool them all," Rose tells Li, on a whim. But it's a whim she believes in. "I'm going to leave this place to *you*."

The Good Guys never helped anyone that much. Other than a lady who'd let them load up her car with groceries in the Waldbaum's parking lot, the Good Guys never really helped anyone at all. Vin said they tried, but no one wanted helping. Even the lady with the groceries, Vin said, probably just felt sorry for them. So the Good Guys took to drag-racing up and down Beach Channel Drive. Then Vin came home to Sunday dinner to alternately sweet-talk and criticize Rose. *My favorite flower. You call this turd a meatball? My soft, sweet Rose. Lazy bitch can't go to Bensonhurst for some decent bread!*

"It was that and more, and I took it until the day he says, 'Rose,' he says, 'do me a favor. Don't serve this grease when my cousins come from Calabria.' In front of our Jewish friends, he says this, in front of the Baums! He calls my sauce grease!"

Li can't possibly understand the story, yet he tilts his head at its tone of hurt and even stops eating while Rose speaks. If Gary and his atheist wife ever showed her half the deference Li does, Rose might not mind them moving in, having someone to listen.

"That night, I burned the table leaves," Rose says. "This table here. I dragged those two heavy planks one by one across the floor—see these long scratches? That's from dragging them, and, mind you, by myself while Gary and Vin were upstairs watching their shows—detective stories and professional wrestling. Nothing that would interest a world traveler like *you*."

At that, Li tries to give Rose the wad of bills from his Ziploc bag and she pretends not to notice.

❧

Once she finally got to the garage, she saw that all the chairs and cushions she'd paid the grandkids to stack at the end of last summer had been tossed across the dirty floor, and still the officers were going at it, knocking over beach umbrellas, tossing paint cans. What would they do if they actually found a person? Rose's father had come over like this, on a boat from Sicily. And Vin had arrived in an Armani suit on a plane. But those were known journeys. To imagine the suffering of some poor Chinese soul crammed on a freighter for months was beyond her. And when they got here? Forced to kick for survival in the frosty June chop? Hunted down by pigs like rabbits? The thought convinced Rose that she heard that croupy cough again, that someone was there.

"Someone's here," Kevin or Kieran said, but he meant Rose. "Hey. Hi, ma'am. You really shouldn't be out."

"At my age?"

"At this hour. With that chest cold." One of his blue eyes was lazy, drifting.

Rose thought to cough again to cover for the stranger. She wondered if the wok she'd long ago ruined had wound up here in the garage. She'd cleaned it wrong and it had rusted or —

"You should get back inside," the officer insisted, grasping her still-burning elbow. "Mrs. —"

"Don't you even remember me? Gary's mom?" The way it came out, it sounded like begging. Of course, it had been years since Rose had been Gary's mom in any meaningful way. She touched the bulge in her sweatshirt. It had been years since she'd been in her own garage, let alone had a car, driven a car, ridden a bike, fired a gun. How quickly the briny, mildewed stench took her back to mean Vin and all his sticky cousins, the endlessly boiling pots, gritty towels, crumbs, bones, and water rings that had ultimately led her down to the sand dragging those two heavy planks that signified company. *Two leaves, two meats, the vegetable side* —

Kevin or Kieran claimed not to have grown up around here. But, too bad, he'd *kill* to inherit a house like this, on the beach. At the door, he gave her his card. In case Rose saw anything unusual. She stuffed it into her sweatshirt with the gun, for safekeeping. Then Sloane whistled for him to move on to neighbor Tim's house, setting Blacky off yapping for real now.

"Fires on the beach are illegal," said the policeman who had arrived that first time, smacking his nasty nightstick on the smoldering table leaves. "Burning some good wood there—oak, is it? I should give you a ticket. I should haul your crazy ass in." When he'd finally gone, it had taken Rose hours to bury the rest of the charred planks in the sand. And still some animal had it partially dug up by daylight. Vin saw it and raged. Here was the proof of what he knew all along, his wife was "the redheaded devil spawn." Then he drag-raced his moped into a Green Line bus.

$\backsim$

Kids on the beach never stopped trying to dig a hole to China. And once, for a few months somewhere in the '70s, Rose had fashioned a hair ornament out of chopsticks, like she'd seen on that actress, what's her name, in that film, what's it called?

"Other than that," she admits to Li, "when it comes to things Oriental, I'm one big dummy."

Li starts to nod but an involuntary shiver overtakes him. His eyes close. Bits of Fiberall dribble from his lips. He whimpers, backstroking into the table's pedestal. Rose imagines Li's mother teaching him to swim. A river, it must have been, not a curly, raging ocean. A safe and manageable river.

⌒

At first, he looked like some kind of sea monster, soaked through and wrapped in the moldy shower curtain. You could see his chest heave, but when she got up close, the rusty, tentative sound panicked her. Each breath might erupt into coughing or nothing. And the shower house was no place for him—a dank, cobwebbed lair, slick with dog pee–scented wet leaves and the butts of the Marlboro Lights she suspected her ten-year-old grandson was smoking.

"I can help you," Rose said. "My daughter-in-law is a doctor."

The stranger lurched up onto his hands and knees and puked up a gush of ocean.

"You come into my house," she insisted. "I have a nice house."

⌒

"Ma! Ma! You would not believe the traffic! Big whoop, that *Golden Venture*, every single—Ma? Why are you under the table?"

Rose opens her gluey lids; blinks. According to the window, it's morning—low tide. A short, wide man with a graying goatee and a Yankees cap is wheeling in two Samsonites. "Thought I'd start the move-in process. Since I was coming anyways. Oh, look here, that explains it." Gary gives a swift kick to the empty Sambuca bottle. "Tell me you didn't drink that whole thing. Ma!"

Rose shields her face. "I thought she was dying. I thought they were closing the beach!"

"Will you quit yapping about that dopey whale? Ten men just drowned right out—"

Li! It really happened! Rose finds him beside her, under the orange crocheted blanket. But his cheeks look all wrong—too flat and waxy. "Get Maureen, Gary! Hurry!"

"What's Maureen gonna do about a dead fucking fish? A truck already took—Jesus! Not again!"

Now Gary's spotted his father's cowboy shirt. "You keep telling me you don't need taking care of, so how come every time you get blicked, you gotta carry this shit around?" Grabbing for the fringed sleeve, he discovers—"Aah!"—there's an arm inside. There's a man attached to the arm.

If Li weren't so pale, Rose would crack up. If it weren't for the whale dying. "You should see your face, Gary!"

"Who the hell—"

"This is my friend Li...*Li?* Oh my God! Call nine-one-one!" Adrenaline pumps Rose the strength to cradle Li's head, to search in vain for breath or a pulse, but no. Rose crosses herself. "Call a priest."

"Are you out of your fucking mind?"

"He's a Christian."

"He's a *criminal!*" Gary pulls on his own hair, pacing.

"Father Flynn, call. The number's in my pocketbook."

"I'm calling the cops is who I'm calling once I figure out—"

"The *white* pocketbook. Upstairs—"

"Would you shut your fucking trap?"

Vin used to say that. And though Gary has Rose's strawberry-blond coloring, he looks just like his father now—the superior purse of his lips, the neck stubble, his fly slightly unzipped.

"You think you can kill me and get my house?" Rose asks, calmer now that she's decided. For once, Gary *will* take his mother seriously. Inside her sweatshirt pocket, the soft wood of the old revolver handle is reassuring. "You think you can kill your own—"

"I said shut up, Ma, Christ! I'm thinking!"

Rose cocks the hammer with her thumb the way Vin made her practice before trusting her to mind the store. *Don't forget to aim, now.*

"Holy shit! What—"

The kick of the gun slams Rose back to the floor, where she stays, wincing, eyes on her son. So strange, the way his body writhes before it thuds, slow twist up, accent *down*. Like those Indian dances she saw years ago, when the Indians came to Rockaway to entertain. Of all things to think of now! That's how foreign Gary's body seems, falling and now slumped over his bulbous luggage, leaking. Another mess for her to clean up. And the throb connecting Rose's elbow and neck is so all-consuming that she misses the screech of the back door somehow. It's the odor that tells her that neighbor Tim's arrived, his unique blend of vodka, envy, ocean, wet dog.

"Get out!" Rose yells, and as his firefighter boots blur past her toward Gary, she quickly thrusts the gun into poor, dead Li's hands. Fingerprints, right? She did not endure years of *Columbo* for nothing.

"I saw that! I saw you," Tim squeals, giving up on Gary and lunging pointlessly to try and revive Li. "What did you do, Rose?"

Once more, she reaches into her sweatshirt pocket, desperate to make the message clear. "This is *my* house!" It relieves her to see the detective's card does not, after all, say Kevin or Kieran, but Vadim. He'll be the one to help her. Vadim Volistaya. Not from around here.

# ONE

# RING AND RUN

*Friday, June 14, 2002*

"EIGHTY-ONE YEARS old." Tim Ray is telling his ex-firefighter buddies how at "eighty-fucking-one" his neighbor Rose started smoking. "Found a stash of her dead husband's stale stogies, and *blam!*" Burn holes everywhere, the new neighbors report. All the places she bumped into things, lit-end first. Tim has spent the last nine years waiting for the brick house to ignite and, with it, his own wooden Cape. What one ember on a sea breeze on a dry night could manage... All heads in the yard nod, concurring. Point is: Tim sleeps better since the Murder House sold. He lost a nostril not long ago! (Surgery.) And still, he sleeps so, so much better.

If the rhododendrons weren't in hysterical white bloom, they could see across the shared beachfront lawn and in through the picture windows of the notorious dining room. There, according to everyone, a Chinese dude shot Rose's son. Too late for Tim to correct them. Too risky too. He'd worked (and drunk) hard to forget what he'd witnessed. And, fuck it, Tim rationalized, who'd even care now?

Fifty-nine locals just died on 9/11. Two months later, a plane crash took out five more, along with some two hundred and sixty on board. The *Golden Venture* disaster is now "so last century" that it's only even mentioned in connection with the Impoliteri house.

Almost nostalgically, Chris D. recalls one corpselike teen Asian who'd tied a bucket to his waist, thinking it'd help him float. Then the conversation swings back to Tim and his new neighbors, the Glassmans.

They're perfect. Scratch that. Compared to Rose (not to mention his own skimpy clan), they're as ideal as possible. A mom and a dad, a grumpy stick-figure Gramps, two red-haired daughters and a third kid on the way. If they hadn't been escapees from an apartment near Ground Zero, Tim would have wondered what the hell they were even doing here, in Rockaway.

True, he barely knows them. Even after five months, this is the case. Only four-year-old Sage has logged any real time outside. They just let her out the back door, same as Tim does with his mutt, Blacky, when he's too lazy to walk him. Lately, Blacky, the girl, and her imaginary pirate friend, Ed, spend whole afternoons in search of buried treasure. Rose's mutant-looking cherry tree is home base.

"Down there." Tim points his Fresca twelve-ounce to where a chest-high brick wall runs parallel to the beach, separating sand from yard, city from private property. In the middle of the wall, partially obscured by cherry branches, a small wooden door is flapping open to let in the little gang. "See 'em?" First Blacky, toting treasure (garbage) in his jaws. Next, tiny, orange-haired Sage, fisting a jumbo plastic ketchup bottle. Finally, presumably, the imaginary Ed.

The kid hauls her invisible pal and that Heinz around every-where. "Oh yeah."

"Oh yeah?" Bean palms his bald spot in disbelief, a quarter-size patch of skin, flushed from his coughing.

Smiling tightens Tim's scar tissue unpleasantly, but how to help it? "Finally some new blood around—"

"Whoa, Butter, your ears are blushing. Is it the mom or are you a pedi?"

All three of the next-door females—with their bony limbs, big joints, and orange frizz—might have been drawn by Dr. Seuss. So it's nothing like Bean McMoron imagines. But the Glassman family as a whole does make Tim feel kind of...buzzed. And he's the only sober guy in the yard—eight months, three weeks, five days. So what's that?

Mark (no last name), his AA sponsor, insists Tim should be avoiding his old friends ("Friends? Ya sure?") Bean and Chris D. Two middle-aged 9/11 heroes who still regularly chug a six-pack apiece, laugh at farts, and call women "stains."

"That Glassman mom's old but she's no stain," Chris D. opines, cupping his hands in front of his buff pecs to describe her. "Medicine-ball tits."

Chris D. got a BS in PE from BU.

"Because she's pregnant, dickhead," Tim says, only fueling the guy's rant.

"My point exactly! They're extra-horny knocked up. More blood flow to the—"

"Is that true?" Bean's got two kids to Chris D.'s one, so how come he never heard of this supposed phenomenon?

" 'Cause you're a fag?"

Mark No Name *is* wise. And yet. These are the same guys who coach Little League and T-ball, plan memorial paddle-outs, and head up programs to take wounded veterans jet-skiing, and that's when they are not rushing into burning buildings, working second jobs in contracting, or donating bone marrow. They would never be less than impressive to Tim. But they cannot save him no matter how hard they try or how often they stop by under the guise of coordinating visits to the fire widows.

Not that Tim entirely minds this. Imagine the general happiness if everyone had a place like his yard to come, sit, check the waves, decompress. And the calls to the widows are, to Tim's mind, a basic tax owed for surviving. It's humbling to follow Denise McClary as she sews sock monkeys for 9/11 charities. It buoys *him* to see Maggie Shannessy organize trips to Washington, pro bono lawyers, and comedy clubs. When Trish Shea rants about "revenge enlisting" in the army, all Tim has to do is listen and she always eventually calms down and shuffles the cards for hearts. As for his old friend and new lover, Peg, each visit makes Tim pine for the next. How tempting it is to exploit her manic stockpiling of supplies for the next disaster. *Too* tempting. He could fuck her daily just by showing up with cases of bottled water and batteries, like bouquets. Conscience *should* dilute his lust. Peg's husband, Chowder, had been Tim's first and best buddy. Peg herself was second and second-best. A sludge of sadness clogs his chest. Tim is godfather to Peg and Chowder's two young children.

"You do have a way with those widows," Chris D. says. Coincidentally? (Tim is sure he's been keeping the affair on the QT.) "Maybe you should get ordained and be our fire chaplain."

"Not this again." The brotherly vibe dies as soon as they start in nagging Tim to return to the Beach House—Engine Company 268.

"Time's up, Butter. Back to work. Whaddaya say?"

What *do* you say when they're still calling you Butter (short for Butterfingers) fifteen years after one lifeguarding mishap? *Figured I'd quit firefighting before I get a worse nickname.* What do you say when even the widows (except Peg) cringe at the sight of your mashed-in nose hole? *Don't you dare pity me while I'm pitying you.* Tim's still got eight years until his twenty-year retirement, so what the hell do you say?

You don't say no. So why did they make him keep saying it? "No. No, thank you." He will not go back to the FDNY, especially as a chaplain (what the fuck?), or as a chauffeur (yesterday's brainstorm). He will not have a beer. Or, please God, no, date one of their single or divorced sisters or cousins. He's alive-on-sick-leave-count-his-blessings not going back. And though Bean, a lieutenant now, keeps calling him King Coward—bottle cap flicked at Tim's head—it's the eighth or ninth time they've stopped by since Tim was sprung from Peninsula Hospital.

"What guy on sick leave can teach driver's ed, reel in a twenty-five-pound striper, and surf Hatteras?" Chris D. keeps on.

"Meaning?"

"You're only thirty-six, Butter. What else ya gonna do?"

"Whatever scares you is a good bet," Mark No Name advised. Flash on a carful of teenagers taking turns at the wheel, and Tim shrugs. "Keep teaching for Steer-Rite Auto, I guess. Otherwise, I don't know...let my beard grow? Garden? I just bought these really cool Malibu outdoor plant lights."

Tim's friends ("Friends?") screw up their ugly mugs in unison. "*Garden?* You're not even Italian!"

Which is when they hear a car pull into the neighbors' driveway. It's too early for Dad and Gramps to be home from work running their locksmith *empire* (*#1 in the Tristate Since '58!*). And teen June has no license (which Tim plans to remedy). So it's a guest, a contractor, a Con Edison meter man, or just your average outsider making a U-turn. You learn to expect a dead end in Rockaway.

᠑

It's *that* house—an ivy-choked brick square where city street meets city beach. Its windows are pocked with BB holes. The ceiling's moist, dripping. And yet it's not the state of disrepair that disturbs Sue. It's the way the house has enchanted her family. Four-year-old Sage spends all her free time taking orders from an imaginary pirate. June, sixteen, swears that ghosts live inside the bedroom walls. Sue's husband, Dan, has developed migraines and an aversion to the dining room, the very spot Sue most enjoys.

Southern exposure.

Good acoustics.

The Atlantic Ocean through two large (albeit dirt-streaked) picture windows.

Here, with her feet up on a big oak table, Sue can simultaneously listen to her new iPod, mind Sage out back, and review Genesis. Not the band (though she was a major Peter Gabriel fan, early years), but the book, in which God turns out to be a cross between her father-in-law, Mozart, and Eloise. Possibly bipolar. A tyrant. Absolutely a wit. The master of understatement. When the doorbell rings, *He's* just created "all there is," and appraised it as "very good."

Sue decides to ignore the bell. June's on the beach. Dan's on the golf course. Chances are it's those ring-and-rip kids again. Sue would just catch another look at the crumbling stoop, cracked sidewalk, and sandy trash blowing around on the dead-end street. Then again, who knows? What if? Another emergency? A lifeguard needing the bathroom? A housewarming gift needing detonating? FedEx with anthrax? Apology daisies from Dan?

Dan believes Sue will forgive him for anything if he just sends daisies, since, once, as newlyweds, she lied and said that they were her favorite flower. Back then, Sue thought it possible to curb her husband's extravagant nature. Or protect herself from it. To change him. And if not, so what? Back then, Dan, conversely, thought Sue'd stay the same. Suzanne Ainsley, the spacey musician Dan met on a midnight locksmith call ("The keys to the car *and* my apartment are in there!"), would never have demanded he stand up to his daddy the way Sue did in their latest fight. *That* Sue had barely known herself, let alone Dan, let alone his father, Sy, the source of so much future strife.

Dan works beside his father at Glassman Locks & Keys (*What Have You Got to Lose?*). Sue assumed Dan's salary would ascend with the years. Yet nearly two decades later, and even though Dan now technically *owns* the company, it's Sy's gifts that still keep them afloat, infantilized—a dishwasher here, a college fund there, orthodontics, an iPod. And now that Sue finally agreed to convert to Judaism, the big prize, a beach house.

Craftily, this latest bribe was made on 9/12 even as Sue and Dan argued over who had left all the windows open in their cramped Tribeca apartment. And though Dan had never before interfered in his parents' quest to convert Sue, in a few weeks, he was begging her to say yes. A bit unhinged, Sue guessed. In an unrelated crisis, Dan's seemingly healthy mother lay dying in the ICU at Brooklyn Hospital—heart attack. How desperately she had wanted a Jewish daughter-in-law Dan reminded her.

"Sorry, but that won't work on me."

Ever smooth, Dan switched tactics. "Well, we can't stay *here*. What do you think we're breathing in?"

"People, metal—"

"That was rhetorical. Oh, Su-zy. Who loves the ocean more than you?"

"We can move without your father, Dan."

"When we sell our apartment at Ground Zero?"

"We'll figure it out."

"You're in denial."

"*You're* in shock."

"My mother's dying. And without a Jewish —"

"Sorry, but that won't work on me."

These words were repeated often, in the same order and also rearranged with the occasional add-on insult or plea. Then, for a time, Sue and Dan stopped saying anything. Dan's mom died, and his dad gave him ownership of Glassman Locks & Keys. Dan sent Sue daisies and they made up (sort of), avoiding the subject(s). In the end, Sue discovered she was pregnant again...at forty-two. And caved. Blame hormones or love or the post-terror downtown stench, but moving suddenly seemed the only option. Within an hour of her assent, Sy had the whole conversion arranged with his rabbi and golf buddy Larry Gutman. An early-summer date was set for the ritual. As June loves to say, Sue sold her soul for a sea view and a few extra bathrooms.

If Sue were converting to Christianity, she could confess and be absolved. Instead, there's only punishment. First, the catch: her father-in-law was going to live *with* them. (So Sue could take care of him.) Then, the rub: other than Sy's own bottom-floor suite, the old wreck would be renovated piecemeal. (It's high time Dan got handy.) Next, the revelation that the Murder House was not a name coined by witty children but the result of a shooting death here in this room. Perhaps worst of all is the doorbell itself, now again chiming "For He's a Jolly Good Fellow."

Sue rises; head rush. The digital tune was clearly chosen by Sy to drive her, a lapsed music teacher, insane. And it's working. As she zigzags down the front hall, faded forms on the peeling pink wallpaper shift from roses to skirts to tiny uteri to cupcakes.

Sue swallows. She spits. Yet the saliva keeps returning, overflowing on her tongue, an eternal maternal fountain. This merely the latest in a tall list of pregnancy indignities — the bulging vein in her crotch, the dizziness and hemorrhoids, the itchy belly and startlingly graphic dreams of sex with Philip Glass, the Good Humor Man, and her own husband! "For He's a Jolly"—

If only it were possible to conjure a person bearing baked goods—éclairs, crullers, doughnuts. Sue would take a Pop-Tart, so severe is this sudden, almost nauseating need for frosting. The neighbors she's met so far—retired firefighter cum driver's ed teacher Tim Ray, with half his nose missing, and the always-yelling Mole-Kacy family—don't strike her as people likely to bake. So Sue's pleased that the peephole reveals a curvy Indian beauty swathed in lemony silk. (The fact that Belle Harbor homes aren't sold to brown people Sue is still too new to have grasped.) When she opens the door, she finds an additional guest, below eye level, in a wheelchair. Elderly but solid, with a mustached smirk and a puff of no-color hair. In the lap of her flowered housedress sits an enormous, white, cracked leather pocketbook.

"The lady's come home," the aide announces.

"Excuse me?" Sue asks.

"Excuse *you*, Mommy? Do you speak English? I *said*, 'The lady's come home.'"

"There must be some mistake."

But the gorgeous helper just shoves the wheelchair over the threshold. Sue backs up to protect her toes.

"Careful, carrottop!" The senior laughs, donning bifocals from a beaded chain on her neck. She peers up at Sue through newly googly, magnified eyes. "That your real color?"

"I don't know who you are but — "

"Well, I know *you*, Red. You're, she's — "

"Suzanne," prompts the aide, as though they've studied up. "I gather this is Suzanne, married into the Glassman family." She reaches out and pats Sue's bulge. "Twins? At your age?" Two insults in four words! As if on cue, the baby (singular) wakes and begins jabbing at Sue's ribs in syncopation.

"Suz-anne," the old woman says, thrusting out a hand. A zing of window light electrifies her gaudy gold bracelet.

Sue has to force herself to lean down and shake. Sure enough, the reptilian skin transmits a steady bolt of dread.

"Rose Camille Joan Russo Impoliteri."

"Ohhh." At last, Sue (partly) understands.

The daughter-in-law, Maureen, who handled the house sale, told the Glassmans that the elderly seller was "incapacitated," "lingering" in a nursing home in Forest Hills. But this old gal with the loud housedress, powder-blue hoodie, and fuchsia lipstick appears, if anything, overly animated. When Sue offers to hang up her things, she clamps onto her bag with a tissue-stuffed sleeve and commands the aide, "Move it!"

Instantly, the chair is hurtling down the hallway. "This is my hallway," Rose narrates, pointing out the obvious. To the right, "my graaand staircase." To the left, the door to "my living room." Farther down, "we have my half bath — "

"Can I get you…anything?" Sue asks, a bit breathless from keeping pace. They've arrived at the end of the corridor, the doorway of Rose's "famous kitchen." Back in the day, Rose would right now be breading the Friday-night fish while figuring out her big Sunday meal. "That's the antipasti *and* the pasta, two meats, a vegetable side —"

The wheelchair veers off into the dining room/murder room, where Sue just assumes they will stop. But on they roll (the aide as if also on wheels, gliding), past the big round table piled with Sue's books and CDs, over the long scratch in the tile floor, toward the back door.

"Push hard. It's broken!" Sue calls, idiotically. Rose obviously knows about the door. She moved out only five months ago, after…eighty years? Ninety? To all but the Glassmans, this is still the Impoliteri house when it's not "*that* house" or "the Murder House."

"The Impoliteri house? That old wreck'll be work!" said Dr. Mole next door, first day.

"So you're the plucky ones who moved into *that* house," chirped Sage's preschool teacher, Miss Katy.

"The Murder House? People live in there? Ya sure?" This from the pizza guy before agreeing to deliver.

Not to mention the ring-and-rip crowd, who chant, "Scary Impoliteri, Scary Impoliteri," as they race away, shrieking.

The Impoliteri house is rife with spider corpses, loose doorknobs, saggy ceilings, broken locks, and sweating walls, for starters. It's a money pit with a weird oregano/shoe polish/moldy smell that no amount of Ajax will obscure. Like a third (or fourth or ninth) kid, it's so used to being neglected

that it acts out even when it's paid attention to. An opera
of a house is how Sue regards the heavy, dark, Old World
mustiness. Fat, ornate furniture legs plot to trip you; worn
velvet cushions sigh out clouds of melodramatic dust; drafty
old windows turn ordinary sea breezes into hysterical arias.

It moves Sue, despite everything, the overblown dynam-
ics. She's settling in. By the ocean, nothing can corner you.
The appearance of the old lady confirms it. Sue already
feels...attached? Attacked?

Sue retreats to the kitchen, spits into the stained, oversize
marble sink, and scarfs down four Fig Newtons before picking up the phone to call Dan on the seventh hole.

"She's come home!" Sue says, her mouth still jammed with
fig. "Whatever that means." Then, flashing on the huge white
pocketbook: "I think she might have brought a suitcase."

In the background, Sue can hear her father-in-law, Sy,
barking at Dan to "wrap it up! We're in the middle of a meeting here."

"Hello to him too! Will you...hurry back, please?"

"On my way," Dan promises.

"Like hell you are," Sy rails. "How dare you skip out on a
dying man in the middle—"

"You're not dying, Dad."

Sy did have bone cancer. Fifteen years ago.

"Gimme that phone!"

"No!"

"Hand it over!"

Sue paces, half listening to them wrestle for the cell. The
corner kitchen has windows on two sides—one facing her

driveway and the Mole-Kacy garage, the other fronting the rhododendron hedge and, past that, the neighbor Tim's house. He's out back, as always, with his cronies, all in Adirondack chairs. But their eyes, usually fixed on the ocean, now stare into her yard.

Sue pivots to see where exactly they're looking. Beyond the doorway connecting kitchen to dining room, there's a straight view across a strip of scuffed, sunlit tile and out through half a picture window. In the available frame, the aide's graceful brown hand slices a piece of blue sky. Following her yellow dress downward, Sue can make out, in receding order, windblown greenery, a stretch of brick patio, some anemic grass, and, down at the bottom right corner, a miniature silver sandal—Sage! Her little girl is out there with strangers! "Gotta go!"

"So you do!" her father-in-law bellows, having apparently wrested the phone from his son. "Shabbat shalom, Sue. Don't forget to put in the brisket."

⌒

Tim's primed for the screech of the Impoliteri back door. On his feet as soon as he hears it, he tucks then untucks his T-shirt, sits again, stands again, sits. Which Glassman will emerge and what can he think to say to any of them? Then the house spits out *Rose*, and Tim feels, at once, paralyzed.

During her absence, the old lady has acquired a wheelchair and a hot brown chick in head-to-toe yellow to push it. "This is my yard," Rose says as they clear the weedy patio

36

and plow onto the patchy grass. The long lawn is contiguous with Tim's own save for a thick, dividing row of rhododendrons. Anyone can see that this was once a single property. But Rose insists that her companion "picture it!" back when her father owned the entire plot. No lawn at all then, just the best victory garden in the U. S. of A., spanning the beachfront between two soon–to–be–New York City streets.

Apparently old Rose is still too proud for a hearing aid. Tim easily makes out every word.

"One day, I'm a little girl playing on my private acre, and the next I'm a madwoman staring down a bulldozer."

Tim and his mom weren't the ones to buy the parceled-off lot. They didn't build the house on Rose's Eden. They weren't even the first people to live in it. Yet the Impoliteris have always liked to blame the Rays for their dip in fortune. The way Tim heard it, Rose's father sold the land after his shoemaking business went bust. With the money, he imported Rose a husband from Italy and set the guy up with a store on Rockaway's main shopping street: 116th. What little time remained, he spent on what little garden remained.

"I've kept a lot of his plants alive," Rose goes on, showing off a small tree by the back door. "This is his yew. That's *yew*, not *me*, get it?" Tim waits anxiously to see when she'll notice... "It's shedding all its needles!" And beneath it: "Dad's fool's parsley! Flattened dead!" The little hoods on the monkshood resemble Rose's own droopy purple eyelids. It's worse than Tim even realized. In the five months since Rose left, her garden has totally tanked. Tim braces himself for the scowl now swiveling toward him.

"And over there," Rose tells her helper, "is one of my neighbors, drunk Timmy."

*Wrong!* Tim wants to shout. *Eight months, three weeks, five days wrong, bitch! Don't make me glad I killed your plants. FYI — I'm not Timmy (or Butter), I'm Tim! Tim Ray! Tim-Remember-It-Ray!*

But what if one of the Glassmans were to hear? They'd never want to get to know him then. And what if Rose's return is his fault? What if crowing to his friends about the great new family next door has in some way invoked her? How foolish of Tim ever to have believed that he was free of Rose simply because she'd moved. She was his burden. And he forever part of her tour.

"Timmy and his jolly band of firemen —"

"Firefighters," Yellow Babe corrects, then brings a hand up to her glossy lips to — hey — throw a kiss.

Chris D. mimes catching it on his flushed cheek. "Wow." Bean reaches back and slaps the side of Tim's head. None of them have quite gotten used to their sudden social upgrade. Easier to get laid than to sleep these days. And what with the wreck crew finally dismissed from Ground Zero in May, there's time to fantasize. Not that they don't love their wives, not that they'd ever — but, oh, to be unattached FDNY at the onset of the summer of '02! Why isn't Tim out nightly, banging supermodels?

*I prefer widows,* Tim thinks, again afraid they know he's sleeping with Peg, widow of his best friend, Chowder. Add to this heavy secret the reappearance of Rose, and Tim's body goes as rigid as Jill (his old lifeguarding partner Sloane's

Doberman) when she's tensing to rip out some flesh. Tim could sic that bitch on Rose for how she scoffs at the Glassmans' new lawn chairs, some kind of fancy wicker treated to withstand the salt air—*"As if!"* It *is* an unusual first purchase for a house in need of a new roof. But to Tim, it only makes his neighbors more intriguing. He tosses out one of his mother's go-to warnings: "Judge not, that you not be judged."

Rose just snorts. "What's Irish and lives in the backyard?"

"What?" Chris D. wonders. He *would*.

"Patty O'Furniture!"

Yellow Babe looks down at the ragged tan grass. (Tim's cropped, hydrated side of the lawn glares green.)

Bean laughs himself into coughing.

Encouraged, Rose goes back in for a knock-knock joke. "Who's there?" she asks herself and answers, "9/11."

"Enough!" Yellow Babe insists, shaking her unshakable hair, a tall, braided, layered (maybe varnished?) creation. "These jokes of Rose's, I don't know. It's like Tourette's."

No prob, no biggie, the guys explosively assure her. Chris D. even spits out a "9/11 *who?*" But the question is swallowed up in the old lady's sudden agitation for "the hose! The hose! Get the hose!" The withering yard was already upsetting to Rose but now with her glasses on, it's "devastating." Her bracelet trembles as she points at a mopey purple mound, her "poor, poor lobelia!" And—"Holy God!" Beside that: "My climbing sweet pea! What *was* my sweet pea! The hose, please! Someone help me!"

Tim feels hot. At the very least, he could have recommended a gardener to the Glassmans. The exuberant health of his own flowers in comparison embarrasses him. Dahlias in five candy colors. (If you stand at a distance and squint, you can pretend they're fireworks.) Loud, pink fringy dianthus that smell spicy enough to bite. Sprouting, ruffled stalks of lemon geranium that glow at dusk and make the air taste like citrus. To Tim, this has been the biggest revelation of sobriety, how all is more, not less, vibrant, amped up, full. On a good day, Tim feels almost like he's gone back to Sage's age, constantly bugging out on flowers and insects, on the way people move, on the words they use.

"That red, that's my bleeding heart!" Rose wails. But it's the ravaged cherry tree that truly ignites her. She tries to rise from her chair, then swats the aide with her pocketbook for daring to restrain her. You don't need to know Italian to get the gist of what she's shouting. Tim's friends promptly remember they have stuff to do; they're off. Later, man. Under the tree, little Sage, with her eyes squeezed tightly shut, believes she has made herself invisible.

⌒

Queens has thirty cemeteries, but Rose's father long ago decreed that the family ashes be sprinkled out here, on the cherry tree. "Of course, as a Catholic, he'd have preferred burial, but laws are laws. And for eternity, look it, you can't beat this view." Southwest, there's Sandy Hook. Southeast, Far Rockaway. Straight ahead, the magic horizon, able to hold down the whole Atlantic with one single thin line. Most of the time.

Best not to ask what Rose means by that, Tim warns Sue. He grew up in the next-door house, so he knows. "Rose has seen more nor'easters and hurricanes than you have time for." And: "Better watch your feet around that wheelchair."

Sue's bare feet feel as bulbous as the rest of her—knees, belly, boobs. Wherever they move, they're in the way of the dressy aide laboring to push big Rose there and there, and "not there, there!" while the old lady brandishes the hose gun, apologizing to her cremated relatives about the sorry state of the yard. "The foxglove and castor bean might rebound with a good soak, Daddy, but the horse chestnut is just too paaarched! I heard that! Don't you start, Vin..."

Tim leans in toward Sue, his pointer finger revolving by the side of his head in the crazy sign.

*And what's* your *excuse?* Sue resists asking. The guy may share their lawn and wall, the door to the sand, and, for all she cares, that mangy cherry tree, but does that give him the right to stroll over with his half a nose every time she appears? Between Tim and the Mole-Kacys (with their four wild look-alike boys), Sue's had more neighbor contact during five months in Rockaway than in all fifteen years in Tribeca. Not to mention Tim's rank dog, Blacky, who pees against her shower house hourly. Even Rose asked what Tim and his mutt thought they were doing when they sauntered around the hedge.

"Helping?" he asked, looking down at his chest. What appears to be mustard obscures one arm of the red cross on his faded lifeguard T-shirt. Now he scratches at his already raw, stubbled chin, adding, "That tree seriously needs some fungicide. I can run down to the store?"

"What a doll!" The aide exhales, clearly smitten. She scans Tim's exaggeratedly V-shaped torso with a shiver. It's the presence of a firefighter, even a past-tense one, that enchants her, enchants June, Dan, the whole country at this point, the free world. Which brings Sue to the question: What the hell? What exactly is she missing? It's a familiar sensation, sitting grimly in an audience uproariously laughing, or the reverse, cracking up alone like a kook. That's Sue. And though she'll never admit it to her father-in-law, she suddenly longs to be back in the dining room, feet up, eyes closed, iPod cranked, listening to *Shabbat Prayers Made Easy*. Track five features a surprisingly versatile alto.

"Maybe Rose would like to be alone with her thoughts?" Sue tries.

"God forbid."

"Well then, anyone for a Fig Newton?"

The aide reels back as if the cookies might infect her. Rose accepts one, then, while chewing, demands to be parked at the cherry tree. The strange hunched specimen was planted in memory of Rose's mother, who died birthing her. (All eyes magnetize to Sue's belly.) Sprinkled on top are the ashes of both her parents and her husband, Vin. And now — Rose interrupts herself, lifting her bifocals to diagnose "fungus." As if Tim hadn't just said as much. "We need the whoozit spray, with the yellow label —"

"Spray?" Sue asks. Don't they see that Sage is playing there? That's where she plays every and all afternoon with her imaginary Ed and Tim's incontinent dog. It's an endless quest to find "the shiny treasure"—shells, sea glass, select trash. "Spray chemicals? *There?*"

The aide reaches over and gives Sue's bump another demeaning pat. "Don't worry, Mommy. Human beings flourish on toxins. Like cockroaches."

Bibi's the name. Not Indian but Guyanese, with a line from the Koran tattooed on her dainty forearm.

"What's it mean?" Tim asks as if he would really like to know.

The aide dabs a tissue at a wet spot on her yellow linen. Already her matching espadrilles have been "decimated" by grass stains. "There are so many meanings."

Rose hoots. "Is 'jihad' one of them?" She blasts the tree with the hose gun. Sage leaps up and runs for Sue, hugging the big ketchup bottle she uses for comfort in lieu of the usual bear, blankie, or chewed-on thumb. "Another ginger! You're lucky you're not in Calabria. In Calabria, you see a ginger, you spit and cross the street."

Bibi drags a manicured finger across her throat. "Kill me, now!" You see what she puts up with, day in, day out from this jokey, paranoid senior? "It's getting worse too." Rose has been refusing her meds. Not to mention that she "parties like it's the end of the free world."

"It *is* the end of the free world," Rose says.

"Well, it will be if you don't mind your pressure."

Sue might commiserate if Bibi would stop touching her.

Pat, pat. "Another girl, Mommy?"

"Don't know," Sue lies. Dan insists on being "surprised," as if a bloody five- to ten-pound creature squeezing out from your wife's vagina isn't shock enough. It's a boy he wants. Or his father does, so Dan does. Even a second girl elicited sighs from the many Latino technicians employed at Glassman Locks & Keys. A third and they might send condolence cards.

"See the way she carries? Low and pointy, that means girl." The aide will not stop. "Has your belly button popped? A lot of pressure on your bladder?"

"What?"

"You have the heartburn?"

Heartache is more like it. In nineteen years of marriage, Dan has never once missed following up a fight with daisies. All around them, the still-overgrown but newly watered garden drips.

"If you don't have the heartburn, it's a baldie."

"Can we please not—"

"Have a seat," Tim says, having hauled down all the new furniture. A chair for Sue and Sage. A chair for Bibi. A side table for the Fig Newtons. An umbrella. And, unless he's intruding (yes, but she can't say so), a chair for Tim too.

Tim compliments Sage on her Heinz. It's from their old apartment's fridge, a detail that seems to charm him. "People don't think enough about condiments, do they?"

Sage just looks. First at Tim's stubbly chin, then higher up where the right half of his nose should be—a shiny red patch like strawberry fruit leather. According to June, it was melted in the North Tower. So Sue knows she should be grateful. Sue *is* grateful. Still, does he have to be so...*present*, constantly offering his sunscreen around like a joint?

"I was a lifeguard once upon a time, so —"

"We're fine, thanks."

"You think that but you're all so fair. That one especially." He gestures with the lotion toward the beach and...June!

*Eyes off my daughter!* Sue wants to say, wondering how long she's been down there and why Tim knows about it. The teenager already seems overexposed on the windy shore in that short navy skirt without some weird neighbor guy watching. June sags under the weight of her red backpack. Her long copper curls blow around, tangling. Then her pointy elbow bends. She's throwing something into the sea. "Oh no, not the egg!" Sue says. "Tell me my daughter did not just throw an egg."

Aside from taking her Regents exams, all June has to do to advance to the eleventh grade is pass Health at the local high school. That is (1) attend class, and (2) carry an egg (labeled with a pink number *3*) for a month without breaking it. Alas, Sue failed to consult her daughter before brokering this deal. A single class, she thought, how bad could that be? Very bad, apparently. Extraordinarily *bad*. In hindsight, Sue admits she was wrong, over and over she's admitted it. But June refuses to forgive her.

"In hindsight!" June shrieked at Sue just this morning. "In *ass*-sight?" She dangled the egg out Sue's bedroom window. (Her own being encased in ivy.) "I *will* drop it," she threatened. "I *will*." At issue, that "prison of a school." Metal detectors and cops! The gym turned into a nursery for student mothers!

Dan would have instantly let June skip the day, the week,

the rest. (Thankfully, he goes to work early.) But Sue called June's bluff. She knew the straight-A-minus student would not really risk it all. And so it was. The tantrum passed. June returned the egg to the nest of maxipads she'd fashioned for it in her backpack and rushed to catch the Green Line bus to school.

Not to say Sue has any illusion this constitutes victory. June might like the break from her old school, Stuyvesant High (windows overlooking the Ground Zero rubblescape, EPA air testers chirping ominously in the classrooms). But that in no way guarantees she'll finish the year here. What if even this one class is so awful that June would rather chuck the egg into the sea and be done with it? Has she? A bit nearsighted, Sue is forced to rely on Tim.

"Not an egg," Tim says. He attended and dropped out of that same local school when it was better but not that much better, then as now a tense meeting place for segregated Far Rockaway blacks, Rockaway Park and Broad Channel Irish, Belle Harbor and Neponsit Jews, and a smattering of bused-in Ozone Park Italians. Later, he took the equivalency plus the exact minimum of college credits needed to become a firefighter.

As he tells Sue this, Tim becomes aware that she is inching away from him. Her arms cradle her belly protectively. This is the most Sue's ever spoken to him at one time. He *would* go and tell her he's a high-school dropout! Better not add that it's a bottle June's tossing into the water. Better not tag his new neighbor's daughter a litterer.

At least the girl can't throw for shit. Even these mushy waves easily return the trash to her. Again and again, it washes up in the suds at her feet. Her beat-up blue Pumas kick the wet sand in frustration. No socks. Tim tells Sue he can offer June the extra spot in his weekend driver's ed car, if she's looking for an activity. (He could really use the cash.)

Sue turns away, massaging one of her ankles. June can start the course tomorrow, Tim hears himself babbling. She's hardly missed a thing. "Kenny Mole-Kacy from next door is in the Saturday car so June'll have a familiar face. Why not? Think about it."

Sue thinks. Sue thinks: *Perpetually enraged daughter driving around with not one but two creepy neighbor males? Cue some eerie music—minor chords and screechy violins, unusual plucked instruments.* It's a soundtrack that also suits Rose, now calling Sue's attention. Crossing herself with the hose gun, Rose mutters loudly in Italian. To the dead? The aide? The tree?

At four feet tall or so, it's clearly a dwarf variety, grown misshapen toward the sheltering wall, branches cracked from weather and salt. Slender leaves cocooned in fuzz. Nonetheless, hard clusters of fruit drip down in voluptuous defiance. The trunk bark glows a deep, dried-blood red. According to Rose, there's no rational reason it's not dead. "It's a miracle."

This pronouncement hangs there awhile, no one daring to challenge it. Sue fingers the teeny bones in Sage's hand. (Bigger ones have already grown inside her.)

"Then again," Rose adds, "ground bone *is* the superior fertilizer."

Tim laughs nervously. "When the time comes, I'll be sure to sprinkle my mom back there on the rhododendrons."

Naturally, everyone turns to take in the hedge of shrubs

and the houses that flank it: Sue's ivy-covered brick square inlaid with tile; Tim's small, white peeling Cape. Both structures are in total disrepair, but whereas his gives off a homey vibe — its back porch crammed with surfboards and fishing gear — hers could have acquired its haunted rep sans the murder. Every other window is strangled in ivy. The back door, left open, hangs on its rusty hinges. If these aren't good enough horror-flick images, just pan out to the viny, neglected yard where a strange, wrinkled woman in a wheelchair intermittently rages, and Sue should want to run like hell. But the opposite has happened. The house belongs to her now and she, somehow, to it, bewitched by this ruin on the skinny peninsula between ocean and bay, Rockaway.

The rhododendron in question is thriving even without the help of ashes, so furry with flowers it looks set to crawl over the lawn, past the new chairs, and out the open door to the sand. Sue's not sure whether Tim was joking about tossing his mother's remains on the hedge. What if crematory gardening is some kind of quaint, dark local practice?

"Well, that'd be fitting," Rose scoffs, raising her several chins. "Since your mother planted those as a fence to exclude us Impoliteris."

"You know that's not true," Tim argues unconvincingly. Scary Impoliteri.

"I know it's pretty humdrum, rhododendron," Rose sniffs.

Sage likes this. "Humdrum rhododendron," she repeats, drumming out the rhythm on Sue's thigh with her ketchup bottle. "Humdrum rhododendron. Humdrum —"

"Of course, she never was one for originality, your mother. Take a chance, I kept telling her. All you gotta do is prune some, fertilize, mind the pH."

"Well, you know *my* mom," Tim says. "She probably thought *pH* meant 'pray harder.'"

"Humdrum rhododendron," Sage keeps on, as if hypnotized.

"My mom prays harder than anyone," Tim translates for Sue's benefit. "Even harder than her sister who's a sister, Sister Agnes. Since you're also religious —"

*"Me?"* Sue asks, following Tim's gaze to the pocket of her dress. "Oh, this?" The little Bible she'd been reading earlier! "This is nothing!" She must have put it in there when the bell rang, in the fog of pregnancy. "I mean, *I'm* nothing. I mean, I am converting, but it's nothing." She pulls out the book and tries to Frisbee it onto the table for emphasis but it sails past, thuds onto the grass.

Bibi gasps. "You just *threw* the Bible!"

"Not intentionally."

"Says Miss Nothing!" The aide recovers and examines the book, pronounces it "vandalized," and shows it around for all to see "the travesty."

On the inside cover, on the occasion of Dan Glassman's bar mitzvah, the Ladies' Guild of Temple Beth Shalom wish him *an enormous mazel tov.* Under and over this inscription, a green Magic Marker scrawl details the P.O. box, et cetera, to write away for *Golden Hits of the Seventies* on eight-track.

Sue loves the image of young Dan scrambling to capture the address before it scrolls off his Brooklyn TV screen. (The

Bible was evidently the only paper within reach.) But Bibi's appalled; distressed, even. She clucks, shades her eyes.

"You're a Muslim. What do you care?" Rose asks. "If you had any Jewish friends, you'd know that lots of them are loose that way. My Jewish friends the Baums, well, Jewish *ex*-friends, they're loose that way."

Bibi peeks out from under her hand to see if Tim's watching her display of moral outrage. *Sorry, babe.*

"Humdrum rhododendron," Sage chants on. "Humdrum rhododendron. Humdrum—"

"Shhh!" Bibi reaches out and tugs a pigtail.

The freckles instantly bleach off Sage's small face. Then they're gone altogether, hidden in Sue's dress.

"Will the florist-delivery guy look in the yard?" Sue asks, hoping to lighten the conversation. Cremation, dead plants, religion, really? She is also curious. "There *is* a local florist?" Since Rockaway has no bookstore, shoe store, or movie theater, it seems a fair question. "I'm expecting some daisies."

"You can eat those," Rose says, blinking furiously at the tree. "Daisies, nasturtium, *sage*—"

The child looks up at the sound of her name. She and Rose exchange pouts.

"Healthier than Fig Newtons?" Sue asks, stroking her daughter's still baby-soft hair, the color of orange sherbet. "Is that what you mean?

But Rose doesn't seem to know. What she means, where she is, anything. *"Che cosa? Che cosa?"* Her voice has dropped a full octave. "Where is your mother, Timmy? Off with my husband?"

"Tim. I'm Tim now. You're not making any sense."

"The nerve of her, to call herself a Christian."

"Rose," Bibi soothes. "You're confused, Rosie."

Sue is too. The old lady's face has gone all pinched and twitchy. Is she having a stroke?

Bibi blames it on the medicine she won't take. "Somebody please tell her to take it. I'd be —"

"Take it," Sage says.

"That's your mother's house that you're living in, Timmy. Where is she? Where did you put your mother?" Tim drops his mangled face into his hands but Rose will not stop. "Answer me, Timmy, where is she, Timmy, Timmy —"

"Akron!" He finally breaks. "Since September. You know that, Rose. You all at the church had that good-bye thing right before she went home."

"Home?" In Rose's trance, the word sounds alien.

"Ohio."

Which is when Dan, in his plaid golf wear, appears, booming, "Buckeye State!"

In slow motion, Tim rises and the two men shake on it.

❧

Bibi's Ford Fiesta is parked diagonally mid-driveway as if to take up the most space possible. Consequently, the rabbi's station wagon juts into the street. Sy's reaching over from the passenger seat and leaning on the horn. The continuous B-flat lifts Sue from her chair and around the house to the car. On the way, she reflects on the all-too-common scenario in which she tells a student to play a B but a B-flat keeps sounding.

"Are you out of your mind, Sy? We have neighbors!" As if on cue, Kenny Mole-Kacy skateboards past, holding up his fingers in a peace sign.

Sy clucks at Sue. "We've been waiting. What's the matter with your hair?" He touches his own badly dyed comb-over. "We're waiting ten minutes now. Didn't Dan tell you?"

"There's a lot going on back there."

"Well, I wanted you to meet Rabbi Larry. Rabbi, Suzanne. Suzanne, Rabbi. He'll be doing your conversion on Sunday."

"I know," Sue says. "Hi again."

The rabbi nods. They've met before. You don't forget a werewolf in a yellow crocheted yarmulke. The first meeting was only a few months ago, the setup the same, with Sy, in a car, post-golf. So why are they pretending otherwise?

"Finally netted her, Seymour?" the rabbi asks through his mat of graying facial hair.

"Took nineteen years. But, woo-wee, one goy down." Then the two men actually high-five.

"Don't look so solemn," the rabbi tells Sue, holding out a moist hand, furry all over, even the knuckles. "We're just goofing around." She takes his paw, invites him in.

"Yeah, come!" Sy seconds, squinting at Bibi's pristine Ford.

Rabbi Larry taps his Rolex. "Thanks, but Mindy already calls herself a golf widow. If I hit any traffic on the Belt—"

"A rabbi can't spare five minutes for a dying man?"

"Sy! You stop with that." Sue helps her father-in-law out of the car. His cancer did leave a few range-of-motion issues, but the rabbi's right. "This absurd insistence that you're dying! It's killing me!"

The rabbi waves. "See you at Sue's Jew party Sunday."

"Shhh." Sy bangs the side of the car.

"It's a surprise," Sue says, laughing.

The station wagon backs up, turns into the street, stops. The rabbi's arm shoots out the window with a sheet of paper. "Forgot to give you this," he calls merrily. "Fill it out and bring it with."

Sue hurries over, forgetting she can't hurry. Halfway down the flagstone path, she stops to let the baby finish an Irish step dance on her pelvic floor.

"Never mind," the rabbi says, rechecking his watch. "The form's optional."

Enter Kenny Mole-Kacy. He zips over on his skateboard, swipes the paper from Rabbi Larry's hand, and rides it smoothly to Sue.

"Thank you?"

"No prob. Tell June I said yo."

❧

Sue knows it's useless to call but Dan can't help it. Fridays are the worst. Nothing like that first attempt at weekend home repairs to stoke his sense that chaos is imminent. One mess with the caulk and he's crouched on the far side of the bed, stabbing his doctor's number into the cordless. In the background is the soft burble of the radio he's kept on every waking hour since Bush color-coded the threat level (yellow). To "stay alert," Dan feels, is his patriotic duty. But how alert can he be if he fails to notice his own hugely pregnant wife filling up the doorway not two feet from him?

Total concentration on Dan looks like this: The tip of his tongue pokes out between his thin lips. Heavy dark eyebrows scrunch. Eyes cast down. Under his breath, he wills his neurologist to pick up, pick up the phone. Not because he has a migraine. (If he did, he'd be in bed with the shades drawn, immobile.) Rather, this call is all about the migraine-to-be, its unknown properties. As with pleasure, the anticipation of pain is often more material than the real thing.

Dan stares down at the planks of—oak? Pine? Ash? Neither of them knows squat about wood, only that a floor should not resemble a ramp. If this worries Dan, it's his own fault for allowing his father to monopolize the contractors. Sue said as much in their morning spat. (The old man would have his own suite of rooms with faux stone paneling and Jacuzzi bath even if the floor above collapsed in the meantime.) Sue imagines Dan is taking a break from stressing about his impending headache to worry about the floor instead. What lies beneath but rot? He's panicking. Rot and corpses. The whole thing will, any second, drop, releasing a cache of dead bodies to rain down on the dining/murder room below. But the actual scenario in Dan's mind is surely darker. There is no one better at scaring himself than her sunny husband.

Sue also suspects June's been playing him, playing up those sounds in the walls. Just the house settling, Sy keeps telling them. Whatever that means, Dan says he's glad of it. "Since *unsettling* pretty well describes the place now."

Apparently, the doctor's answering machine has picked up again. "Dan Glassman here." He sighs into the receiver. "The meds don't work. Nothing works. I've cut out all TV, nuts, aged cheese, red wine..."

Sea breezes rattle the red paper lanterns outlining the fireplace and all three screened beach views. This and more Chinatown schlock festoon the walls and shelves. Such a stark contrast to the solemn wooden bedroom set, you have to wonder: Did Rose buy these knickknacks before or after a Chinese man killed her son? And which is creepier? And if you're Sue, you also have to indulge your worst self by putting these questions to your anxious husband every time you're lying next to him, below the tomb-shaped headboard. Call it payback for years of putting his father's desires over hers. That he nonetheless continues to beguile Sue is both a comfort and a puzzle.

"...I'd appreciate it if you get back to me right away," he's saying, eyes moving up the wall to where a cheap print of a snaky Chinese river hangs crookedly. "Please call me ASAP, *please.*"

"Oh, quit begging," Sue says and grabs the phone from him. "Get another doctor if she won't answer."

Dan's small, bright eyes glow up at her. Not the Glassman brown you'd expect but turquoise and luminous, offset by his dark brows. One wink from one of those eyes can undo Sue. Yet Dan closes them, wrapping his burly arms around her thighs.

"Sing for me, Suzy? If you sing—"

"Not now."

Dan's been asking Sue to sing ever since she made that long ago late-night call, choosing randomly from the Yellow Pages attached by a chain to the phone booth. Glassman Locks & Keys had a half-page ad and catchy taglines: *#1 in the Tristate Since '58! What Have You Got to Lose?* This was back in Tribeca's bad old days, early eighties. Hudson Street. At the mouth of the Holland Tunnel. Sue's all-girl band, Visitation, had just played a club called Wetlands, and she'd locked her keys in the car. Dan found her out front, guarding the instruments with a can of pepper spray. Sue could tell he had not, as he claimed, heard of the eclectic (that is, pretentious) Visitation—uke, glock, flute, drum. But he was groggy and fun, insisting Sue sing for him before he'd jimmy her car open.

All these years later, and Dan still sulks if Sue won't croon on command. These days he seems put out by lots of things that Sue *won't* do, like convert without a struggle. So much angst can't be good for the baby. Or be friendlier. Would it kill her to chat with a neighbor? Why won't she make just the *tiniest* effort with her hair and what she wears?

Dan fingers the hem of her white maternity dress, a wrinkled hand-me-down from a friend who got it from her sister's cousin, so he's not completely out of line when he asks, "What's this? A mummy costume? Haunted-house wear?"

His image consciousness made sense back in Tribeca, a no-man's-land they watched turn gradually and then rapidly posh. Commercial lofts were renovated for residential use. Vacant buildings morphed into chic spas, restaurants, and shops. On any given day in the 1990s, Dan could score a slew of contracts for Glassman Locks & Keys simply by putting on a suit. But here? In Rockaway?

"You try fashionizing this huge, itchy belly!"

"If you'd let me." Dan reaches a hand up the cuff of her sleeve. "I fantasize you in a red low-cut—"

"Fashionize, not fantasize."

Dan shoots off one of his lethal winks. "So what *is* your fantasy these days?"

Sue slips away, not about to describe the hot ice cream truck driver, how his crotch in the truck lines up right with her face. Not now, anyway. She can't afford to be derailed from the reason she's slogged up all those stairs. The visitors. Dan said he'd deal with them. "Uh! Why can't you ever do what you promise?"

"I—there's so much to figure out—the byzantine way my father runs this business, it's...I can't be having migraines!"

Sue was as stunned as anyone when Sy chose his wife's shivah to announce that Dan would take over as owner of Glassman Locks & Keys. Later, it occurred to her that he might have had some tax incentive. But there, in his Brooklyn Heights brownstone, Sy seemed to make the decision impulsively, as though the old narcissist couldn't bear to cede attention to anyone, even his deceased wife. If it meant transferring all shares of the company to his son, so be it. Nothing really had to change. Sy kept his CEO title, his cushy office and beleaguered secretary. And what a nice bit of drama he'd dished up, tapping a fork on his low stool to quiet the mourners for the big announcement.

"Estelle, may she rest in peace, was so proud of Dan for following in the footsteps of her great-grandpa Henry"—inventor of the first key-duplicating machine. "On this sad occasion, I'd like to add"—snotty tears gumming his throat—"I'd like to say, without my son..."

"Dan?" Sue says now, spitting into her handkerchief. "Are you even listening?"

"What if I start having headaches *all the time?* What if I have one in the middle of negotiating—"

"Focus, Dan. I'm telling you, this woman gives me a really bad feeling."

"She's a world-renowned neurologist—"

"Not your doctor!" Sue points with the confiscated phone out the window. "Rose! I'm talking about Rose and her...person. You promised you'd see them out and you didn't and now look! Get up! Look!"

Outside, the waves, previously absent, bounce up spray. The lifeguard's gone home, inspiring the next-door Mole-Kacy boys to do some illegal surfing. Heaving long boards bigger than they are, the dark, shaggy tribe cut across the Glassman yard and stream through the beach door. Only the pimply oldest brother, Kenny, remains in street clothes—chinos, gray windbreaker. As his brothers whoop and weave toward the waves, he is creeping, creeping up behind June.

"Watch out!" Dan inhales, no doubt picturing their daughter's long, wan face when startled, the gap between her front teeth. And he's unnerved by June's miniskirt. "Not a successful windy-day garment. What is she doing down there anyhow?"

"Smoking."

"What?"

"On the lawn, Dan!" With the phone still in hand, Sue adjusts his head downward to where Rose sits before the bent cherry tree, sucking a cigar and tippling a tiny airplane-size bottle of Sambuca.

Under the tree, Sage (and, no doubt, imaginary Ed) pretends to smoke and drink too. Cherry twigs as cigarettes chased with ketchup.

Personally, Dan says, he's entertained, even *touched* by the solid, ancient figure in a housedress and hoodie who insisted he aerate her lawn with his golf shoes. "Did she tell you about the time the ocean met the bay?"

"Yes, and the time before that and the time bound to be." Not to mention corrupt politicians and bootleggers, tides of hypodermic needles, fires, plane crashes, the star-crossed *Golden Venture* (now an artificial reef down in Boca Raton), "*and* a whole stream of awful jokes, which is proof she's been here six hours too long."

"I-invited-them-for-dinner-don't-kill-me," Dan blurts.

Even the baby writhes in frustration. Not only have no flowers arrived, he's using Rose as a pawn in their feud. "How could you? On Shabbat too!"

"*Shabbat?*" Dan laughs the way only Dan can laugh, a roar that requires his whole head, neck, and torso—which is to say, largely. "*Shabbat?* I had to force you to go to my parents' house every Friday night for nineteen years. Now, all of a sudden—"

"I'm converting! In two days. For you!"

"That's not entirely accurate."

"For your father, then, your mother's memory, whatever." Neither Dan nor his father seems to care, really. It was Dan's mother, Estelle, who pushed all these years. Sue is in the ignoble position of converting for a dead person.

Again, Dan's hand reaches out to grab her, but Sue moves aside. She will not be seduced into relinquishing the phone.

"You want to call someone, call that daughter-in-law, Maureen, to come and get these people. Dinner, Dan? Really? Rose thinks this house still belongs to her."

"That's why I thought dinner—we'll talk."

Sue leans her forehead on the glass. Down below, the vigorously watered garden still looks lifeless, just lifeless and wet now. The slick cherries drop from their feeble branches at random intervals. "Your friend Tim wants to spray poison on that tree; did you hear him? *Poison*, and Rose agrees. Speaking of, what's with Eve? I mean, what did Eve do that was *sooo* terrible?"

"Eve?"

"Aren't the Jews all about education?"

"Look, I'm sorry. I should have asked before inviting Rose but I thought—"

"You always do that!" Sue snaps. "You apologize then go on to explain why you're right. Don't say you're sorry if you're not sorry!"

"But I—"

"And don't think daisies can fix *this!*"

Sue's florid, overheating. It's her temper. It never serves her well. Of course daisies *could* fix this, at least temporarily.

When Dan reaches for her this time, she doesn't resist. But she wills him to notice how her wedding ring digs into her inflated finger, to notice and understand *her*. It's a question of integrity. Who will Suzanne Ainsley Glassman, the Jew, be? If an old lady arrives at *your* house unexpectedly and refuses to leave, you should not be the one who feels like the stranger.

⌒

Rose is still there, jabbering to her dead relatives in the cherry tree. If Tim hadn't sobered up, he'd doubt his own perception. But it's real and it's happening. From back on his own side of the hedge, he can hear the old biddy blasting the Glassmans as thieves and *cafoni*. Bibi, meanwhile, strikes a pose if Tim so much as glances over. So he gets busy unpacking his new Malibu garden lights. But the not-looking is its own distracting activity. And when the phone in his board shorts vibrates, Tim spends an irrational second wondering why Rose would be calling him.

Right away, the connection, as usual, fails. (Fear of brain-zapping waves nixed plans for a Rockaway cell tower. Typical.) Tim sprints into his house and retrieves the now-ringing cordless. Chris D., at the firehouse, wants a surf report. "Fast! A new visual while I'm stuck here cleaning the john."

There on Tim's splintery back porch, all it takes is the slightest lift of his chin to spy whitecaps, veiny as rib eye. A couple of kids bob around on their boards, wiggly, loose black teeth in the big Atlantic mouth. "Southwest winds are putting on some texture and bump."

"I hear a *but*."

"Well, the tide's coming up so it's a bit deep, kinda weak. The better spots might be pulling in some plus peaks, but still I bet they're kinda dumpy."

"You going out?"

"Nah. Friday, you know. Bad luck for sailors and surfers."

"How am I supposed to live vicariously through a total lightweight?" Chris D. asks over the suctioning sounds of his plunger.

"I got stuff to do."

"That sleek black helper chick? Yeah, baby."

"F you." Tim's tense. His face itches. Rose's reappearance has reminded him of things he can't or doesn't want to remember.

The toilet flushes. "Okay, well, guess I'll pick you up at eight. Can't have the widows seeing you in that auto-school junker."

"About that—"

"No way are you bailing on the widows. Denise McClary needs screens and..."

Now it's Dan Tim spies, freshly showered and khakied. Holy crap! Quarterback? He glides out the tricky back door balancing an hors d'oeuvres–laden wicker tray. In his whole life, Tim's never served anyone anything more complicated than a pizza bagel. And he probably dropped it on her lap. Whoever *she* was, which he was too wasted to recall.

"Hey, you still there, Timmy?" Chris D.'s asking.

"The name's *Tim*."

Rose and Bibi flutter to attention at Dan's approach.

"Tim. Timmy. What's the diff?"

"The diff, *Chrissy*, is that Timmy would hang up on you, whereas Tim is just going to say, 'Later, dickhead.'"

How Tim misses the old days when you could really slam down a phone. No matter how hard you press an Off button, it's just not gratifying.

Timmy, Timmy.

Timmy would be over there distracting Rose so as to drain all her miniature Sambuca bottles. Timmy would have his own bottles, too, of course, stashed all over his mother's house, much larger bottles of Stoli. Timmy visited his mother often, so often he wound up living with her after Alicia, his wife of two months, chucked him out. Last straw: He'd left Alicia stranded during a hurricane to "check on my mother." In the end, even Tim's mother had moved away from Timmy.

Eight months, three weeks, five days—longer than his marriage.

"Hello. Um, Tim, hey," Dan calls. Who knows how long he's been standing there, electric-blue polo and matching eyes, the tray held out to him over the hedge.

Tim smiles, rising. His knees ping from squatting over the Malibu garden-lighting cables. Walking over, he pictures himself through Dan's eyes—baggies and flips, unwashed, unshaven, prickling, damaged face ablaze. Tim positions his elbow to cover the mustard stain he's just noticed on his shirt, which only spurs Dan to ask if his arm's injured.

"Oh, no. Just fell asleep," Tim lies, shaking his elbow hokey-pokey style.

Dan can't be more than six or seven years older, but he's got the steady eye contact and thin, braided leather belt that clearly makes him the adult in this scenario. Even his neck is thick in just the thickly authoritative way Tim used to daydream his absent dad's would be.

They chat about the Malibu garden lighting — manly voltage and wattage — while Tim devours all the remaining fancy blobs from the tray. Then Dan flicks his GI Joe jaw. "Quick question?"

"Sue already asked."

"Sue?"

"Yeah, yeah, no worries; I'm certified to teach driver's ed and also to drive government vehic —"

"Ah, you scared me. I was inviting you to Sue's conversion party. It's a surprise. I thought she found out."

"No! No!" Bibi's voice interrupts from across the hedge. "I won't touch that." Tim's heart revs. It's ridiculous how nervous Rose makes him. The aide scoots her slim yellow hips backward, away from the old lady.

"Maybe the aide's sauced too." Dan laughs, mimicking Bibi's movements with the tray balanced on his head. You can tell he's the rare large man who can dance well.

"Just listen," Rose pleads.

Tim strains to decipher the conflict but Dan's loud rasp wins out. "It's my dad's party, really, not that he'll help with it. What I'm even serving? No idea. The house looks like a war zone. Sue —" As Dan says his wife's name, his smile collapses. You can see he'll have his dad's mouth before too long. The grooves for Sy Glassman's puppet-like jaw are all there, if faintly, framing his skinny lips. That Tim's own missing father could right now be walking around wearing Tim's future face has never even occurred to him.

"So you'll come?" Dan asks. "Sunday, noonish? No circumcision required."

An invitation from the Glassmans? "Are you kidding me?" This was the last thing he'd expected. And the most welcome. "Yes!"

Dan seems startled by Tim's enthusiasm. "Oh...it *is* a great excuse to get to know the neighbors. Let you all inside the Murder House to see there are no poltergeists. Am I right?"

Tim contemplates the familiar brick monstrosity looming behind Dan's head. The starlings that nest in the ivy sound miked but even they could be phantoms. They're nowhere in sight.

"Am I right?" Dan repeats, more tentatively.

Tim holds up two empty palms. The sky weighs a ton. Aside from his infancy in Ohio and the two-month marriage spent in Dayton Towers (Far Rockaway), Tim has lived his whole life here, next door. "Honestly? I've only been inside once."

"You're not serious?" Dan hugs the empty tray to his chest.

"Yes. I am."

"And that time?"

"Some other time." The night of the *Golden Venture*. That's twice it's appeared in one day, after Tim has pushed the scene from his mind for years and years. "Let's just say I wasn't invited." *Let's just never say I busted through the back door after hearing a gunshot to find Gary falling onto his suitcase, blood spurting from his eyeball, while Rose put the smoking gun in a dead Chinese man's hands.*

"*Mi casa es su casa,*" Dan says, too heartily, looking away at the surf casters leaning against Tim's porch. Does Dan fish? Before Tim has a chance to ask this, the neighbor reaches into his pocket and whips out a fifty. "Um, one more thing," he adds, casual-like. "If we could maybe use your driveway Sunday? For the overflow?"

So that explains it.

Tim pretends not to see the money. Or at least pretends he didn't see Dan see him see it. For once, he's glad to spy his dog peeing against the next-door shower house. "No! Blacky! Get!" It gives Tim something to do while Dan shoves the bill back into his khakis. Despite the mounting evidence, Tim refuses to let the Glassmans disappoint him.

Muttering about "something on the stove," Dan heads off, twirling the tray expertly on two fingers. *Never, ever, leave your cooking unattended,* the firefighter still inside Tim shouts silently. His audible voice is offering its millionth apology for the dog pee.

What Blacky has against (or for) Tim's own nearly identical shower house is hard to fathom. Tim's mom used to credit the large crucifix she hung in there, now mildew green. And Tim factors in the sacred vibe forged the summer he and his first girlfriend, Alex, lost their virginities to each other inside, over and over. But both of them know the animal is likely just attracted to something scent-worthy growing in the Impoliteri yard. Dogs are ruled by odors and sounds humans barely perceive, and while their loyalty may be a given, their discipline is a reflection of their owners' own.

Blacky has none whatsoever. Doesn't listen to Tim, never did. In his own time, the mutt saunters, not home where Tim's calling him, but back to the cherry tree. There he barks once at an invisible intruder, circles the ground, and lies down, done. Inches away, the women are too absorbed in their mysterious argument to acknowledge the animal. Rose pushes her white pocketbook at Bibi, who absolutely refuses to take it. The aide situates herself out of reach, one delicate brown hand on her heart.

Straining to hear more over the racket of quietude — ocean, birds, breeze — Tim begins walking down his side of the hedge. Step by step, he feels his mood changing. Tim's psyched to be included in the Glassman celebration even if parking concerns drove the invite. They'll get to know him and then they'll like him and then he'll always be included. But Tim's uneasy on account of Rose standing in his way. He'll stay on the outside of the family so long as she's around, bad-mouthing him. Psyched, uneasy, psyched, uneasy, uneasy, psyched. The closer Tim gets to the women, the more the balance tips, what with the anticipation and the damp garden smells — flowers, cigars, herbs, cherries, old flesh. Psyched, uneasy, uneasy, psyched, uneasy, uneasy, uneasy. Scary Impoliteri.

Tim really had intended to water Rose's plants until the

Glassmans had a chance to get settled. He even bought an extra-long hose attachment. But he kept putting it off, so strong was his distaste for next door, a sense fostered long before the night of the *Golden Venture*. Mr. Impoliteri, a hulking monster in a suit, needed only Frankenstein bolts in his neck to complete him. Gary, a squat ghoul encased in hair gel, was his fitting sidekick. As for Rose, the woman they regularly abused, Tim guessed she was more like a pitiful fiend, a victim turned killer in delayed self-defense. At least that's what Tim had convinced himself of while mostly avoiding Rose and the incident all these nine years since.

But now, clearing the end of the shrub, Tim suddenly views her anew, that is, soberly. The way she's pushing her pocketbook on Bibi recalls the gun she forced into the Chinese man's hands. Difference is that dude had croaked and couldn't object. Bibi is ultra-alive and vivid, holding five sharp, sparkly fingernails high in forceful protest. "This is not part of my job description!"

"And who pays your salary?"

"Maureen."

Curious why Rose wants so badly to give Bibi her purse (sending the woman to buy her more booze?), Tim reaches out and intercepts the bag, basketball-style, and, whoa, what a load! His arm drops from the weight of it.

Step One of the Twelve Steps: To admit he's powerless in the face of Rose's (apparently many) tiny bottles of Sambuca. They're sooo cute! Unluckily (luckily?), she claws Tim's arm, regains possession of the bag.

"You packing, Rose?" Tim jokes but the funny snags in his

throat as he considers—could she be? Tiny bottles of Sambuca are not *that* heavy.

A long smear of pink lipstick mars Rose's too-white smile. She wags her head, slowly, no.

"So, whatcha got in there, then?"

"A dead body."

Bibi sighs and plucks a tissue from the old lady's hoodie sleeve, then leans in to wipe at her stained teeth. Such an intimate gesture makes Tim want to bolt. Instead, he turns his face away and allows himself a good, hard scratch. It's a torment, this facial hair he's trying to grow—he can *feel* it growing. But the hope is to divert attention from his missing chunk of nose. So he is willing to suffer.

On the sand, June is now heading home. She holds the bottle the tide had returned to her up high, like a torch, away from Kenny Mole-Kacy. Kenny jumps, grabbing at it. That is, unless he's going for her bra strap, a black slash against her freckly shoulder bared by the weight of the red backpack.

"My bracelet!" Rose says, patting her wrist. "Where is it? Bibi? Give it back!"

Ignoring the accusation, the aide begins searching the grass.

"Give it back! Give it back!" Rose hollers again before turning her frustration on Tim. "What's with *you*, gawker? Go buy my fungicide."

"I can't," Tim says, regarding the pitiful tree. Fermenting fruit and dusty, curled leaves (which Sage calls "not-treasure") plop down on obliviously sleeping Blacky. "Without permission from the Glassmans."

*"Permission?"*

"It's not your house anymore."

Bibi accidentally (or not) backs into Tim, then lets loose with a waterfall of minty giggles.

Tim does nothing. It's a practice he's perfected for such instances when women come at him with their hair and nails, flexible limbs, dangling jewelry, *feelings*. (Men are generally bigger but much more contained.) Doing nothing is almost always effective. Case in point: Bibi quickly gives up the flirt and resumes combing the lawn for the missing bracelet. Tim can check out his dog in peace.

In his sleep, Blacky whimpers and cringes. If dogs share their owners' recurrent nightmares, Blacky's a lifeguard on that far-off July 4th when the big sandbar bursts and all the guards are swimming themselves numb saving body after body from the sudden, violent riptide. He sees the girl come up for air in the swirling water; he's got her; she's coughing but he's got her. Her thin limbs hold on. Then she's gone, replaced by a desperate old hairy guy, pulling him under. Below it's all green-gray mush. His eyes sting. He glimpses the last of the kid, her little heel being yanked by the current, away.

Tim's supposed to "start from empty," Mark No Name and his ilk all say—that is, put a lid on thoughts like these. Not only has Tim replayed the tragic moment too often for too long but he's also exhausted every alternative version: He slips from the man's grip, catches up to, and saves the girl. He hangs on to the man and saves the girl too. He loses them both, et cetera. In one scenario, Tim even drowns himself.

It's essential that he think of something else, anything else, that Blacky might be dreaming—about a pirate ship, say. The old dog sentenced to walk the plank for peeing against the shower house one time too many.

"Ahoy," Tim whispers to imaginary Ed, described to him by Sage as "brave, brown hair, my height." As an afterthought, Tim digs some coins from his pocket to drop onto the treasure pile. "Spend wisely."

"Are you talking to me?" Bibi wishes.

On the beach, June's now close enough for Tim to recognize the bottle in her hand as one of his own Fresca empties. A piece of loose-leaf floats within. Aha! A message in a bottle! He should have known a Glassman would never litter. Besides, how many of those notes did his own sorry young self chuck into the surf in vain, in vain. As the teenagers approach, Tim can hear Kenny trying to guess at June's note.

"'Dear Kenny, there are things I'd like you to do to me. Put it in, Kenny, my hero, put—'" He halts, losing color at the sight of the three adults. "Mr. Ray. Ladies." A slight, jittery bow.

June nods at them and hurries on toward the back door. Her thin, cold legs look purple where the veins show through translucent skin.

"How do you start an argument with a redhead?" Rose cracks. *"Say something!"*

The old lady's phlegmy chuckle gives Tim the chills. If Kenny heard her, he doesn't show it. He stares forlornly at the back door, hands shoved into his windbreaker pockets. The image of June and her legs lingers in the boy's mind, Tim

senses. In his own self is an odd, mounting pressure to protect June, protect all the Glassmans, from—what exactly he
can't say. Cursed Rockaway in general? Kenny Mole-Kacy
in particular? Rose or his own paranoia of Rose? Tim tells
himself he's being irrational. The old woman is not toting
her dead husband's gun. And even if she were, such an old
weapon wouldn't fire. And even if she were and it would, she
hasn't the strength, at her age, to lift it. Besides, the heavy
thing in her white pocketbook could be anything: Six pounds
of espresso. Hand weights to combat osteoporosis. Gold!
Rose won't show it to him simply because she's a mean, stubborn, mistrustful crone. And that's all.

"Okay, then!" So how come Tim can't stop recalling the
weapon? Small, gray, pitted barrel, wooden handle. If something should happen to a Glassman...Rose must leave *now*.
To that end, he offers a "special ride" in his driver's ed car.

"Get out!" Bibi pushes on his chest. "You're a firefighter
*and* a teacher? Get out!"

"Ex-fire—"

"He's a drunken bum and a drunken bum." Rose snorts.
"I wouldn't get in his car for all the tea in China." Then she
dons her sweatshirt hood, transforming herself into ET with
lipstick. "A guy named Timmy walks into a bar! *Ouch!*"

"Sticks and stones," Mark keeps advising, a phrase only
slightly less moronic than "the luck of the Irish." Words can
fucking harm you! The words *I know Rose Impoliteri murdered
her son* could put her in prison. Well, could *have*. To begin
only now to sort out why he failed to say them is like hauling out some rusty-wheeled thing from the garage and trying

to make it go. Words not said also suck. Love means *having* to say you're sorry. A lot. All the time. Which Alicia, his ex-wife, failed to do, ever.

Soon the sun will begin to lower and smear into its slot behind the water. The widows will be expecting him. Denise McClary, who needs—what does she need again? The power to sew new sock-monkey husbands? Faith? Screens? To stop saying, "I shouldn't be laughing," every time she laughs.

And Trish, with the death wish, en route to Afghanistan. She'll need someone to mind her four cats while deployed.

Only Peg needs something from Tim that Tim needs back, but it seems wrong to need it. In survivalist mode, Peg asks for sex in the same tone in which she requests carbon filters or, now, respirator masks small enough to fit her two kids. That's another one for Step Four. Saying yes to her. Saying no to her.

Step Four of the Twelve Steps: To make a searching and fearless inventory into the morality of screwing your best friend's widow. Kind of biblical, Tim thinks, by way of shaky justification.

Then, spurred on by the image of Peg's ass in her snug park ranger uniform, Tim suggests a car service. Hell, if Rose won't go on her own or let him drive, he'll spring for a limo.

But Rose just stares at her cherry tree, dry, round, brown doll eyes and wrinkled silly mouth wide.

"Damn," Bibi says. "You are spooky."

∽

In the kitchen, Sue grins by the Shabbat candles. Sy's just handed her a matchbook from a place called Topless Tony's. "So you're going to strippers now?"

The old man shrugs, no apologies, a desiccated string bean wearing the same gray sweatpants and black leather vest he's had on since his wife died. For some reason, Dan's chosen today to notice.

"This is what he wore to meet our new suppliers. Three strangers flew in from Tianjin to meet him in *this*."

To Sue's mind, Sy's home-dyed hair is the bigger problem. There are stains, black stains, on the back of the man's neck. And Dan's distress merely animates Sy. He paces the worn linoleum, taunting. "Did I embarrass little Danny in front of the Chinamen? Did I forget to kiss the Asian ass? Why should I care! It's *your* business now."

"It's a disorganized mess is what it is. I should fire you."

"Like you have the guts. It's high time those people learn what it means to live in a free country. I can wear my jockstrap to the meeting if I—"

"That's what you think it means to live in a free country?"

"Free expression, free speech—"

"And the right to bear arms." Dan moans, holding a kitchen knife to his own throat. When no one protests his suicide, he turns back to maniacally stirring the gravy. The shit-brown sauce pocks the tiled backsplash.

No wonder not even the doctor will answer his calls. Dan stands up to his father over work attire but ignores misogyny, mind games, questionable ethics. Finally, he's been given the business, and nothing, not one thing, has changed. According to his mother, Dan was seven when he picked his first lock. He's a natural. Whereas Sy learned the trade only after he married the boss's daughter. (Eventually taking over and renaming Reliable Locksmith after himself.) Those Chinese suppliers have to know it's the polite guy in the clean clothes to whom they should listen and not egomaniac Sy with his Mets tie and bialy breath.

"You married into what I deserve, now you deserve what you married," Dan once said to Sue at the height of a fight. The sentence lingers in her head like a good country-music lyric. Words so plain, they fool you into thinking they make sense. But the entitlement piece, she gets, truly. They don't *deserve* a thing.

"What about the right to eat?" June asks, roaming around, shaking sand from her hair. Living in Rockaway requires that you accept a certain amount of beach on your body, underfoot, in your bed.

"Religious freedom first," Sue says, striking a match. Up pops the image of the backyard on fire. Rose has fallen asleep and dropped her cigar while Bibi slinks off with Tim. That's ridiculous. Rose loves her house too much, so much she won't leave. Sue actually asked a ninety-year-old woman to leave. Surely that has to be a spiritual low even for a superficial convert. Instead of feeling remorse, Sue muses about ousting Sy along with the women.

"People! People!" her father-in-law calls, meaning Sue. "Is it asking too much to get the candles lit before the first pitch? Do the words *subway series* mean anything?"

"No," June says, though Dan's radio has been hyping it all

week. Mets versus Yankees. Clemens versus Piazza. The first time the two will meet since Roger threw a 98-mile-an-hour fastball into Mike's helmet.

Sue's hand shakes, lighting the candle. She mentally replays *Shabbat Prayers Made Easy,* using the tick of Estelle's avocado-shaped kitchen timer as a metronome. Sy has moved in with the entirety of his Brooklyn kitchen. His belongings add a bright note to Rose's scarred countertops and hanging rusty pots, but it's a grace note at best. It's Sue who will have to sort through all of it—the lifetime's worth of things Sy brought with him, the other lifetime's worth of things Rose left behind.

That is, *if* Rose left them. Now that she's back "home," who knows? To Sue and Dan, fleeing their own possibly contaminated possessions, the furnished house had seemed like a godsend, its many stuffed drawers and closets like a series of time capsules awaiting discovery. Ha! Sue's sigh contains enough worry to blow the candles out.

"Make a wish!" Sage says, hopping past her en route to June. Once at her sister's side, she pogos in place, asking, "What's a stripper, Junie? Junie? What's a stripper?" Seated at the table, June gazes through the screen overlooking the driveway and the Mole-Kacy garage. A scruffy blond kid is banging his skateboard on Kenny's popular basement window. "Yo, Ken Doll. Open up!" Everything about the Mole-Kacys is amplified, even their guests. Sy calls them the Yellers.

"What's going on over there with the Yellers?"

Kenny deals Cipro, June informs him matter-of-factly. For anthrax. Given the current level of hysteria, it seems plausible. Letters containing spores have already killed five people and infected seventeen others. The antidote is in short supply. Not to mention Kenny's father is the kind of doctor who offers to *bring over* pills for Dan's migraine.

"That little Poindexter, a dealer?" Dan's having trouble believing it. He strolls over with his wooden spoon to check out the scene for himself. "Oh, I see, yeah. That is definitely a buy in progress. But Cipro?"

June offers to score them some. "I can probably get a discount."

"He does like you." Sue's noticed. "From day one." On day one, Kenny shot June with a BB right in the butt! Not that Sue knows this firsthand. She overheard June bawling on the phone to her best friend, Jake Leibowitz. "It hurts to sit! What if there's, like, a piece of BB still in there?" And no fucking way would she be telling her parents. "Don't be dense, Jake! What if I still want to hang out with him?"

June claps a mosquito dead on her thigh, examines the resulting smear. Sue figures this is in lieu of smacking her pesky sister.

"What's a stripper, June? Junie? June?"

"Someone who takes their clothes off for cash, okay? Shut up."

"Treasure cash?" Sage can't believe her good fortune. She quickly shoves the ketchup bottle between her knees, yanks off her purple sundress, and stands, palms raised, waiting for the easy pay. You can see the slight sunburn where her clothes weren't—fluffy cheeks, arms, shins, and the tops of her small flat feet. "June? Junie?"

"Ask Grandpa," June says.

"Grandpa's busy," says Sy, wresting his nine-inch TV from a cardboard box marked KITCHEN MISC.

"Radio *and* TV?" Sue whines. Dan's trusty transistor has been murmuring on the counter this whole time.

Sy knocks on his liver-spotted forehead. "Call me superstitious but I'm gonna catch every second of this series come hell or high water."

"Hell *is* high water," Dan points out, "in Rockaway." And to Sage: "C'mon, babe, get dressed."

Sage shakes her unraveling pigtails and holds out a palm. "Money, please?"

Candles, prayer, *baruch atah*. Sue wills herself to focus. All those Friday nights when Dan's mother, Estelle, performed the ritual—where had Sue's attention been? She'd like to say it had been on music—Stravinsky's genius use of the bassoon, the autobiographical opera she planned to write someday, or even the slow progress of the concert band she directed at M.S. 250. But if she's honest, back then, as now, her mind was probably on dessert. The warm, gooey Godiva inside Estelle's architectural meringues; honey-cardamom apple cake, so light; butterfly-shaped crisps that dissolved on your tongue in a sweet, lemony mist.

Perhaps if Sue herself had baked, the prayer would come back to her. She'd done her best to replicate her mother-in-law's Sabbath table—silver candlesticks and kiddush cup, bone china, a braided challah, which she had to cross a bridge to find, under a square of heirloom velvet. But everyone refused to eat in the "haunted" dining room, and

Estelle's lace cloth, too big for the kitchen table, is puddled on the floor. Without owner or context, her mother-in-law's possessions are fast draining luster. Estelle's decorative whisk broom is nearly indistinguishable from Rose's actual whisk broom. Her collectible tins blend a little too well with the rusty cans stamped with expiration dates going back to the 1960s. What were stylish antiques in the Glassmans' Willow Place brownstone—the leather trunk, the china doll, the barber pole—have here all been subsumed by and demoted to clutter.

On the open shelves, Rose has left chipped service for twenty, a glass for every beverage from malted to shot. In the cabinets, all manner of platters and pans are crammed in with molds, whisks, funnels, and skewers. Peering into a coffinlike freezer filled with mysterious cuts of meat, June swears she sees a pinkie. Can she please be excused?

"No," Sue says, loudly enough to drown out Dan's "Yes."

Only the silverware is conspicuously absent. Sneaky Maureen must have decamped with it, just as Sy sold Estelle's set before moving.

"Oh, let him do it, the old miser," Sue had said when Dan complained. "He gave you his entire business."

"And that's somehow my fault? You're saying it's *my* fault?"

"I'm saying let him sell the damn silver. Who cares?"

Dan cares for the same reasons he's crouched in front of Sage. Because silver looks more proper than stainless; clothes more proper than nudity. Because a boy is what you *should* want to get after two girls. Or so Sue supposes Dan

79

thinks. Dan holds the miniature garment by the shoulders, jostling the phantom child inside. "No one gets paid for being naked here. Sage. Put this on!" Then to offset a sternness even he must realize is out of character, he adds, "Put this on and I'll give you a quarter, sweetie."

"No!"

"What about Ed?" June butts in, clearly out of boredom. "Is Ed wearing anything?"

"Brown hair."

Ed too came with the house.

"Well, maybe Ed will light the candles," Sy grouches. Though free of its box, his TV is still in need of a working outlet. "Or how about you, Dan? You're looking rather femmy over there by the stove."

Dan's shoulders heave but, as usual, it's Sue who reacts. "Did you honestly think I'd start cooking just because I agreed to convert?"

"Worth a try." With the heavy TV under his arm, Sy sets out across the room.

June says, "Don't worry, Sue. No one wants your food."

As if in response, the back door lets out its rusty C-minor chord and Bibi calls, "Hello? Hello? What's cooking, Mommy?" Then there's the creak and hum of the wheelchair traveling over the dining-room tile.

Sue quickly lifts Sage into her arms. "We're going for a ride. Where are the car keys?"

"*Now?*" Dan asks.

Sage invites Ed to come too.

Sue: "We need milk."

"*Now?*"

June's on her feet. "Can I drive? For practice? I'm in driver's ed as of tomorrow so—"

"I don't know about that."

"No. I *am*. Dad said—"

"Driving? On Shabbat?" Sy heaves in disapproval. As if *he's* so devout! Lighting the candles two hours before sunset. "We need milk."

Sy regards Sue from his crooked height, head to toe, and, in the dismissive tone he's perfected over years as the boss, says, "Well, I suppose you could use the walk, pudge."

June dives to the floor, scooping her backpack (the egg) to safety ahead of Sue's temper. Sue is tamping the feelings down, down. The blob of rage settles in her sinuses, blurring the room, which now includes Rose, dozing, and Bibi, tilting her hat of hair leftward. "Feeling a little hormonal, Mommy?"

That's it. Even Dan understands that Sue must go. He extracts the car keys (and a fifty) from his khakis and places them, somberly, in her open palms. Then, over her own objection, Sue tosses them to June.

⌒

Parents aren't supposed to mind about being liked. "I can't be your friend *and* your mother," Sue's own mom, a divorced linguistics professor, had too often said. But their entire relationship has now boiled down to seeing each other for Christmas, every other Thanksgiving, and the rare NYU-area lunch. So fuck that—Sue's minding. If this means letting June drive with her forearms down 116th Street, well...Rockaway's main commercial strip is already like an outer-borough version of the Pirates of the Caribbean ride. Even a teenager can see you have to slow down or risk hitting something.

Grizzly, bug-eyed heads pop out from SROs and Irish bars, sunbathers whoop and weave toward the A train, minivans loop the block as if on a track, their back windows open for panting retrievers, or closed, kids' faces smushed against the glass. A tan panhandler sporting a puka-shell necklace tries to clean their windshield with his filthy Corona towel. The show has Sage, in the backseat, clapping, and Sue begins to sing.

"'Oh-ho-ho, a pirate's life for me'! And Ed!" She's tickled by her own analogy. And though they don't actually need milk, who can resist a shop with the preggo-friendly name of Pickles 'n' Pies? "That's for us! We're stopping!" Raspberry rhubarb for Sue and, while they're here, chocolate chips, more Fig Newtons. Chocolate pudding.

After that they really don't require anything but to suck in the warm, sugary dusk streaming through the Camry's four open windows. Sue was silly to worry. June's doing fine. Oh, to be sixteen again and know everything. When every sentence starts with *I*.

"I feel like I'm in a parade." Sue smiles as they exit down the peninsula's main drag, Rockaway Beach Boulevard. American flags festoon the median, the windows of homes, the street lamps and tree fences. "I feel like waving."

"You having some kind of glucose rush?" June asks, breaking the spell. "What number cookie is that for you to-day, Suzanne?"

Deflated, Sue passes her half-eaten snack to Sage. Lashed to her car seat, the kid's busy lecturing Ed on Miss Katy's preschool dos and don'ts. "Friends and ketchup *do* stay in the cubby." Sage's magenta Barbie underpants are already coated with crumbs but she happily accepts the chocolate chip. When it refuses to balance on the Heinz bottle, she tries it on her nose, the top of her head, and so on, until it's resting beneath the driver's seat. (Six months later, when Sue finds it there, it will, alarmingly, still be as soft as today.)

But for now, Sue can't help holding the waxy bakery bag close to her face, inhaling. June's confirmed what Sy said — *pudge.* She's a cow; it's established. Delusional of her to think she'd be able to drive even five blocks without being re-minded of that old man! After all, it was Sy who leased them this car (so Dan could be his driver). Sy who had the dream of living in Rockaway (near ocean, Shea, and his best friend, Bob Baum). It seems to Sue that Sy will have to die for Sue to get her husband back (if she ever truly had him). But what kind of person thinks that? Sue is waiting for her father-in-law to die.

"Hands at ten and two, please," she reminds June. "Safety."

"You're not my driver's ed teacher."

"Hands at ten and two."

"What you are is..." June glances at the place on Sue's dress where the fabric *pop-pop*s from the baby's rhythmic kick. (This is what it must feel like to be possessed.) "You're a professional breeder."

"June!" Sue covers her belly reflexively. "Was that necessary?"

"Um...was it *necessary* to have a third kid because you couldn't think what else to do?"

"Oh, fuck you!" Shit! How could Sue say that? "I can't believe I just said that."

Sue had quit teaching when they moved, vowing to finally compose *StuyTown*, her opera about growing up in Peter Cooper Village with its twelve playgrounds and encircling gangs. That Sue has so far written only half of one aria really makes June's comment sting. Still, you don't say *fuck you* to a kid, *your* kid, ever. "I am so, so sorry."

June shrugs her narrow shoulders. Huge tits like Sue's, poor thing. Soon the backaches will start. Is she unfazed or numb? Hard to read. At sixteen, she's nothing like the earnest pothead Sue had been. Nor was she ever like any of Sue's Upper West Side music students—uncertain but diligent girls with blow-dried hair, mouths crowded with braces; greasy boys sucking on reeds, dreaming of blow jobs. At sixteen, June seems more like a twenty-five-year-old genius who just happened to find herself in jail.

"Red light," Sue says as the car bucks to a halt.

"Ed threw up in his mouth," Sage complains.

Across the street, St. Francis de Sales sits on the corner with its sweet, yellow pentagonal face. Sue blinks at the silver cross atop the roof peak. At this distance it appears delicate enough to wear around your neck on a chain. Not that she's ever worn one. (Her parents were lapsed WASPs, academics. The closest they had ever come to belief was a stint of proselytizing for Esperanto in the '70s.) So why does the gory, concrete symbol resonate with Sue more than an abstract Jewish star? To review: There's Sue's favorite cousin, Dale, who became a pastor after gambling away his wife's inheritance on fantasy sports. There's her passion for chocolate Easter eggs nestled in bright green plastic grass. There's tinsel—the word alone fills her with a shivery gladness. And the clean smell of evergreen. After that? Nothing.

"I'm not having a bar mitzvah," June says, following Sue's gaze to the church. "Just to say." Her aggrieved green eyes, ringed in liner, keep reminding Sue of two tiny flat tires.

"*Bat* mitzvah."

"Well, I'm not. Did Jesus?"

"What?"

"Have a bat mitzvah?"

"*Bar* mitzvah. No."

"You just said *bat!* Stop changing everything!"

"I'm—"

"If I didn't have one when Grandma nagged me for two years straight, I'm not about—"

"You loved Jake Leibowitz's bar mitzvah," Sue reminds her. At the ice-skating-themed affair, it snowed indoors and they all got chocolate trophies. "You went on about it endlessly."

"If you say so."

"You get chocolate," Sage mimics, bribing Ed. "Stay in the cubby like Miss Katy says and you get chocolate. And presents."

June turns to squint out Sue's window and on through the church schoolyard chain link. This is where they brought the bodies after the plane crash, said Sheila Kacy from next door. At the moment, the space is occupied by four middle-aged guys shooting hoops.

"They look like Tim's friends," June observes dreamily. "Do you see him?"

Sue laughs. "Like he ever leaves his backyard."

"He leaves! He leaves to surf, fish, grocery-shop, teach driver's ed! What *did* he say about me again?"

"That there's room in his Saturday class. But I'm not sure I feel comfortable —"

"That's all he said? There's room?"

A three-pointer crashes through the rusty, netless basket. "That's what I'm talking about!" says the shooter's teammate. The two run at each other, smash chests, then loudly regret it.

Green light. As the car leaps into action, a round fetal part — skull? heel? butt? — presses on Sue's bladder.

"I told you, Ed. Miss Katy said —"

"Tim asked for me personally?"

"I don't know!"

"Can't you just say yes?" June hisses from the gap between her front teeth. "Can't you *ever* make me feel good?"

"Miss Katy's dos and don'ts —"

"Screw Miss Katy!" June accelerates. "Screw that controlling bitch!"

Actually, Dan's admitted to having this very daydream while watching the young teacher's pretty British tongue poke out from her thick wet lips to bat around a juice-box straw.

Dan loves reporting these reveries, and no wonder—they're inspired. After nineteen years he still excels at this, their secret game. In return, Sue often feels compelled to fictionalize. Faking a fantasy is way harder than faking an orgasm but sometimes easier than telling the truth: ice cream man.

"Slow down, please."

As June veers onto their dead-end street; one wheel rides up and over the curb. Sue stomps on an invisible brake. The red backpack slides off the seat, onto the floor.

"You know you look like a total spaz, Ma?"

All right, Sue deserves this. For the *fuck you*. She deserves way worse. June's right. She's too old and nuts to be having a third child. There *was* midlife panic in her decision to keep the baby. Parenting has many downsides but it rarely feels like a waste of time. She stares into the red backpack, which the commotion has left partially unzipped. There's egg number 3 (swathed in maxipads), a wad of gum-encased coins, a Fresca bottle.

"Please slow down, please," Sue repeats, trying to sound as nice as possible. "You don't want to kill someone."

June laughs. "There you're wrong. I'm gunning for a Mole-Kacy, or a Yeller, as Grandpa would say."

Through the open window, they can indeed hear yelling, a lot, followed by gunshots, more yelling, more gunshots. "Kenneth! Stop that!" "Stop that right now!" The Mole-Kacy parents stand between the morning glory–festooned pillars of their front porch. Dr. Mole, the bald dad, wears his white medical coat juxtaposed with tight cutoff jeans. Ms. Kacy, the taller and platinum-haired mom, sports a maroon-pantsuit-and-pumps ensemble. Though divorced, the two apparently still live and yell together. "Kenneth? Are you listening?" "Cut that the hell out!"

Ignoring them, Kenny continues to pump BBs into the DEAD-END STREET sign. Only when he sees June behind the wheel does he drop the air rifle and salute.

"Can we move again?" June asks, but the reckless way she swings into the driveway is obviously for Kenny's benefit. She shows off further by leaning on the horn to blast away his younger sibs.

Like Blacky and Tim, the Mole-Kacy boys are magnetized to the Glassmans' home. When not ringing the bell and running, they're using the property for a beach shortcut or falling (up and down the stoop, over the flowerpots, off their bikes), wailing, "I'm gonna sue! I'm gonna sue your daddy!" at poor confused Sage, who keeps thinking they're referring to her mother, Sue.

Tonight they've found a new game—dancing on the roof of Bibi's Ford Fiesta.

"They're not still here?" Sue moans, hauling herself out of the car. "They're still here?"

The boys scatter, not understanding that it's Rose Sue wants gone or why their new neighbor has tears in her eyes. "They're still here?"

"Who's that?" one of Tim's friends yowls from the other side of the hedge. Sue immediately ducks. Those blockheads are back again? They just left! "Must be the ghost of Gary Imp!" A coughing fit drowns out the rest of his comments, something about "homeland insecurity."

Swell

Behind Sue, June also gets low, listening. Sage crouches behind June. The three of them creep the remaining length of the driveway, beyond the garage and stinky shower house, to the massive rhododendron.

"We shouldn't eavesdrop," Sue whispers and June agrees and they move a little closer.

$\sim$

"I always despised that *paisano* Gary Imp," Bean confesses between more hacking. "Remember when he beat up Barry Lowenstein's dad in the schoolyard? The guy comes to—"

"Let Tim talk!" Chris D. scolds. To Tim's amazement, his friends (friends?) are really paying attention. Even the Mets game they fussed to watch via two extension cords has been turned low. It's like the old days, before Tim got too drunk to be coherent. That is, just the right amount drunk, when he could hold a whole bar full of people rapt.

"Listening to you yak about flowers is worse than listening to my wife tell me one of her dreams," Chris D. said just this morning. But for some reason, he's all ears when it comes to Rose and her aide. First they show up unannounced to visit the old lady's cremated relatives. Next, they won't leave. Finally, they've weaseled their way into the house.

You can see them now, plain as death, across the hedge in the lit square of the Impol—no, Glassman—kitchen. Bibi's curves get snaky as she cracks up at...another of the old lady's redhead jokes? Something more sinister? Either way, Tim "smells danger."

89

"I called it!" Chris D. hoots, twisting his wedding ring around and around his finger. "Didn't I call it? Bibi propositioned the Butterman!"

"You called it," Bean admits.

"Give us the deets!"

Tim's disappointed. "You're barking up the wrong tree."

"A lovely tree. Long, with real juicy —"

"Chris, peel your eyes off the aide for one sec? Now check out the grip Rose has on that bag."

"Vice! You think Bibi is fixing to clean Rose out?"

"No! Rose has got —"

"What?"

Tim's stuck. He can't mention the gun — duh! — without mentioning the murder, without... "Never mind. That old loon just annoys me."

But it's his friends (friends?) who are really annoying him. They aren't listening to Tim at all, Chris D. being too busy slobbering over Bibi, and Bean — well, hasn't Bean coughed here enough today? Tim will never seem sensible to the Glassmans with these clowns hanging around, so how will he be able to warn them that there's a deranged woman sitting in their kitchen? "I really need to get rid of Rose, pronto."

Chris D. grins. "Get Bibi all to yourself? Good move. How about we toss Rose into that bonfire?" This a reference to the latest teen rager on the beach. Nostalgically, they've decided to keep an eye on it rather than shutting it down. "The real deal would be even better. Come back to work and on the next five-alarm —"

"Lame try."

"Seriously, Butter, we need you. Peewee's weak mid-hose."

At mid-hose (Tim's station), you can feel the water pounding beneath your hands, through the line, through your thick gloves. Let go, and the rush of liquid or the hose itself can easily knock you flat. For Tim, that made it so hard not to let go.

"Eskimos push their old folks out to sea," Bean says and all three separately picture the wheelchair floating.

To erase this image, Tim throws in, "Poison." Earlier, Rose said the rhododendron fence was toxic *and* a laxative. "Death by diarrhea. But if you think that's freaky…"

Tim relates the strange way Rose referenced his mother wanting to keep the Impoliteris away, God knows why. "And God *must* know, since my mom manages to fit Him into every conversation." Praise Him, she'd probably say if asked about Rose now. Have charity. Vincent Impoliteri was not a kind husband. But it's easy to be loving when you no longer live next door. The most gleeful Tim had ever seen his mom was one night long ago when they watched Rose drag her table leaves down to the sand to burn. "Hell is a lake of fire," his mother said, and she laughed. She could not stop laughing.

Competitive gardening was the one bond between the two women. That is, Rose bragged her garden was superior, and his mom agreed. The meek shall inherit. "But come to think of it," Tim says, "they did have an uncanny lot in common. Same church, same lawn, one son apiece."

On the word *son*, everyone gets quiet, thinking back to Peg's kid during tonight's widow visits. Ryan's booger-smeared face when he came down from his nap looked so much like his father's that Peg herself said, "His son, his twin," meaning, of course, Chowder.

"Why are they called twins anyway?" the boy had asked. "If one of the towers is bigger?"

"*Were* they called towers, ditwit," said the older sister, Bridget, obviously sick of the topic. She flung her mom's park ranger hat.

Peg reached out and easily caught the Stetson. (All-state in softball and basketball *and* swimming.) She was pissed at the guys for showing up without the respirator masks she'd requested *twice*. Like, what's so difficult? She already had to score the Cipro for anthrax from some high-school kid. "You guys are beyond pathetic."

Which is when Tim clutched her unwashed blondish ponytail. Told her: Cut the shit. Time to stop playing survivalist and hold the long-delayed paddle-out for her dead husband. Of course, Chowder had already had a church memorial. But a lost surfer is owed a floating ceremony as well. Chowder would bust Tim's balls if he knew how long they'd lagged. "This weekend," Tim hissed into Peg's ear. "Say you'll do it this weekend."

"Let go of her!" Bean said, stumbling on a box of dehydrated apples en route to rescue Peg. "Let her be! She's busy preparing for what's next."

"She's busy acting mental!" Tim shouted, though he was clearly the one who was acting, acting like he wasn't falling for her, a girl he'd known since nursery school! "What's next should be Chowder's paddle-out. It's been nine fucking months!"

"Let her go," Bean repeated.

And all the while, Peg was breathing into Tim's neck. "No, don't let go. I like it. Harder."

It's terrifying how sexy grief makes her. Peg now seems an altogether different tomboy from the one he'd always known. Only her kids—the fact of them—keep him halfway contained.

And even more frightening is that Tim can't recall the last time he saw Chowder. No surprise, Mark No Name blames substances. Whole swatches of memory evaporated along with the stale bong water. Nothing but reek left. Could this also be why Tim had never once considered the strangely hostile dynamic between Rose and his mom?

"Hell, no." Bean coughs, standing up from his Adirondack chair—to exit? Tim can only hope. "You were just too busy obsessing. Bugs and Alex, it used to be. Now it's flowers, the Glassmans, and Peg. Same diff. Face it, Butter, you're OCD-fucking-oblivious!"

This had the sickening sound of truth to it. "Oblivious?"

"That you need to come back to work, man."

*Bugs still interest me*, Tim's about to say when he spots June and her red backpack slipping through the beach door. Minutes later, Kenny Mole-Kacy materializes, following. "Maybe it's time to break up that party," Tim says instead.

Rose is turning him into a busybody neighbor, the kind of butt-sniffer he could never bear. Another look into the Glassman kitchen window reveals Sue entering the room from the hall. She freezes, a bakery bag clutched to her chest. In the foreground, at the table, Rose, with a napkin draped over her hair, bends over the Sabbath candles. Two candles, Tim thinks longingly, like two melting towers, each week resurrected anew.

⌒

Rose knows all the words. *Baruch atah Adonai*…She knows to cover her head and the circling motion to make with your palms. Doing so, her hands tremble, as if she's resisting an urge to pass through the flame. Even more jolting to Sue is that Dan's the one on his knees by the wheelchair holding up the candles for her. The prayer competes with Sy's little TV, now propped up on the meat freezer; bottom of the third, no score, man on first. Sy has the whole braided challah held vertically between his hands. His sepia eyes dart from game to Rose and back again. The old woman seems to know all those words too. "Swing and a miss!" "Stuck it in his ear!" Spaghetti has materialized on the table, some kind of olive sauce in a bowl unfamiliar to Sue. Also, a box of assorted Band-Aids. Between Sage and the empty space for Ed sits Bibi, probing a blister on her heel with a car key. In the face of this strange tableau, Sue can see only one option. Sing. Sing the prayer.

Automatically, this relaxes her. Her shoulders drop; her spine aligns. It's a trick she discovered early on to block out her warring parents. Sing in bed, in the bathtub, out in the hall when necessary. And the prayer melody's in her head, after all! Sue always gets a melody! The rush of air pressing up from her diaphragm even calms the baby. She feels as if she's breathing sound. When it's over, she's left with a familiar raw ache, like hunger.

"*Ah-mein,*" Sy says, picking up the kiddush cup.

Then the blessing over the wine, over the bread, every word of which Rose knows too. Turns out she was a Friday-night regular at the home of her Jewish friends the Baums until Bob Baum stabbed her "in the neck." Saying his name, Rose's lips contort as if tasting something heinous.

"Whoa, back up," Sue says. "*Bob* Baum? Is that *our* Bob Baum?" Sy's business associate/golf buddy/best friend. It has to be. Bob lives only a few blocks over. It was he who first told Sy about the house.

"Small world." Sy nods at the screen. "Let's eat."

Dan rushes to the oven to remove a pan of sliced brisket he's been warming. The room fills with the enticing and repulsive smell of beef.

"I know what food is," Sage says. "Dead animals." But she eagerly holds out two plates.

"Bob and my daughter-in-law were in cahoots from the get-go," Rose insists. "They said the house was in dire need of repair, that it was hazardous, which I guess it was—" She scans the peeling walls of the corner room. "Is."

They told Rose not to worry, Maureen and Bob did. Her move to Forest Hills was temporary. For her safety. They'd take care of *everything.* All she had to do was sign. On "sign," Rose slaps the arm of her chair too hard and then grasps her elbow, wincing. "You see what they did there? I thought I was signing a renovations contract! But they sold my house! You see?"

Sue begins to eat, to gobble, really. Unlike Dan, fluttering sympathetically around Rose, Sue doesn't automatically buy this sob story. Unlike Bibi, rolling her eyes, Sue doesn't immediately discount it. She just chews and swallows, calculating the myriad of possibilities and keeping a steady eye on Sy.

"The way they treat us old people..." Sy tsks, still gazing at the screen.

"You think I'm some kind of dummy, Glassman?"

Sy pats Rose's veiny hand with his own. "Oh, no, no."

"Your pal Bob tips you off to a beach house and you never wonder why it's such a steal?"

"A fixer-upper. You said yourself—"

"A swindle and you knew it."

"With all due respect," Sy says, at last turning to Rose. "The place had a certain reputation." It's the Murder House, in other words, a detail Sy neglected to tell Dan and Sue.

"All my stuff's here," Rose says, surveying the jam-packed kitchen. "Why would I leave all my stuff if I knew I was moving?"

Sue had simply assumed there was no room for Rose's things in assisted living. But Sy's leg is jiggling. Sue watches Rose watch Sy's leg jiggling. "So Bob never mentioned me, then?" Rose keeps on. But the fire's gone. She sounds depressed.

Sy turns the TV volume down. Clearly it's dawned on him that he's got to work a bit harder. "To be honest," he tells her, "I'm not sure. I mean, it's embarrassing but—my brain's still a bit foggy from the chemo."

Sue groans. She can't help it. Sy's last cancer treatment was in 1987.

"Cancer?" Rose asks, guardedly sympathetic.

"Bone," Sy whispers. "But I'd rather not...I think I need more noodles." He holds the bowl up to his nose. "What the hell is in this sauce, woman?" Really pouring it on. Wow. You can actually see Rose's face twitch from her effort to resist him. When Dan chimes in, calling the dish "magic," Rose is lost.

"I'll have you know, I made pasta six days a week for forty years."

"And on the seventh day?" Sy prompts.

Bibi shifts in her seat, bracing herself for the familiar litany. "On a Sunday" — the aide mouths along with Rose's words — "on a Sunday, I'd serve the antipasti *and* the pasta, two meats, a vegetable side, salad, dessert —"

"Oh, now you're making my stomach growl," Sy says, theatrically dumping the rest of the spaghetti onto his plate. By this point, it's too much bullshit even for Bibi. Bouncing the car keys in her palm, she tells Rose, "Time to go home."

"I am home."

"C'mon, Rosie. You know that's not right."

So Bibi was only humoring Rose with her introduction "The lady's come home." Bibi uses the same singsong voice for both Sage and Rose. "If we don't go now, you'll miss your program. You don't want to miss your program."

*Survivor*? *CSI: Miami*? Kudos to whatever TV show compels Rose to give in; she gives in; she'll go! *If* the Glassmans promise to fix up her father's garden.

"Done!" Sy claps. "On it! Rose, I owe you a tremendous apology. Had I known the yard was in such disarray...Of course, in my condition, I don't get out much."

Sy in action. Sue's so disgusted, she momentarily forgets

that the uninvited guests are finally leaving. Rose crosses her arms imperiously as she's wheeled from the room. Ever the gentleman, Dan assists.

On TV, masses of gulls mill about the outfield, so many they've paused the game to try and figure out what to do. Laughing gulls, the announcer explains. "They're shooting them at Kennedy airport. Maybe the commissioner —"

"What's he talking about?"

"They get sucked into the plane engines," Sy tells her. "It's not safe."

"You knew about this?"

"It's all over the media."

Inexplicably, Sue begins to weep.

Alarmed, Sage runs and hugs her. "Don't worry, Mommy; it's just a dream."

"You're not actually blubbering over those birds?" Sy asks.

"I don't know," Sue says. She really doesn't.

"Stupid birds, shoo!" Sy says.

"Shoo! Shoo!" Sage mimics.

Sue thinks of the blessing over the children. No one remembered to say it, though it had been Estelle's favorite Shabbat ritual. Still leaking tears, Sue places her palm on her daughter's warm head. Baby Sage. Any day now she'll be usurped. June still hasn't forgiven them for having a second kid. On some level, she never will. As only children who yearned for siblings, Sue and Dan were late to understand. Onlys have their own pressures — *Just don't die on us, we have no backup* — but it seems easier than a lifetime of jockeying for position.

"What's the blessing over the children again? Sy?"

"Not now." He wiggles his fork at the birds on TV.

"Just tell me —"

"Shoo!"

Now Sue's extra-determined. Still holding on to Sage, she twists her bulk to block the screen.

"What are you doing? Move!"

"Mommy —"

"Tell me the blessing!"

"Later."

Sue snatches the end of Sy's fork. One shove and she could spear the tines right into his barrel chest. She's that furious.

"Mommy, let go —"

"You don't give a shit about any of this, do you, Sy? You just want to convert me to ... win!"

A grin percolates across Sy's grooved face as he considers the accusation, that sparkling word — *win*. Meanwhile, a TV commercial blares the "Star Spangled Banner." Buying motor oil is so patriotic.

"Mommy. You're hurting me!"

"My God." Sue's been pressing too hard on the poor kid's head. Parenting strike two (after the *fuck you*). "Sorry, Sage."

"And Ed."

"And Ed."

Sy's so entertained. "Before you say the prayer over the children," he says, laughing outright at Sue, "you might want to locate them all. Uh, *where's* June?"

☙

June's pretending it's a movie. It feels safer. She's *that* girl, the gawky redhead who drops her books but is secretly gorgeous behind glasses once hair products are applied. Maybe she's cool in her old school, the competitive Stuyvesant, but at Beach Channel High, she's still a yet-to-be-labeled problem. It's the kind of movie June and her best friend, Jake Leibowitz, prefer. Not too much thinking required. At the end, there's redemption. Or at least a makeover.

The movie opens here, with June standing on a dark, windy outer-borough beach. Acoustic guitar is omnisciently picked. She's about to throw a message in a bottle. *Not the good kind of bottle,* June wrote in her daily e-mail to Jake. *Not the kind sealed with a cork and black wax—prop budget? If only I knew how to skim a shell, I wouldn't even need a bottle. I don't even know what shell's best for skimming.*

The daily e-mail to Jake is in place of the daily phone call since June caught her mom eavesdropping. Thrice.

To think of shells as containers where animals once lived can really, really make you tired.

It's take number two zillion, so June's tired. It's not just shells; no one taught her, a girl, to throw anything. A wave rolls in (city-puddle gray), then folds and breaks. White froth carries the bottle back to her. June kicks the sand in frustration. The camera shot widens. A little ways down the beach, where the boardwalk starts, other teenagers sit by a bonfire. Does June care that she's not there with them? Her wistful expression leaves this open to interpretation.

And there's no need for the cheesy voice-over either. Just the fact that those kids can get a fire lit in this beach wind shows the difference between her and them, locals and new June. She'll bet every one of them can throw a bottle far out to sea, not to mention skip shells, body-surf, differentiate a surf clam from a razor clam. On their scratchy radio, P. Diddy is singing "'Yeah, c'mon. I need a, I want a...girl'"— further driving home the schism. None of them would ever have a best friend like Jake, a gay hockey player who speaks four languages (one of them his own invention).

June will have to break it to Jake soon. Their summer beach/movie plans are nixed. He is not what you'd call a believable character, not here in Rockaway, anyway. If he insists on a role, he'll have to hide miserably beneath a flannel shirt and board shorts. Then, depending on the focus-group feedback, the story will end with him drowning himself or meeting a merman and living happily ever after.

Again, June throws the bottle. Waits. Again, it returns. Throw. Wait. Return. It's like a game of fetch with Blacky, only no joy. If the script were to take a more allegorical route, June could *play* Blacky, fetching a Frisbee thrown by Tim, petted by him, good girl. Or misbehaving, jerked by her collar, a loving slap, bad, bad girl, naughty girl. Luckily, it's dark, the quarter moon as cloudy as her dead grandma's cataract. June removes her backpack and walks up a bit to place it on the dry sand. Maybe she'll throw better without having to worry about the egg. Maybe if she turns sideways, like boys do, and really concentrates on reaching her achy arm back.

"Boo!" Kenny Mole-Kacy pounces. His loud windbreaker rustles all around her for the second time today. He's her neighbor, at her bus stop, in her health class, and now he's touching his thumb to her cheek, saying he heard "cool news!" They'll also be in driver's ed together starting tomorrow. "Don't look so excited, June."

Actually, with his pimples and thinning hair patch erased in the dark, Kenny's sort of, well, not as hideous as usual. "You know," June says for something to say, "you shouldn't carry your egg like that. Loose like that in your pocket."

"Tell me about it. I already failed Health once, fall term."

They laugh for no reason.

"I'm surprised Tim let you in," Kenny says. "I mean, the class is half over. Regina and I are pretty advanced."

"I've driven a lot," June lies, tonight having been only her third time. "Who the fuck is Regina?"

"You'll see." Kenny reaches for the bottle. "Still can't get this thing to float?"

"I can...I just—I decided to change my message."

"Too derivative?"

"Time to dial back on that SAT prep, Kenneth."

He moves closer. His hair smells like burned wood, but how? June looks from him to the party and back again.

"Yeah, I was just over there making a delivery."

"Of Cipro? Why would they want—"

"Not Cipro."

"You deal pot too?"

Kenny squeezes his face as if pained. "Do you really think I'm that common?"

"Um." June doesn't know what to say. She doesn't know the difference. Dealing this or that; who cares? Here she had Kenny cast as the stock nerd character and now he's turning into someone with...layers. Plus, it seems to be getting warmer even though it's night. Her heartbeat synchronizes to the pulse of the lighthouse. Not really, but it's a nice line. Words matter. She bailed on what was Friday dinner and is now Shabbat. The lighthouse is named Ambrose. Kenny says it's called a bonfire from the days when they burned bones.

"*They* who?"

Abruptly the party radio stops, which jacks up the ocean volume. June has to lean in to hear his whispered reply. "I don't know, June. Let's go back to my garage lab and research."

"Think again, bad-dialogue man. You shot me with a BB from that garage window!"

An accident, Kenny claims. Or, alternatively, "That was my brother Ritchie." Kenny strokes her collarbone, smiling. "Did you just call me bad-dialogue man?"

"I have a boyfriend," June lies. Kenny's fingertips are surprisingly callused.

"Oh yeah? What's his name?"

"Jake." It's the first thing to pop into June's head. Luckily, Kenny can't see her best friend's Friday-night uniform — tuxedo shirt, skintight red jeans, glue-on rhinestone eyelashes.

June heaves the bottle once more, aiming for a small silvery puddle the moon is making. Once again, after a few bobs, it's riding the next wave in. They both dive for it, legs zingy with cold, tangling in the shallow, bubbled surf. June cannot let him get it. If it wound up at the party, if her message was passed around the fire for all those local girls to read —

Being popular means never having to say you're sorry.

Bottle in hand, June races up toward her backpack, but

her waterlogged Pumas are so slow. When she's halfway there, Kenny catches her skirt and they tumble. Cool sand molds to June's limbs. Her wet feet and shins are numb.

"Let's make Jake jealous," he says as she struggles unconvincingly beneath him. So he believes her fib? Perf! Knowing more than the antagonist makes the audience feel smart, ergo invested.

Kenny probes the gap between her front teeth with his tongue, says, "I expected you to taste like cinnamon." Whether this means she does or does not is unclear. *His* flavor is beer-and-barbecue-potato-chip-ish.

"Bite me!" A stray voice carries from the party. This gives June the idea to do just that, bite, then run. A much-needed bit of drama? But then a second, more commanding voice — Tim's? — shouts, "Listen up!" and she imagines being here with Tim instead of Kenny, underneath Tim and his big hero hands, her mouth on his Adam's apple, rashy with stubble.

"Vampires turn into redheads after death," that old lady at her house all day said.

"So that explains you." Kenny pulls out a pack of glow-in-the-dark condoms. He's working through a case of them, a gift from his dad for his perfect GPA. Well, almost perfect. Like he said, he has to repeat Health. Unzipping his pants, he mimics the horrible Queens accent of their teacher, Nurse Riva: "Leave a half inch of space at the end and slowly unro*lll* to the base of the *pea-nis*."

June pictures Nurse Riva's corpselike complexion, white as the chalk dust that smudges her vast polyester suit and settles into a fine sediment lining every surface from the

hot-pink plastic fallopian tubes to her stained GOD BLESS
AMERICA coffee cup.

In the back row, stoner types fake know-it-all boredom.
In the front, embarrassed innocents blush. In the middle, the
"immatour majority," as Nurse Riva calls June and Kenny's
ilk, disintegrate into silliness. "*I* wanted a zucchini." "Your
cuke's thicker." Then come giggle fits, vegetable duels, condom balloons.

June's giggling now as Kenny's hands push under her
skirt—short, navy, pleated. A hip look, back in her old neighborhood. But Kenny informs June "as a favor" that around
here, people confuse it for part of a Catholic-school uniform.
And that thought makes June too weary to move, though her
mouth says, "No, cut it out, stop."

"Don't say that." Kenny breathes heavily. "If you say that,
you'll be letting the terrorists win." He yanks aside her sandy
underwear, taking advantage of her laughing fit—that comment! She's rolling around, practically gasping. And before
she can either push him off or summon the fantasy of Tim
again, it's done. Too clumsy to hurt. Too quick to protest.
Over without the O(rgasm).

The essence of anticlimactic.

"I made a mess inside June-ie!" Kenny crows, scooping
up the bottle and chucking it jubilantly far, far into the sea.
There's that, at least. It's on its way. "I made a mess inside
June-ie!"

This reminds them both to check on their eggs.

❊   ❊   ❊

"What the fuck?" Kenny says, suddenly on his feet, pants zipped. A bulky shape totters toward them, calling June's name. "Is that—fuck! Is that your *mother?*"

In the dark, the globe of Sue's belly appears eerily detached from the rest of her. And there must be some new kind of special effects, because her voice seems like it's coming from her navel. "June? June? Are you here, June?"

"Go away," June shrieks, thankful no one can see her whole body blushing.

"Ah, you *are* here...why didn't you—oh, hello, Kenny."

The way Kenny bows and says, "Good evening," makes June go back to hating him. She already hates her mother, hunting her down in a way she'd never dare in Manhattan. Because? "You're a psycho! Go!"

"Aren't you hungry?" Mom asks. Behind her, a second shape moves toward them. God, not Dad too! No, Tim!

"Tim! For Chrissake! Are you following me?" Mom has the idiocy to object. "You are everywhere!"

Well, yeah! Of course! He's the protagonist! Come to rescue her from no-good dealer/player/nimrod Kenny Mole-Kacy. It's Mom who's in the way. Not even a plot-advancing minor part, just some fat extra, slowing down production.

"I was just, um, checking on that bonfire," Tim says, turning to look behind him. Oddly, the party seems to have gone the way of a Scout meeting. Ten or so kids now sit or lie on the sand, holding hands, doing what?

"Burning the bones," June says, turning to Kenny. Alas, the dark schemer has slipped into the night. She wonders if it's something bad like heroin or truth serum he's dealing. At least that virgin thing is over with.

"Looks nice," Mom says of the gathering. "Are you going?"

⌒

It's not just June who doesn't want Sue around. Sage also dismisses her. She wants Daddy. Only Daddy can put her and imaginary Ed to bed. "Only Daddy and Ed also love sparkles."

So Sue retreats into the dining room to sit with the cross at her back. Or the contour of the cross. Rose must have taken the object with her to assisted living, leaving the dark shape on the sun-bleached green wallpaper. Without turning around, Sue can see it there, burning, over the hideous marble sideboard. Meanwhile, from the table, Rabbi Larry's completed questionnaire stares.

*What do you know about Judaism?*

One God. Persecution. The Ten Commandments. Holiday basics.

The broken door is distracting. The wind blows it open, then partly shut, with a sound like someone tripping up stairs. Out there, the fire and a weak comma of a moon are the only lights.

*Why do you want to be a convert?*

Home ownership. (If she has to be a fraud, she'll at least be an honest one.)

Because I promised.

Love.

*Are you being pressured to become a Jew?*

Yes.

Her answers probably won't stun the rabbi. "Given our history," he said that first time they met, "we can't afford to be exclusive." Then he drove off to his Friday golf with Sy, Dan, and...Bob Baum. The rabbi had to remember this encounter. If the fact that she's Sy's daughter-in-law weren't enough, her red hair should have clinched it. Sue regularly has to pretend she recognizes people who remember her from "the hair."

She folds the paper and lays it atop her stack of books— Dan's bar mitzvah Bible, Midrash texts, *Jewish Conversion for Dummies*. Studying them has unexpectedly brought her pleasure but a competing impulse says to torch them in that beach fire. The hubris of men! She'll show them! If it's a Jew they want...

Sue gets to her feet to try and fasten the door, then sways, momentarily losing her footing. For a second, she actually forgot she was pregnant. Impossible. When did she last feel the baby move?

A starling unleashes a lengthy song—pure tones, assorted clicks, bits of melody, and even mimicry of the back door knocking open, banging shut. Sue thinks about how she'd score these sounds. Castanets, piccolo. A wooden stick attacking a timpani? Out on the lawn, there are no birds, but, dimly, she can make out other fluid forms. Blacky coming through the hedge, plants pushed around in breezes, Tim's friends taking off again. "Later, Butter." "Take it easy, man." They toss a—ball? Hat? Keys?—casually between them, gliding in the limber, uncomplicated way of boys, the boy Dan vainly craves. Vainly and in vain.

Sue prays for her unborn daughter to kick her.

TWO

# TODAY IS YESTERDAY
# TOMORROW

*Saturday, June 15, 2002*

NEVER MIND THAT an asteroid just missed hitting the planet. The radio report was cut short for "Breaking news: President Bush on the White House lawn urges Americans to exercise!"

"What kind of exercise?" Sue asks, completely missing Dan's point. When there is space junk zooming toward you, it's nice to have a heads-up. (Ditto rogue waves, hijacked planes, pandemics.) Dan wishes he had brought the radio out here onto the stoop. Sue said she only needed his help "for a sec" and now it's been at least fifteen minutes.

But someone needs to hold the instructions if she's going to hang the mezuzah properly. "Shoulder-high on the doorway." Whose shoulder? Hers. At the bottom of the upper third of the right doorpost. So-and-so inches from blah-blah. Let her just cut away some more ivy. The plant is enveloping the house like a net.

"Or maybe it's what's holding the place together," Dan says, still distracted by the idea of an asteroid big enough to destroy a major city yet small enough to avoid detection.

Sue suggests he make himself useful, so Dan adjusts his stance, shielding his bikini-clad wife from the sporadic parade of beachgoers, dog walkers, and haunted-house geeks who travel down this city street. Warm day; warm for June. Every head does a double take at the profile of the pale baby bump ballooning between the two halves of her swimsuit. Not sure whether to wave or swear at the rubberneckers, Dan alternates between both while Sue hacks away at the plant.

"That's a very good knife you're wrecking—is that...from the set Aunt Ruth gave us?" A wedding gift he still feels is too nice to use, almost two decades later.

"No," Sue says. "Not that I'd care." She despises Ruth (famously overheard saying "interfaith marriage is doing Hitler's work") and is indifferent to objects in general. "I found this one in a drawer." Perhaps the mezuzah is like a prophylactic charm meant to protect them from the next time Rose and Bibi appear—tomorrow? The day after? The day after that? Because they're back. And Sue is not happy.

At seven thirty, Dan heard the Ford Fiesta rumble into the driveway; everyone else was still asleep. First thing Monday, he planned to find a new doorbell (what was Sy thinking?), but first thing Monday is far away when you're listening to the digital "For He's a Jolly Good Fellow." Dan rushed outside to greet the pair to spare the sleeping people more of it. With all the sand in his bed, the shuffling in the walls, the birds in the ivy, and pre-party nerves, he'd been up for hours already. He'd shaved, made coffee, and was two items into his shopping list—ice, cheese...

Dan opened the door still holding the pen.

"Ready to sign up?" Bibi asked, standing before him like

a glam fortune-teller—dark hair swirled into her usual turban, full makeup, sheer mauve tunic, and harem pants. At the bottom of the stoop, Rose sat in her wheelchair, glaring up at the aide. Dan could see straight down through the no-color hair to her hot-pink scalp—*Like a baboon's butt* is what came to mind. Nonetheless, Rose's outfit killed. The highlight: an old red cowboy shirt whose white fringes matched her white pants, oversize white sunglasses, white pocketbook. "Aren't you looking smart today, Rose? I think you're getting younger."

You could study how the comment unfolded her, could see her posture improve, a flush rush to her cheeks, a gleam of teeth. "So far this is the oldest I've been!" Only Rose's round brown eyes messed with the good vibe, fixed unblinkingly on Bibi, a few menacing beats too long. "No beauty help from Sticky Fingers over here. First my bracelet, now my lipstick." Rose's dry, colorless mouth puckered. "Consider yourself warned."

Naturally, Bibi denied all charges. What would she want with Rose's bracelet or used cosmetics or any of the other ridiculous things she's been accused of stealing—a hunk of Gorgonzola, a cheap Chinese fan! This house! "Do you see me moving in here? Maybe if you'd stop spitting out your meds and put in your hearing aid, you wouldn't be so paranoid."

Determined to stay out of it, Dan gathered the rolled-up newspapers lying at his feet. Not the *Times* and the *Journal* (he had never got around to rerouting them) but the *Post* and the *Wave*, both addressed to Vincent Impoliteri.

"Did you hear about the asteroid?" Dan asked, picturing the president being briefed on the threat and calmly continuing with his one-handed push-ups. Were there newspapers piled high in their former Tribeca mailroom? he wondered. For sure, the real estate agent would clear them when showing the place. But who'd be looking at it? Secretly, Dan had begun to hope no one, finding comfort in the option of returning. Against all reason, Dan had felt... safer there.

Descending the stoop, he was struck with the fun-house sensation that the stairs were separating themselves from the house. On closer inspection, the concrete was, in fact, severely cracked and gouged.

"Might be the Mole-Kacy boys smashing them up with their nunchucks," Rose says, as if this were a real possibility.

This launched Bibi into a play-by-play of yesterday's struggle to carry the wheelchair up the stoop — Rose nearly toppling to her death and Kenny Mole-Kacy to the rescue. "To be clear, that is not part of my job description. There'll be no heavy lifting today."

"Today is yesterday tomorrow," Rose sang. "But okay, wheel me round back. I want to check how my garden's coming."

Fast-forward three hours and ten degrees and the stress over this, plus the house and the impending party (bread crumbs in the oven! He completely forgot!), and Dan's really not feeling this mezuzah thing.

"Some day of rest," he says, envying all the neighbors passing the house en route to the beach — "We should do like those people!"—toting striped umbrellas, wheeled coolers, inflatable whatnots. Instead, Sue has him grunting over the intractable ivy. The stuff may look romantic, but, they've discovered, it bores through the grout between the bricks, not to mention serves as a convenient highway for all manner of small creatures. At their feet, a pile of the shredded vines oozes with snails, ants, and aphids. "'Six days do your work, but on the seventh'..."

"I *was* resting," Sue reminds him. "Until I saw those women. At least you could have warned me." First thing in the morning, there they were again—Rose and Bibi by the tree. Sue was so startled, she splashed steaming tea on her thigh. And with Dan gone (to the store), she had to literally fight off the aide's medical assistance.

*Should have taken it,* Dan thinks, scanning the cockamamie bandage Sue has fashioned for her burn from toilet paper and duct tape.

"Look, I don't know what went down with this house and Rose and Bob Baum," Sue says. "But after yesterday? Why, *why* would you let them back in?"

"I'm a decent person?"

Already Dan can hear Rose invoking her Jewish friends the Baums if and when she sees this mezuzah. Any mention of Judaism leads Rose right to her "double-crossing" Jewish friends, the Baums. Had that dweeby Bob with his corduroy bow ties really helped Maureen trick Rose into selling her house?

Sue wipes a sweaty hand on Dan's polo shirt. "If I had seen Bob at temple, I—"

"*Temple?*"

"Temple, synagogue, whatever. I assume the Baums belong to the same one as Sy."

"You skipped your OB appointment? For *temple?*"

"Bob would know who I am, wouldn't he?"

"Who *are* you?" Temple? Mezuzah? Up half the night reading Dan's old bar mitzvah Bible with a mug of tea and a highlighter like it's a college text on which she'll be graded? (Sue is the daughter of two professors, after all.) "The question isn't rhetorical." Dan really doesn't know. Factor in Sue's bikini and bandaged leg, the explosion of rusty curls, sun-bleached eyebrows, and a glitter-mermaid forearm tattoo (courtesy of Sage), and a Jewish pirate is what she most resembles — "Just slap on an eye patch, grab a parrot, and you're ready to set sail to Israel with Ed."

Sue waits for Dan to complete his riff, holding her pointy chin high, fisting the knife. Yeah, he probably went too far. She thinks he's making fun of her. He *is* making fun of her, but —

"*Are* there Jewish pirates?" Sue's actually curious.

"The Baums?"

Sy's been buying lock picks from Bob Baum for thirty-eight years and he's golfed with the guy most of that time. You'd have better luck convincing Sy to switch allegiance to the Yankees. But Dan always tried. It was no secret that he was wary of Bob, wary of all the vendors for and employees of Glassman Locks & Keys. A family business has more in common with a kingdom than a company, and Sy's reign was deviled with cronyism, backward and opaque. "Where's our oversight?" Dan has been asking since his first proper post-college day on the job. "Why aren't we sending out RFPs for bids on our hardware? Installing window guards? Leading in electronic keypad locks? R and D, Dad! Innovate or die!" Now Sy has finally given him the power to change everything and it's so much, too much. All Dan really wants to do is cook. Specifically, clams oreganata. Rose has agreed to share her secret family recipe.

It's too hot to think. Also too windy. Oh, but better look whom he's talking to. Someone who's thirty-seven weeks pregnant is always hotter, hungrier, more tired, more suspicious.

"How could you instantly buy Rose's story?" is the question that's been bothering Sue. "Last night when she claimed Maureen and Bob tricked her into selling the house? How could you not at least wonder? Unless you know it's true? Is that why you let her back in? Scared she'll sue us?"

The question shocks Dan so thoroughly, he stutters when he responds. Did Sue actually think him capable of conning a senior citizen? Not to mention of lying to her, his wife?

"No. No." Sue sounds almost disappointed. "You're too worried about being liked to do that. Sy, though. Sy might." Here she starts slicing at the ivy in double time, in sync with whatever's streaming into her head from her iPod. "What is it?" Dan points at the device. "What's on there?"

Clearly put out, Sue retrieves the iPod from somewhere within her massive baby-primed cleavage and holds it up for him to read: "'Disc two, *Havdalah Prayers Made Easy.*' Are you fucking kidding me?" He'd assumed her playlist was eclectic, but—

"*Golden Hits of the Seventies* would be funkier, it's true." This a reference to Dan's bar mitzvah Bible in which he'd long ago scribbled the info to write away for the eight-track. He'd come across the book while bagging his mom's things for Goodwill. Zero memory of defacing it but the music came right back to him. "War." "Fame." "Billy, Don't Be a Hero." Dan had played that shit till there were no more devices on which to play it and by then didn't even care, so deeply were the songs grooved into his brain. "Who Do You Think You Are." "If You Don't Know Me by Now."

Aside from June, Sue is the one who can best appreciate this, precisely because she understands great music, which pop is not, so why compare? Pop is all about the hook and its ability to yank you at twelve, thirteen, forty-two, through some nasty shape-shifting murk. Dan physically cringes recalling his luck-of-the-draw Torah portion: Leviticus 15, the rules regarding menstruation.

"I mean, what kind of sadist asks a kid whose voice is cracking to write and deliver a speech about that? Rabbi Larry Gutman, that's who!" The same guy set to convert Sue tomorrow. "Hairy Larry, beware."

"I thought he was your golf buddy."

"Sy's buddy. I just go along."

"You just go along," Sue repeats, leaning back on her clogs to assess a little patch cleared of greenery.

"Meaning?"

"You just go along." Her swollen calves resemble bowling pins. "Either that or you stay out of it."

Birds chatter explosively in agreement.

"So, then." She sighs. "Are we done? I think we're done."

For a nauseated minute, Dan thinks she means them, their marriage. But then Sue swaps her knife for a hammer, and he exhales. It's the ivy-cutting that's finished. An empty planter holds the tools, the mezuzah kit, plus all her usual supplies — tissues and Fig Newtons, water and hat, the aforementioned Bible. Dan reaches for the book, astonished. In the few weeks Sue's had it, she's undone decades of pristine neglect.

The spine is cracked. There are food stains in the margins. Dan had been about to toss it into the donation bag along with Estelle's Scrabble dictionaries, inspirational gift crap, and back issues of *Architectural Digest,* but, naively, he'd thought the Bible might make Sue laugh, a real laugh, with her gums showing. If he got really lucky, she might even sing — a scrap of a Golden Hit in her golden voice. "If you don't know me by now, you will never, never, never know me."

Fanning himself with the pages, Dan can smell the old leather and paper and, more faintly, his mother's closet: suede, mothballs, an orange-jasminey scent she wore — Fracas. Just yesterday, he'd walked in on Sy crying into one of Estelle's still-perfumed scarves. He had passed it to Dan, and Dan had smelled it deeply and passed it back and they had taken turns, trying to breathe her in, their grief a private, faintly unseemly thing in a neighborhood reeling from far bigger tragedy. Estelle had picked a bad time to die, Sy

said then and not for the first time. Even back in Brooklyn Heights, where Estelle had started a food pantry, served
as temple treasurer, and volunteered to teach adults to read
every Monday, Wednesday, and Friday, the meaning of her
life was de facto minimized because it had not ended in either
an act of terror threatening the entirety of Western culture
or, second best, the second deadliest plane crash on U.S. soil.

Sue wedges the hammer between her long, pale legs, in-
serts a tiny nail between her teeth, holds the mezuzah up to
the door frame. "Are you sure you want to go through with
this?" Dan asks.

"All set!" The nail bobs up and down between words.

" 'Cause you know it's still your choice...in the end. When
I urged you to do it, I didn't realize—even my mother
wouldn't want you converting if..." It's like the opening of
one of Rose's terrible jokes. A wife walks into the weekend
as a secular humanist. Only there's no punch line in sight.
"I was thinking that it's not too late to reconsider this
whole...we do still own the apartment."

"But I love it here!" Sue says. A beefy dude passing by on
the street halts at the sound. Dan salutes him as if to say, *All's
well with us, move along, pal.* Also because the guy's pretty impressive, with two kids, a boom box, and two beach chairs
strapped to his torso.

"Rose is not getting her house back," Sue adds. "Did you
hear me? Repeat that."

"Rose is not—but Sue, what if it's true and she *was* fooled
into moving? Shouldn't we at least—my God, what's with
that dude?"

Superdad is still standing in front of the house as if in a trance, kids and beach gear hanging off him.

"What dude?"

Sure enough, the man vanishes the moment Sue looks over at the street. To hell with the oglers and with his linen shorts; Dan needs to sit. The air is too white or something, too moist, squawky with seagulls, not to mention the planes, big ones taking off and landing at Kennedy Airport all day long, small ones with banners advertising Z100, Hawaiian Punch, and ten-week-old fetuses courtesy of Go Pro-Life. In no time Dan finds himself worrying abstractedly about a pair of young moms pushing strollers and talking shit about someone named Pam. What is wrong with them? Dan can hear every word! What if Pam or a Pam friend is near? More treacherous still is the fact that their toddlers are barefoot while the street all-out glitters with glass, and the sand ahead is scorching. They are not thinking clearly, these women. Flesh is gathering under their transparent beach cover-ups. They are not having enough sex.

No, it's Dan who's not having enough sex. The advanced pregnancy, yes. But Sue's anger is even harder to work around. Obviously, Dan is not thinking clearly. In truth, he can't tell whether he's angry back at her or simply angry that she's angry. His mother would know. Dan reaches in his shorts for the phone — oh, right, he can't call his mother anymore. Just as well. There's no reception in Rockaway. And even if he could, calling Estelle would irk Sue even more than his calling his neurologist. Best to focus on his squirming unborn son (son?).

Sue has "dropped," according to the OB (last week), and the view of her from below is straight out of the aquarium. One, two frantic undulations, then the baby resubmerges. One, two ripples of her skin, and again a pause; like that. It occurs to Dan to blame the impending birth for his wife turning inward, away from him. It happened with their other kids, in a less extreme version. Yet so much else also seems to be conspiring against them—9/11, Judaism, the iPod, Sy, Rose, the house. Dan's ghost sightings might have all turned out to be dust motes, but he'd still swear the place is...influential. Even now, craving connection with Sue, he can barely resist an urge to be back inside the womb of the kitchen. There, mercifully, Rose has offered to assist in all his party prep. "If you really want to know how to feed a crowd..."

"Are we almost done? Sue? I'm in the middle of something."

"Your life?"

"What?"

"The middle of your life, Daniel."

"Daniel. Is that my middle-aged name?"

"Biblical name. It means 'God is my judge.' Don't look at me like that. I read it in the baby-name book."

Here's the prompt for them to argue about whether it's better to choose names before the birth (Sue's opinion) or after, so as to meet the kid (Dan's). But New Jew Sue doesn't argue. Instead, she informs Dan of her own brand-new Hebrew name, Bat Sarah Imenu, and Dan surrenders to the fact that he has no clue what Sue will do, think, or say next.

"Instead of putting up the mezuzah, I'm just gonna write God's name here with a Sharpie," she announces, adjusting her strained bikini top. "That's the commandment, isn't it? Write God's name on the door? Whoever decreed we had to put it on a scroll in a box?"

"Scroll makers?" Dan guesses. "Box makers?" Perhaps Glassman Locks & Keys should bring out a line of mezuzah security. Liturgical dead bolts. Judaica-inspired closed-circuit TVs. The little housed scrolls are, in his experience, just bait for the door-to-door Orthodox. In a moment of weakness, after Dan's mom died, Sy paid a few of those black hats to pray for her soul, and they never stopped ringing his ("Send in the Clowns") doorbell. Till he moved, they kept ringing. "Like stray cats you feed or—"

"Rose?" Sue quips. "Just you watch. She'll be coming back tomorrow and the next day and—"

"Stop!" Fooled into selling the house or not, the old woman was born, raised, and lost her son here. "How can someone religious like you begrudge her a couple of visits?"

"Why is everyone calling me religious?"

By now Estelle's soul, no longer buoyed by prayer, must be hurtling downward, mistaken for an asteroid. But she's free, at least. It's Dan who's left to pay for all her sins. Her sins: dying before her "dying" husband, insisting Sue convert, insisting Dan make Sue convert, insisting Sy make Dan make Sue convert.

The Sharpie talk was only hypothetical, turns out. Sue/Sarah steps back to admire the garish tube hanging on its sanctioned slant.

JILL EISENSTADT

"God bless," Dan says, standing. "Now can I get back to my—"

"Shhh," Sue says. "Kiss." She presses two fingertips to Dan's lips, then touches the box.

"Go ahead," Dan says. "Give my love away."

Then, wouldn't you know, there's bald Dr. Mole, pretending to mist his morning glories but really setting up to tell the whole neighborhood that the Glassmans are getting very Jew-y now, very Old World, so don't bother inviting them to any lobster bakes this summer. Mole takes Dan's nod as an invitation to stroll across the driveway, spray bottle in hand. A frilly ocher guayabera accentuates his potbelly, over which his white physician's coat blows open in the breeze. Mole forms his thumb and pointer finger into a gun, shoots Sue's bandaged thigh, then plops himself down on the stoop next to Dan. "How's the cranium, big guy?"

"Still attached." Dan tries not to judge the man on his too-tight sweatpants and PVC sandals. Unlike Dan's big-shot neurologist, Mole listens carefully to all of his complaints and has, over these few months, offered not only standard migraine medications but a whole host of other strategies. Allergy testing. Acupuncture. Craniosacral massage. Even color therapy.

"Did those last pills help?" Mole asks. "The blue?"

"Helped a bit," Dan says. Before he puked them up.

"We could try something stronger."

"Like Cipro?" Sue cracks.

"Excuse me?"

"Just wondering why the mail hasn't come yet."

Dan smiles down at his sneakers, trying not to laugh. Sue used to be this funny on a regular basis.

"Am I missing something?" Mole asks.

"Your son—"

"Oh, by the way, I approve."

"Approve?" Dan's still incredulous that a brainiac like Kenny would deal anything, let alone Cipro.

"Approve of my son with your daughter. Hot stuff!" Mole turns to leer at Sue—the exposed abdomen, huge breasts. "I know all about you wild redheads."

Dan clutches Sue's hand. "The oven! Excuse us!" He lets the unseen forces suck them back into the house. Shoulder to shoulder, they charge down the hall as if Mole were pursuing them.

She's smiling. No gums yet, but still. To be on the same side with her again, even superficially, feels so right, Dan can almost quash the image of his daughter with that zitty loser from next door.

"That's a major step down from Jake Leibowitz," Dan says. "Am I right?"

"Jake's gay."

"I know. Too bad. Love that Jake."

"Did you invite him to the party?"

"Party?" In the kitchen, he races for the oven, his bread crumbs. "What party?"

"You're really going to do that?"

"Yes!" The blast of heat to Dan's face feels like a blessing. Before him lies a crispy golden-bread-crumb landscape.

Rose's antique appliances have saved him from rubble. "Now for the clams!"

"Clams? That's shellfish."

"Yeah."

"Your mother didn't eat them."

"Yeah."

"If I'm going to be Jewish, a kosher home might—oh!"

Rose is here, sitting in the corner, her wheelchair backed into the shadows. She's holding a boning knife; assorted other blades are piled in her lap.

"Someone took my good French knife! I looked every-where!"

"Are you trying to scare us?" Dan asks.

"You don't need me for that."

This is true. Sue looks faint. "This is too...too—"

Rose points her weapon at a tub of clams Dan's pulled from the fridge. "Those'll need a good scrub."

Sue grabs a rattling plastic bag off the counter and starts to flee.

"Why won't the clam share her lunch?" Rose says.

As Sue brushes past, Dan sees that her bag is *full* of mezuzahs, mezuzahs for every doorway in the house.

"Because she was shellfish."

࿆

June has no buff hockey-defense boyfriend from her old school; Tim's sure of it. There is no Jake Leibowitz who nick-named her Swoon and gave her that fancy gold bracelet a grandma would wear. Maybe June has been inspired by her sister's imaginary friend Ed. Or she's bored, insecure, joking. But the other driver's ed kids are buying it. As the car barrels down Newport Avenue, the questions fly.

"What color eyes?" asks amber-eyed Regina. She's in the backseat with June, yanking the new girl's feral red hair into something called a fishtail.

"Gray," June says, wincing.

Kenny drives into a pothole, then whomps on the gas to get out of it. Up ahead, a frightened power walker in coral velour leaps onto a nearby lawn. In the rearview, Tim spies June checking on the health-class egg in her backpack.

"Is this Jake any relation to Dennis?" Kenny asks. "Dennis Leibowitz?"

Turns out a last name like Leibowitz really ups June's believability. Now there's room to elaborate. Still ignoring Kenny (no way is Jake any relation to one of Kenny's friends), she specifies, "Gray eyes." (Kenny's friends are all druggie science geeks.) "Walnut-shaped." (Whoever drives after Kenny has to do all kinds of seat adjusting.) "Longish lashes."

Tim wonders if June's in over her head.

"Did you say walnut-shaped?" Regina presses.

With the egg probably still in mind, June amends this to "Oval, you know, like...oval." And asks about the rumor that their health-class teacher raises hens in a shack down in Arverne.

Kenny laughs. "I'll bet she grows the veggies too." For in-class condom practice, there's a choice of zucchini or cuke.

In Tim's day, the class was called Sex Ed. "No food props. Separate classrooms for boys and girls."

No one's interested.

Regina, who has already passed Health by safely hard-boiling, is moving on. "Jake's hair?"

"If it's anything like Dennis's, it's humongous," Kenny says, lifting his hands off the wheel to mime a 'fro. "Like a hedge."

Tim says Kenny looks like "some kid about to mow you down with his Big Wheels. Quit messing around, Mole-Kacy, I mean it."

"Big Wheels! I had those!" Kenny crows. "Big Wheels, Hot Wheels, slot cars, Go-Karts."

"Boys get comfy with all the vehicles young." That's June's observation. She's sure her dad wants a boy baby so he can "relive his childhood smashing toy planes into Lego skyscrapers."

"Not funny," Tim says but wonders…about Dan. Personally, he'd be cool with a kid of any gender. Back when he was still hitting the bottle, his then-wife, Alicia, had an abortion without even telling him she was pregnant.

*Sandy* is the word June picks for Jake's brand of blond. "Sandy?" Regina repeats. Her own pale hair is too short to even describe. "Sand…*aaaah!*"

Tim grabs the wheel. Kenny has drifted into the wrong lane and a bus, almost.

"Righteous!" Kenny's eyes shine. Tim must admit, adrenaline becomes him. But when he starts in boasting, "Our vehicle scared off the enemy vehicle," Tim has to call him an asshole.

"If I'm an asshole," Kenny says, "you're the whole ass." Then he disinvites "everyone" to his séance tonight on the beach.

"Why would I go to a séance?" June asks. "I already live in a haunted house."

"That's exactly why. I'm gonna purge it!"

"From the outside?"

"You think I'm going *in?* With the ghosts of that murdered Gary and a dead Asian roaming your halls?"

"You don't know shit," June says. "They're in the wall!"

"I heard the shots. When it happened. The night of the *Golden*—"

"You live *there?*" Regina gasps. "You *live* in the Murder House?"

"You were seven," June reminds Kenny.

"I had ears."

"Small ones." Kenny's ears are still small and part of the lobes are attached to his head.

"So what'd you do?" Regina asks him.

"Called the detective. Well, my dad did. The guy left his card before that, when they came by to check if we were hiding refugees."

"Were you?"

The detective had been snooping around Tim's house then too. And with him, wouldn't you know, was Mike Sloane, Tim's old lifeguarding partner. Back in the day, Mike was the self-appointed master of cruel ceremonies—hazing, death kegs, you name it. That he'd grown up to become a cop was, well, troubling. Tim told Mike to get the fuck off his property. Of course, that was before the gunshot that sent him stumbling upon two corpses in Rose's dining room.

NYPD hadn't immediately notified FDNY about the beached freighter. By the time Tim's crew arrived at the scene in Breezy, six refugees had already drowned and countless cadaverous others were leaping off the ship's bow. Tim had rushed in, fully clothed, flashlight in hand. But instantly, his old lifeguard instincts returned. He dropped the light and dove under, feeling the familiar blast of cold salt water rushing into his sinus cavity. Whirling around, grabbing for limbs in the dark, he pulled in half a dozen men within minutes. Onshore, one had no pulse. Another vomited, then cheered, "U.S.A.," genuflecting. A third, Tim discovered mid-CPR, was a female—eighteen, nineteen tops—wearing men's clothing, her perfect tits flattened under a dirty, tight Ace bandage.

Tim drags his mind back to the driver's ed car. Tells Kenny to make a left at the light. Best to steer clear of the desolate, sketchy parts of Far Rockaway and the charred Belle Harbor block where the plane had dropped. First responder turned first preventer? Were that possible, Tim would gladly go back to work. But how many dangers come to light either too late or after the threat's passed? (Take the asteroid that just missed Earth by a mere seventy thousand miles.) To imagine what unknown horrors they right now face—man-made and natural, from within, from without...Tim grabs a plastic fork that's poking out between two seat cushions and *whisk-whisk*s his itchy face. "Ahhh."

"Wait till Kenny spazzes again and Tim pokes his eye out,"

Regina says. "Then he'll be symmetrical. One eye, one nostril."

"Yeah, but," June points out, "we'd already be history if Tim's feet weren't always hovering over that second brake." Defensive driving, the real thing. He must get wicked cramps in his calves. And (talking more softly) he must be embarrassed by the car (a '94 Honda Civic) when he "goes to pick up dates."

"Does he? Have dates?" Kenny joins in the speculation. "A date tonight?" Reasons for their suspicion: Tim's collared shirt, clean hair, sport coat.

And it's Saturday!

Amazing how they talk this way. Forget he's there. Or they don't care, maybe want to provoke him? If so, his refusing to get riled only makes the speculation wilder.

Maybe Tim climbs up on the car roof after work to unscrew the yellow light-up Steer-Rite Auto School sign and burns rubber to *her* house...

Does it unscrew? The sign? Could this be his weekend ritual? Stash those permit books in the glove compartment. Cover the extra brake with sheepskin. Air out their teen odors or blast them with the brown, jiggling, triangular car perfume that came with the lease, mysteriously attached to the back dash alongside the tissues.

Kenny predicts Tim's woman smells of small dangling airfreshener trees—pine, coconut, green apple. She's a cabbie with mace stashed under the seat; an ace mechanic-ess, nothing on under the jumpsuit but grease; a slutty-mouthed monster-truck-circuit mama performing at the Meadowlands every weekend this month. She's a racy race-car driver, a leggy car-show blonde, or some pixie jailbait driver's ed protégée. She's Regina.

"Ha-ha," Regina says. "Anyhow, he might ride a horse or a ten-speed on his time off."

Tim works hard to keep his reactions to himself. That way, he can retain some authority. But when Kenny misses the turn, all is lost.

"Christ! No!" The kid's driven straight to the plane-crash site, the very spot Tim was navigating around. Now he's melting down. "Keep driving! Kenny! Go!" As if he could shield them from what they're not seeing—the houses that *had been* there. Another hole in the skyline writ small. Tim knows that Regina and Kenny saw much worse rubbernecking postcrash. And Regina's got June reined in so tight by the hair that she probably can't see much more than a slice of burned tree and cyclone fence. But Tim still feels uncomfortable, responsible. Disregarding his instructions, Kenny drives extra-slowly past the plywood barricade.

The Wailing Wall, Peg calls it. The thing's covered in carnations, photographs of victims, teddy bears, and good-bye letters written in Spanish. Through the cracks, you can glimpse grass planted by the airline—four feet high already, obscenely green. No one is allowed over there, not even the people who own the property.

"I changed my mind," Tim tells Kenny. "Pull over. Your turn's up."

"What?" The kid slaps the wheel edge with an open palm.

Like Tim's ex-wife did in traffic. Or for effect. "I can man this sled better than them!"

Regina objects, "Don't lump me in with Ju-ne! It's her first day!"

"I hate the way you say my name. 'Ju-ne.' Like 'Eww, new girl, new Jew.'"

Kenny: "Are you converting too?"

"What's it to you?"

"We're invited to the party."

"Who's we? What party?" Regina wants to know.

Tim gives up. "Just please get us away from here, Kenny. *Go!*"

Zero to thirty, Kenny peels out like he thinks he's in an action pic. They slam backward, the guys into their seats, June into Regina's lap.

"Seat belts, ladies!" Tim knows he sounds mean, but sad is all he is. As they speed past the Sunset Diner, he can't resist narrating, "Picture a sleepy female park ranger" — Peg — "on the morning of the plane crash. She's sitting by the window —"

"Is she hot?" Kenny asks.

"It's been two months since 9/11. Two months and one day, to be exact." A few streets down, at St. Francis, they'd recently held the last of thirteen funeral masses. "She's a brand-new widow."

"That's hot."

Dropped the kids at her mother's, gassed up the car, stopped at the diner for breakfast. First bite, sip of black coffee, second bite — *boom;* the whole restaurant was shaking! An Airbus 600 roared past the window. Tail! On! Fire!

"What was she eating?"

"Kenny! What the fuck?" June sounds about to cry.

"Oh, you know you're curious too, Juuune." Kenny's way of saying June sounds like gargling.

"Greek omelet, rye toast," Tim says because, weirdly, Peg had told him that very detail when she visited him the next day in the hospital. While she and the others ran toward an exploding house to try to be of service, Tim had lain in bed, uselessly watching the catastrophe unfold on TV. Mayor Giuliani. Matt Lauer. It was later that night—after Ox, with burns over 40 percent of his body, was wheeled in to share his room—that Tim decided to quit firefighting. He was tired of saving people and failing to save people, of being at the wrong place at the wrong time and the right place at the wrong time and the wrong place at the right time. He was out-of-his-mind (King Coward) afraid.

Tim yanks a Fresca from the glove box, downs it all at once—*glug, glug*—then rolls the empty bottle around his sore face.

Other eyewitnesses swore there were no flames, or the flames were on the fuselage or the engine or the right wing or the left. Pieces came off in the air or didn't come off. The plane wobbled; no, spun. The plane was chased by a missile or was not chased before corkscrewing, almost vertically, onto the residential street. It was terrorism if you believed it. It was not terrorism if you believed it was rudder failure, human error, a poltergeist.

"Ask me," Tim says, though no one is asking him. "Ask me, these planes…well, cars too, trains, boats—they can't cut it. Transportation needs another revolution. Bad."

"Badly," Kenny corrects, squeezing a blazing neck pimple.

"What about Jake's skin?" Regina asks.

Hopefully, it's begun to dawn on June that every one of Regina's questions is actually the same one. That is, how can June nail a boyfriend when Regina can't? But June can't, or why would she need to invent one?

"Regular," June says of Jake's skin, which even Tim knows is meaningless. Back at June's high school, smarty Stuyvesant, *regular* is a shade of chicken satay, whereas here it's either driftwood brown (east—Far Rockaway) or fire-truck red (west—Rockaway Beach).

They drive past the Texaco station where one of the plane engines actually fell, landing two feet away from a tank of gas. Really, it's a CIA storage area, Regina says her uncle says. Really, the CIA put the engine there to make it look like it came from the plane.

"That's insane," Kenny squeals. "Everyone knows bin Laden crashed it as payback for Moran's dis!" Regina joins in to recite the firefighter's now-famous line, delivered on stage at a televised 9/11 fund-raiser. "Osama bin Laden, you can kiss my royal Irish ass. And I live in Rockaway. And this is my face, bitch."

They howl with the manic glee of anxiety. Even Tim joins them, briefly; Moran's bravery is magnificent. But as far as he can tell, the crash was unrelated. It's time to bag the non-stop conspiracy crap: The terrorists were targeting all the

Jews in the neighborhood. The aliens were trying to land. On and on.

"Let's learn to drive," Tim suggests, "A quiz! For ten zillion points: What are you required to do at a stop sign?" He provides two minutes and (switching on the radio) "thinking music." Pink is midway through singing "Get the Party Started."

"Uh! Pink, no." Regina groans.

But the others like it. Their heads bob in time to the beat. Tim slaps on his irritated neck in syncopation. Then: "Time's up!" He chooses June, noticing how her name in *his* mouth shapes his lips for a kiss, then immediately trying to unnotice it. June is already making fun of him, giving her fake boyfriend his every feature—hair to muscles. "Your answer, please? June? At a stop sign you..."

"Gun it!" June shouts. "Is this a trick question?"

Tim decides to ignore her. As they zoom down Cross Bay Boulevard, he moves his shoulders, up and down, side to side, to the beat. Choppy bay on their left (a few seasick boats). Sewage-treatment tanks on the right—bright blue, looming. Smells like egg.

"Stop!" Regina shrieks.

The car skids some, then halts as Kenny brakes. A sound like "heh" presses out from June's chest.

"Bingo," Tim says. Never mind that Regina meant for Tim to stop dancing or for Kenny to stop driving maniacally. He proceeds as planned. "And if there is no stop line?"

Regina sighs, lets June's finished braid drop. "Stop before entering the crosswalk."

"And if there is no crosswalk?"

"Stop before entering the intersection."

Tim's taught Regina well. Kenny too, if he'd just stop messing around. It's June, Tim suspects, who'll be the real challenge.

*Jake wasn't here*, she scrawls on the steamed window, *6/15/02*.

⌒

Sue curses a thorny, overgrown bush at the back of the brick patio. A bloody cross pulses on her shin—same leg, already scalded by tea. She whacks at the plant with her plastic bag of mezuzahs. The thing attacked her right as she walked out that pain-in-the-ass door. *Her* pain-in-the-ass door, she reminds herself. She can replace it *and* the bush and even the patio bricks—in between which, she suspects, those biting black flies with green eyes lay their eggs.

Cheered, Sue begins searching through the clanking sack for a mezuzah light enough to hang on the loose door frame. The temple claimed to be giving her a "major discount," but who knows. They refused to take her cash on Shabbat. Behind her, Bibi sits and jeers while Sage and Ed feed "hay" to their "pony," Blacky.

What Sue didn't tell Dan about temple was how she'd walked in to find his father in back, slumped and seemingly unconscious. In actuality, he'd been listening to Dan's little radio, ingeniously wrapped in a sweater, with one earplug hidden between his head and the wall. "I don't go to temple to be with God"—Sy's defense. "I go to be with my friends."

But Sue didn't see any friends other than Rabbi Larry up on the bimah with a squeaky bar mitzvah boy. "You mean your friends at WFAN sports talk?"

Sy just patted the empty seat beside him. "You're late, Sue." Had he followed her there, sped ahead, and snuck in the side door? She wouldn't have put it past him. When she sat down, Sy took her hand and, one by one, uncurled her fingers to reveal the iPod she thought she'd concealed there. "So alike, the two of us."

Sue looked away, at the stained-glass rendering of Eve and the Serpent. She and Sy "so alike"? Please, no. But their interactions with Dan *were* similarly composed of exasperated bullying and affection, Dan wishing they were more accommodating of others, they wishing Dan were less. As the rabbi's remarks came perilously close to comparing Roger Clemens with Osama bin Laden (an eye for an eye), Sue had no choice but to admit that she and Sy shared a whole host of interests and traits: What they'd dreamed of (a beach house), what they found most irritating (other people), who they loved most in the world (Dan, June, Sage). Both Sue and Sy flew into rages, held grudges, were temperamentally sour people addicted to sugar.

In the backyard, Sue continues halfheartedly rustling through the bag of mezuzahs. Her plan—to get real Jewish and scare the men—had worked on Dan well enough, but "so alike" Sy had plainly seen through it. The bush at her foot could spontaneously combust and start talking, and the old man would shrug and summon Dan to summon Tim to put out the fire. Luckily for him, Tim's retired or he wouldn't have time to do the Glassman bidding 24/7. On today's list: teach June to drive, replant the garden, spray the tree, fix the back door, plus do whatever else they're not telling Sue about for the surprise party she's not supposed to know of. Why Tim's so willing is a question only Sue seems to be asking. He likes us, Dan says. He's kind. Isn't that possible?

Well...

The baby is thrashing from every angle. Sneakers in a dryer are what come to mind. Then laundry—a mountain that needs doing—then chocolate pudding. Sue's mouth fills with spit.

"Too heavy," Bibi says of the mezuzah she's chosen— comparatively light, made from...composite? Wood? A human tibia? "Save your energy, Mommy. That will never work."

With pale purple chosen as today's color scheme, the aide sits with the *New York Post* spread across her thighs, painting her fake nails accordingly. When she's not bossing Sue, she's threatening to "prettify" Sage. Still in her undies (though a fresh pair) in defiance of Dan, Sage flips a coin to determine who will get the first pony ride.

"An imaginary kid on an imaginary horse?" Bibi observes at Ed's win. "You gotta love that. If you believe in reincarnation, Ed could be—"

"Ed is not one of Rose's relatives," Sue says. "If that's where you're going."

Bibi waves around a wet, polished hand. "Actually, I was thinking of the Asian guy, the refugee."

"The boy who shot Gary?"

Bibi pauses. "Well, Rose says *she* did it."

"Did what?"

"Nuh-uh! Back up, Mommy!" Sue's been inadvertently inching toward the aide's chair. "Ve-ry bad for the fetus, this polish, you should know that, ve-ry noxious. You're up next, Sage!"

"Rose said she killed her son?" Sue asks. "Really?"

"Now, you see?" Bibi twirls a pointer finger by her ear. "Cuckoo. Then again, who can know—"

"*We* can know. The cops, the news, it's all been—"

"News? Are you serious? Who believes news?" Bibi slaps at the paper on her lap. Headline: "Rockaway Neighbors Scoff at Theory Plane Crash Was an Accident."

"That's different. The *Golden Venture* story is all done. Everyone knows that the Chinese kid—"

"Oh, those evil Chinese, is it? Watch out for the Russians too, and the Arabs, they're the worst. Never trust one of those A-rabs or anyone resembling—"

"Hold on. That's…that's not—"

"No, you hold on, Mommy. You have no idea what crap I put up with daily. You think the guy who searched my purse at the bridge this morning cares I'm Guyanese American?"

The earned outrage doesn't make Sue like Bibi more but it does make her like herself less. Of all the post-plane-crash photographs, the one hardest to shake shows a dirt-caked back windshield upon which some foul finger has written *Nuke 'em! What are you waiting for?*

"But we're getting off topic," Sue says. "Rose—"

"You try going through a tollbooth looking like me then say I'm off topic! I love this country!" Bibi's on her feet now.

One page of the newspaper sticks to her pants. The rest is falling, falling. "I've been to Gettysburg. Twice! Have you been to Gettysburg?" Bibi's the taller of the two. "*Have* you?"

"We're talking about Rose."

"Oh, please. It's hard enough to get her out of Rockaway, let alone to Getty—"

"No, I mean—she can't really think she killed her kid? That's nuts!"

Bibi sits back down, leaving the papers to the winds. A few sheets gust over and plaster themselves to the side of the hedge. "What do you want me to say?"

"That's nuts."

"Ah, but anything can happen when your child disrespects you. You should know all about that, Mommy. You just lose your shit, can't help it. Before long you...I don't know, say something you regret? Pick up a gun?"

Sue squeezes the hammer. In the quiet, the beach noise reveals itself—waves and shouts, flapping fabric, radio static, all of it twining into incoherent sound strands that won't match up with the orderly patterns of towels and jetties. The ocean, which can be so pacifying, now heaves and sighs like a pregnant woman who can't find a comfortable position. Sailboats lean perilously. If you walked up close, you'd see the churned-up sand has streaked the waves brown. Above it all, clouds are strewn like shredded tissue.

Blacky flattens himself onto the grass; he's beat. Pony ride's closed. Sage throws herself down next to him. Ed, presumably, next to her. Sue tries to vicariously enjoy lying belly-down too. Once you're a parent, most of your deepest pleasures (and pains) are thus outsourced. But Bibi's judgment overwhelms everything. Even though she's in Sue's peripheral vision, the aide is invading her consciousness. Impulsively, Sue turns and nails in the mezuzah, hard, hard. Her insistent hand, red and inflated, could belong to someone else. Stop. Done. The little box hangs for one, two seconds. Then, on the upbeat of three, it smashes onto the brick patio, a chunk of the door frame attached.

"I told you that wouldn't work, Mommy."

Inside, Sue heads for the chocolate pudding. Dan and Rose sit at the kitchen table with piles of vegetables, both cooked and raw, between them. "This blade isn't worth the onion it's cutting," Rose gripes, still miffed about her best knife gone missing. "Maureen doesn't even cook. I bet Bob took it."

Sue pauses in the doorway to consider and reject retrieving the knife from the planter on the stoop. "It's hot in here," she says by way of hello.

Dan looks up. "Hey." Registering the nasty feeling Sue's carried in like a firearm, he wisely turns back to his roasted peppers (slimy, red slabs like internal organs). Neither does he attempt to stop Sue from opening the fridge though it's stocked full of telltale party items: dips covered with plastic wrap, animal flesh floating in marinades, pricey cheeses.

"Personally I love the heat," Rose chatters. "Especially with the breeze...no breeze back in FH."

Dan peels the char off a pepper. "Forest Hills?"

"Fucking Hell is more like it, excuse my Italian." She's down to her last onion; her eyes stream. "If global warming would just hurry the hell up, maybe my grandkids would come to the beach."

"You don't live here anymore," Sue reminds her, grabbing a chocolate pudding. "You just said so yourself: you're in Forest Hills."

Rose shrugs, chopping, hand a blur. "This doesn't feel right without my good, sharp knife."

Sage is crouched under the dining-room table. "Bibi tickled Ed till he threw up!" she tattles.

"Tickled Ed? Or you?"

Wrong question. "Mom-my!" Sage punches Sue's feet. "Ed doesn't feel well. See him!"

"I'm trying," Sue says. But no. There's just one visible kid rolling around on the scratched tile in her underwear. Her limbs look Day-Glo red. Chalk one up for Tim, the sunscreen pusher. "I'm not a baby!"

"Sorry."

"Ed's a scared baby."

"Okay."

"He wants you to come outside with him."

"Thing is, I'm really happy in here," Sue says, secretly a little scared too. Not just of Bibi but of Rose *and* those Mole-Kacy boys. Morning activities: Seeing who can stand the longest out on the broiling sand; sitting on the sidewalk with empty cans "playing homeless"; jumping off their house extension screaming, "9/11." Here in the dining room, everything feels so much safer. "Go ask Daddy."

As Sage runs off, Sue decides to abandon the bag of mezuzahs. It did a good job of flustering Dan but utterly failed to make Sue's point. Conversion, like changing your address, might start from a practical place but once you're in the process, your heart starts interfering, then your conscience, then...Sue's next move? Pretend to pray? Really pray? Shave her head for a wig? Oh, she's sick of plotting. All Sue really wants is to sit here at this table with the view and her pudding, thinking about the good old days back in Babel when all the earth was one language, one set of words. But she forgot the spoon.

❧

This is Regina getting ready or not to drive over the Marine Parkway Gil Hodges Memorial Bridge. Beauty check: Bra strap showing? Bangs in eyes? Knuckle crack; one through ten, in agonizing slow motion. Deep breath. "Hail Mary full of"...it. And a fresh wad of purple gum.

"She's got a decent mouth when it's not saying anything," Kenny whispers, licking his lips. "Grape-a-licious."

*Is he trying to make me jealous?* June wonders, sliding across the backseat to the window so as to "look at the cars," per Tim's instructions. "The traffic, notice it, flow and weave."

"I'm giddy. You giddy, June?" Kenny says. He thinks having sex with her gives him the right to talk to her. June stares out at the bridge that connects Rockaway to civilization. She hasn't left the peninsula since they moved in.

"'People are afraid to merge,'" Tim quotes from a famous author whose name he can't remember. Not a big reader himself, he says. "But my ex-wife—"

"Wife?" Regina perks at the word. June too, of course, but not outwardly.

Oval wet spots have formed under the arms of Tim's dress shirt. If he really is wearing it for some girl, then (1) June hates her, and (2) he should just take it off. June got an eyeful of Tim's torso this morning when she finally made some headway on cutting the ivy from her bedroom window. Not enough, though. She had to come downstairs for the full view, then get in line behind Bibi. In the movie, the aide would be a gorgeous mannequin who springs to life to kill the old woman. Dogging Tim is the only time she seems halfway human, jaw hanging, her numerous gold fillings aglint. Rose stiffened upon seeing this. Midway through Dad's lesson on which herbs to pick for the clams, Rose dug into her white pocketbook and pulled out a photo of her son.

"You wanna gawk, Bibi, come gawk at my Gary!"

"Already seen him." The aide rolled her eyes, the big-lidded kind that never quite fully open. She bent over seductively, plucked up some herbs scattered on the patio, and handed them to Dad, asking sweetly if she could read the newspaper he was holding. Then she made a big show of sitting down to read it. As if Tim would give a shit about that! To get Tim's attention, you have to show him some bug whose name you pretend you don't know or ask something about U-turns.

June joined her dad peering over Rose's shoulder. In the photograph, a squat, thirtyish man stands on the beach with this house at his back. His arms are T'd, like he's being crucified or measured for a suit jacket. Even more distracting than his gross black Speedo is the fact that he's got "red hair!" June had never seen an Italian redhead before.

"My favorite genetic mutation," Dad said, touching June's head. Rose just kept trying to get Bibi to come look.

No go. "You can't actually expect us to compare Gary with...Tim? An unemployed pharmaceutical salesman with..." Tim knelt in the dirt. You could see his broad, tanned back, the way it narrowed at the waist, the elastic of his blue boxers poking up from his Levi's. "Our hero?"

*"Hero?"* Rose laughed at the word till the fringes on her shirt were quivering. *"Timmy?"* Clumps of spittle collected in her mouth corners. June worried that she might fall from her wheelchair or choke to death on phlegm. *"Hero?* Who told you *that?"*

Bibi's sleepy eyes narrowed as she jabbed a long purple nail toward June. "Tower two. That's what *she* said."

"Well, someone else told me," June mumbled uncertainly. Did they? It was one thing to make stuff up, but only a certified kook believes her own lies. When the first plane hit the World Trade Center, a block away from her school, June was standing at a bathroom sink. Only the fifth day back after summer break and already no soap? The impact vibrated right up through the porcelain.

Dan was on the way to the subway.

Bibi on line to vote in the primary.

Rose was right here in the yard, minding the waves, monster swells from Hurricane Erin down south. Which is how she knows Timmy was surfing that morning. "Eyewitness... if you're gonna live here, you need to be minding the waves, Jan."

"Dan," Dad corrected while June said, "June."


"June? June? *June!*" Back in the car, Kenny interrupts, sliding up next to her in the backseat. "Did you hear what I said?"

"No. I'm too hot." June sticks her head out the window, intent on puzzling out Rose's claim that Tim was surfing the day of the attacks. Tim *was* a hero! Rose doesn't know shit. If his nose wasn't burned off in tower two, then it must have happened in the plane crash aftermath or some other, equally staggering inferno. Frustratingly, neither Dad nor Bibi seemed at all troubled by Rose's apparent intel.

"Think he could teach me to hang ten?" was all Dad asked.

Bibi, no longer starstruck, just turned her gaze toward the view.

The waves were glassy, sparkling when the sun hit. They did their best to spit out the pale, invading bodies, already lots of them, though it was still morning, ten o'clock. Bibi pulled a tissue from Rose's sleeve to dab at the tiny beads of pancake-makeup sweat that dimpled her otherwise perfect face. "Let's bring our swimsuits tomorrow, Rosie."

"Tomorrow?" Dad gulped. June couldn't tell what he feared more — Mom's wrath or the sight of Rose in a swimsuit at his party — but he stood there with a clump of herbs in his hand looking petrified. "You know, tomorrow is kind of a big day."

"Sunday," Rose concurred, patting her hair. The funny colorless puff made June think of a just-gone-to-seed dandelion. Make a wish and blow.

June wished herself back in Tribeca with her real friend Jake Leibowitz, grieving for JFK Jr. in Socrates coffee shop or laughing at the bridge-and-tunnel girls in towering heels trying to navigate the cobblestones. But the neighborhood was now called "the frozen zone." Cut in half from Chambers to Rector Streets, from Broadway to the West Side Highway, it was enclosed with twelve thousand feet of chain link. So June can't go back or forward; she's like a car idling, like this car, still idling.

Regina is now cleaning the windshield — with June's sweater! Uh!

When the girl finally, finally gets back in the car, she tosses aside the balled-up cardigan and reaches for the radio.

"No radio," Tim reminds them, as if they weren't just dancing to Pink. And reciting the list duct-taped to the dashboard: "NO RADIO. NO ROUGHHOUSING, NO INEBRIENTS, FOOD, TOBACCO, LIMBS OUT THE WINDOW, OR UNNECESSARY PROFANITY."

Regina gives Tim the finger. This would shock June if she weren't so thoroughly bored. The list of sins should have included: NO IDLING FOR FIFTEEN FUCKING MINUTES WHILE YOU WORK UP THE NERVE TO

CROSS THE BRIDGE. Kenny passes the time by snaking his egg up and up June's leg.

June allows this. Eyes closed, she recalls Tim this morning, his Adam's apple pulsing as he gulped straight from his hose. It was worth putting up with Rose's monologues for such sight lines. Here, in the car, the view of Tim is blocked with a lot of cheap beige upholstery.

*Years ago* was how Rose started every one of her stories, *years ago* being geezer code for "better settle in." So June tracked every little thing about Tim—his tongue running over his cute crooked bottom teeth, the rugged chin scruff, how lifting his arm raised his shirt, just enough for a peek at his flat, tan abs.

"Years ago, before AC," Rose droned, "hundreds of people would flock here from the city. Right over that beach wall, day and night, staring at us, jealous. If you were from Calabria, my father would let you use the toilet. Otherwise: 'Dig a hole, buddy.' In a real scorcher, we slept out here too, with protection."

"Protection?" The word made June think of condoms, Kenny's glow-in-the-dark condom from last night.

"Put on your thinking cap, Red," Rose said. "I'm talking about a gun."

On *gun*, up jerked Tim's head. June quickly turned back to Rose before Tim caught her staring.

"On summer Sundays, between church and dinner, we used to hand out buttered rolls. Ten dozen rolls from Harbor Bakery. Guess who had to do all that buttering."

"You know how to butter?" Bibi taunted.

"Maybe if you'd done some more buttering, you'd have a husband, wiseass." That's how Rose had met Vin, she told them. She'd offered him a buttered roll. He'd come from Italy only days before. He stood out on the sand, the only one in a suit, the only clothes he owned.

"I thought you hated your husband," Bibi said.

Rose shrugged. "Not then. I was old. He was handsome."

Vin helped keep the masses from storming the wall, trampling Paul Russo's precious herbs, his precious flowers. After Rose's mother died in childbirth, the plants were all her father cared for.

"Would have been different if you'd been a boy," June guessed.

"Yes."


Now it's these same kinds of plants Tim hopes to find at a nursery across the bridge: castor bean, foxglove, lily of the valley, et cetera, plus the fungicide spray for the sick cherry. Still rhapsodizing about traffic, Tim trails the scrawled list through the air to mimic a car. June's the only one listening.

"Individual bodies operating individual machines weaving together as if they're one single, smooth, flowing organism."

"Orgasm?" Regina free-associates. "Did you? Do it with Jake?"

"None of your business! Yes," June says. Then, not wanting Tim to think she's slutty, adds, "Just once...before he died." That last part just fell out.

"*Died?* Whaddaya mean, *died?*" Regina squeals. The whole

car, previously zonked, is rejuiced now. "Seriously? That's traumatic! Ju-une. Why didn't you say something? Is that…was that…in like…September?" Not even rude Regina has the guts to ask outright. And when Tim quietly whispers, "Christ!" June has to look back out the window so he can't see her smiling.

The sky's a pulsing 9/11 blue too. The kind of perfect sky that now makes June (and the rest of the city) tense. Two poufy, vertical clouds hang motionless over the bridge, which swings slightly, which may at any moment just buckle, all the beachgoers in their cars plunging, clutching phones, hook-on mugs, linty trail mix, while polluted fish float past the childproof windows to the tune of garbled classical music, irate talk stations, or audio books: blockbuster thrillers, lite porn, *Islam Unpacked*, *The America We Deserve*, or *How to Communicate with Your Ugly, Angsty Teen.* Teach them to carpool!

"Traffic is sociology," Tim concludes. "Cooperate or crash."

So Kenny relents and reinvites them to his séance for Gary Imp, tonight, on the beach. They'll get that ghost to leave June's walls once and for all.

Tim recommends hiring cherubim with a flaming sword "to ensure Gary stays ousted." Not even June understands that.

᠐

In line at Bloomers nursery, Regina leans over with wet eyes to pluck at the gold bracelet she thinks the late Jake gave June. "It must mean so much to you."

"Well…" June found it on her bathroom floor. With Regina still attached to her wrist, she maneuvers the massive shopping cart around a burly man hugging a banana tree. "Hey, Red." The man leers, jiggling his tongue.

Maybe Bloomers is to crowded garden centers what Scores is to strip clubs; Grandpa might like it. Girl employees wear frilly Bo-Peep undies, tight crop tops, big sky-blue hair bows. The guys behind the counter are bare-chested under overalls and have on fake-distressed straw hats. Tim has gone off to find fungicide while they wait. But the line moves quickly. Soon, there are only two people left between them and the register. Kenny grabs a stack of organic morning glory seeds from a twirling rack.

"So, like, what are you doing after this?" Regina asks June, offering gum.

Kenny taps his seed packet on June's ribs. "Sorry. But she's busy." If June had known how popular a dead boyfriend would make her, she'd have killed him off from the get-go. "We have plans."

"Plants," June explains. "My dad's paying us to help Tim fix up our yard."

Regina pouts. "Hire me! Kenny's already rich. *And* the fucker just raised his prices."

June asks if that's so why he can't afford a new windbreaker. Kenny wears that same ratty one every day.

"Ooh, you hurt his feelings," Regina teases. Maybe so. Kenny's lower lip is sticking out. Regina puts her arm around him, pokes at the seeds. "Does this by any chance mean free product at the séance?"

Kenny licks his teeth. "We'll see."

June can tell he's waiting for her to ask, *Product?* How can she not?

And clearly Regina is bursting to explain. "Safe-n-Sound, that's his drink. And Morning Glory, OJ...I forget what else."

"Security Blankets," Kenny chimes in, petting June's arm. "Cocoa, TLC, Teddy Bears."

Above the counter, the bank of TVs switch from the default magnified pansy to Channel 11, the pregame show — Mike Piazza and his droopy mustache times six. A couple of shoppers boo, others applaud. Still others yell for the checkout people to get back to work. A woman buying a stone mushroom shrieks right in June's ear, starting a chant for the Mets to "Retaliate! Retaliate!"

"History in the making." Kenny smirks, admirably uninterested. Up till now, June had chosen not to think too much about last night with and without him. But now she can't help replaying the highlights: Message in a bottle. Kenny's mysterious drug drop. Sex, new, peculiar and brief. Her mother and then Tim showing up. Finally, the silhouettes of all those kids at the fire, turning calm, holding hands — "Oh!" She gets it now. "That was a séance! On the beach last night, right?"

Kenny affirms. "Everyone's throwing them these days. There's a big uptick in people to contact." Then, out of respect for the deceased or simply because there's nothing more to add, they stay silent until the line ends. "Howdy, y'all," says the checkout guy, lifting his straw hat in an obviously scripted gesture. Sweat sculpts his hair to his scalp.

One glance at the contents of their cart and good-bye, Southern accent.

"Fucking A! Poison garden! Cash or credit?"

"What?"

"Cash or—"

"Poison?"

Checkout guy points with his scanner at the long line of people waiting behind them. He must think they know what they're buying. Kenny pays for his seeds. After that, with no more money and no sign of Tim, they're forced to step aside. While Regina and Kenny examine the newly interesting poisonous plants, June is happy for a reason to head off in search of Tim. Not in Pest Control—two whole aisles of skulls and crossbones. Not in Fertilizers or Floral Tools. June stalks up and down, pausing and misreading a sign for LIGHTING as LIGHTNING, though the nearby shelves are full of illumination options. Tim's own beloved Malibu garden lights are featured in many assorted sizes and colors. Past the birdbaths and composting bins, she finally spots him— his feathery hair and checked tie first. He's standing beneath a SAY IT WITH CUT FLOWERS banner, his face smushed into a mass of lilac.

Something tells June not to startle him. He's like a sleepwalker better left alone. She stands a few feet back, squirming as Tim sniffs, sways. With the sport coat and with his melted nose hidden in flowers, he could easily be a model for the display—multicolored bouquets and multishaped vases in which to put them. But for reasons June can't articulate, she prefers him with his scars exposed, in his usual dirty shorts and T-shirt. When Tim finally looks up, his expression is serene, woozy. He holds the purple flowers up to her face. The perfume-y, air-conditioned moment with its faint ball-game soundtrack and fluorescent lighting rearranges something inside June so that long after she remembers why, lilacs are her favorite flower. When it's over, Tim clamps the stems between his teeth and picks up a small can of fungicide.

"Sure that bouquet isn't poisonous?" June asks, but he's already set off. Past the stakes and trellises—Nature Management.

Back at the register, they discover that Regina and Kenny and a handful of other customers have been ejected from the store following an all-out Mets versus Yankees brawl. The scuffle overturned a large display of Stars and Stripes merchandise, leaving the Astroturf floor strewn with red, white, and blue glass gems and wind chimes. Which means, finally, finally, it's June's turn to drive.

                                          ⌒

Sy insists on watching the ball game on the kitchen TV. His suite, he says, still reeks of "pain, I mean paint."

"Interesting slip, Dad."

"Neither is good for a guy in my condition."

"The human condition?" Dan knows his father just wants company but is too stubborn to ask. Sy's eyes widen as he passes the counter where Dan's at work assembling an eggplant lasagna. Rose wasn't lying; she knows how to feed a crowd. After the clams oreganata, she talked Dan through roasted peppers, stuffed artichokes, bruschetta, escarole, roast chicken, veal piccata, and three kinds of pasta.

"This is not Jewish food," Sy bellows. "Thank God!"

Dan can relax a little. The old man is satisfied. And without a brisket in sight. He's sure the Jews would have had a sunnier story if all their food weren't brown or beige — matzo, kugel, gefilte fish. The whole twentieth century might have gone down differently if only for trippy purple eggplants, heart-red tomatoes, fresh green basil. "And it's Rose, not God, you should thank, Dad."

"Noted." Sy folds himself into what has become, overnight, *his* chair by the little TV. "But Sue's right, for once; it's time we ease her out."

"Ease her out?" For some reason, Dan pictures June's hand the time it got caught in that giant-claw game machine.

"We can't have Rose here tomorrow when Bob Baum shows up at Sue's party."

"Why can't we?"

Conveniently for Sy, they're interrupted. "Doorbell!" "For he's a jolly good fellow, for he's a jolly good fellow. For—"

Dan's just waiting for the chime to trigger his next migraine. "*You* answer it, Dad."

"A dying man hasn't time."

Dan whirls a layer of sauce onto his noodles. Sprinkle the cheese, arrange the eggplant, start again, sauce, noodles; so soothing. "You're not dying, Dad, you're lazy, which nobody can deny, just a lazy—"

The back door squeals. Footsteps across the dining-room tile. Here's June, skidding into the room, her usual skirt replaced by cutoff jean shorts, carroty hair folded into a long, sophisticated braid. "Is the bell broken? I had to go all the way around back!" Then she talks too fast to follow—the garden center, Rose, poison...

"Poison ivy?" Dan asks, debating whether to criticize her heavy hand with the eyeliner or compliment her on the braid.

"Poison plants."

"Poisonous? But we just used some herbs in the clams."

"I don't know! The guy at the store said—"

"Wait. Is that—" The doorbell again ringing even though June's inside.

Sy hauls himself up from the chair—"Who's lazy now?" He's standing not for the door but for the national anthem. "Sing it, Junior!"

June rolls her eyes. She loathes that nickname. Nonetheless, she slaps one hand across her heart and belts it out: "'By the dawn's early light.'" Like Sue, June can *sing*. So the question always is: Will she?

Dan slips two fingers under her backpack strap and massages his daughter's bony shoulder. "Do me a favor? Please don't use the word *poisonous* in front of your mother." Then Dan returns to his lasagna.

"Skanky Yankee," Sy hollers as the camera pans over Roger Clemens. "I heard you wear a skirt!"

 ∾

"The door!" Sue yells from upstairs. "Someone!" For he's a jolly good fuckhead. That demonic knell won't stop. "I'm on the phone!" Sue's waiting for Rose's daughter-in-law, Maureen, to pick up (or not) and the two sounds—phone and doorbell—overlap and combine, making the bedroom feel even stuffier than it already does, even with all the windows wide open. She pictures her long-awaited daisies left to bake to dust on the stoop. "Hello? Hey! Anybody down there?"

A series of by-now-familiar creaks in the fireplace wall join the various ringtones. These "haunted" sounds intrigue rather than spook her. Imagine if it were possible, if someone *were* listening? "Are you there?" Sue breathes, pressing her mouth against the cool plaster. *"Who are you?"*

"Yes?" a brisk, nasal voice on the phone answers. Figures. Sue finally gets through to Maureen while she's talking to a wall. "Who's calling?"

"This is Sue, Sue Ainsley." So the conversation is now launched without a greeting from either party. Bad omen. "The wife of one of the Glassmans?"

"Shoot."

"Excuse me?"

"I get it. Go on."

Sue takes a porcelain dragon from the shelf over the fireplace. Red eyes, tongue stuck out. She throws it onto the bed.

"Um, can we speed this up? I'm in Provence at a conference."

"In Provence at a conference," Sue's compelled to repeat. "In Provence at a conference." It's like the opposite of *humdrum rhododendron* but just as musical.

"Excuse me?"

Sue adds a fan and a paperweight to the dragon on her

pillow. She hadn't planned to start collecting all of Rose's Chinese knickknacks, but it turns out to be rather cathartic. She clears the shelves of lacquered boxes while she talks. "What type? Of conference."

"Vet," Maureen says.

"I had no idea—thank you so much. For your service."

"Veterinary."

"Ha. You must get that a lot."

"What can I do for you, Sue?"

"I left a message—"

"You and everyone else in that godforsaken house. If it's the boiler—"

"Someone else called you?"

"Your father-in-law. And someone named Dan."

"That's my husband."

"Don't you people communicate?" Maureen's brittle tone stops Sue from yanking down the strings of lanterns that outline the bedroom windows. Rose probably had to pay to have them hung. No way would this Maureen woman have done it for her. Down on the lawn, Rose appears to be rocking an imaginary infant, but by now Sue knows she's just nursing her bad elbow.

"It's your mother-in-law," Sue tells Maureen, though the boiler is also a faulty, antediluvian mystery. "She keeps showing up at the door—"

"Don't let her in."

"Not that simple. You might have mentioned the backyard's a cemetery."

"Every backyard's a cemetery."

"How so?"

"This is why I hired Bibi."

"Bibi's too busy flashing her boobs at the neighbor to even notice Rose is sitting in full sun. I'm watching them right now and I can tell you she hasn't moved the umbrella all—"

"All right." Maureen sounds jaded. Sue can hear her knuckles cracking. "You're telling me that five of you can't figure out a way to evict a ninety-year-old in a wheelchair?"

"When you put it that way...yes."

"Look, I know she's a wacko bitch—"

"Isn't that a little harsh?"

Maureen laughs. "Evidently, you don't know much about my mother-in-law."

"I know you fucked her over!" Sue blows up. "I know you lied so she'd sign the contract to sell this house and that's why she keeps coming back. I know *that*." Of course, Sue didn't really know or even believe that. But now Maureen's silence all but proves it's true. Holy shit! What a thoroughly repellent woman. Sue lifts the snaky-river print off the wall, flings it onto the pile.

Massed together on the bed, the colorful objects take on a less insane, more thoughtful aspect. That Rose sought out rather than recoiled from all things Chinese after the tragedy could be a sign of strength, of owning it. For the first time, Sue lets herself imagine one of her own children dead or, worse, murdered. A wobbly, trapped feeling descends. She grabs the windowsill.

Flash-forward a few decades and Sue could be the old lady alone in and defending this house. On the phone, June or some June relation will be the one calling Sue a wacko bitch, ticking off her many screwups—who says *fuck you* to her sixteen-year-old kid? Then again, by then, Rockaway will probably be underwater. (There's a reason the city dumps its disenfranchised here, and it's not to provide them with a view.) And the rest of New York? A police state, perhaps. Once all the gulls are gunned down, they'll start lining up Muslims to shoot at Kennedy Airport.

"What you did, that's immoral," Sue tells Maureen, but she meant to say *illegal*.

"That doesn't make it wrong."

A new shuffling noise starts up behind the fireplace. Sue hears it as the bass line for the baby's solo kicking. She's bored in there. Whoever's in the wall is probably bored too. Both are getting ready to bust free. Soon.

"I had to get her out of that death trap," Maureen says. "She broke her leg. The stairs! It wasn't workable." Sue listens greedily for reasons that Rose can no longer live in the house but her conscience keeps overriding Maureen's excuses. That poor woman! "When she started smoking cigars and talking nonsense—"

"About her son?" Through the window, Sue sees, her own fuzzy children are busy with other people, real and imaginary. June passes a flat of flowers to Tim. Sage sprinkles brown grass on Ed (presumably). Ed chases her out through the beach door. Squinting makes all of them shrink and grow, appear and disappear. "Killing her son?"

"That's my husband," Maureen reminds her. "I'm the widow."

"My condolences." Sage turns back and sticks her tongue out at the invisible boy at her heels. Then she sprints toward shore. "Stop her!" Sue says involuntarily.

"What?"

"Not you." With the phone still pressed to her ear, Sue lurches from the room and down the stairs. None of the adults outside seem to be paying any attention.

"Look," Maureen says. "I'm at a conference."

"A conference in Provence."

"What the hell is your problem? Never mind, I gotta run."

"No, *I* gotta run."

◦―

The back door pops another hinge as Sue blasts out, a blur of orange braids, blue bikini, iPod cords. The noise levitates Blacky into guard-dog posture. As she makes her way out on the beach, the mutt barks so insanely Tim has to put down the tank of fungicide to run and grab his collar. Hard not to titter along with Bibi as Sue throws the phone onto the lawn and waddles over the sand after Sage. The little pirate crew have been running around on the beach since they moved in, when a layer of snow covered the sand. Sue has just picked today to notice.

The dog is still barking when Sue returns, dragging the girl by the wrist. (For some reason, Sage has been in her underwear all day, bare limbs brown in places where dirt has stuck to the sunscreen.) Tim throws an imaginary Fresca bottle to send Blacky back through the hedge. The mutt's

as addicted to fetch as he is to protecting his friend. Before
the girl appeared to cure the animal, he'd stare at the fetch
object—bottle or ball—long after, hours after, it had ceased
to move.

"Do Ed now!" Sage squeals, thrilled with her mom's attention. "Pull Ed too!"

But Sue's not playing. Nor does she want Bibi's assistance
in retrieving the beeping phone from the grass. "I got this."
With one hand clamped against her back and the other
straight out in front of her, Sue very gradually squats. Reen-
ter Blacky, charging at her crotch.

"Jesus! I'm sorry!" Tim says, sending the mutt home
again, this time with a sharp slap on the butt. "Bad dog!"
Blacky has forged himself a nice passageway through the
rhododendron. He barrels back and forth so carelessly that
each trip digs a new scratch into his dingy coat, knocks a
new flower onto the grass. The blooms blow around lightly—
small, silent white bells that smell like root beer. When no
one's looking, Tim likes to stand around and breathe it in.

Bells and cups, balls and tongues. The curves and scents
of flowers calm Tim. One creamy gardenia had enough juice
to perfume his entire hospital room. There are roses the
color of bruises. Recovery monotony, self-loathing, the endless arrangements people sent to Ox, the firefighter in the
next bed. Who knows what started Tim lusting after flowers.
But right away, he was avid, driving around to plant nurs-
eries, subscribing to gardening magazines. Soon he found
himself fantasizing about frangipani, ogling orchids. It was
flower porn, essentially. But it got him through those early

post-surgery, post-9/11, post-plane-crash days without vodka, wife, best friend, dog, mom (she can't drive and won't fly now). His always absent father did show up in one of Tim's greasy withdrawal dreams but since the whole nightmare took place on the ocean floor, there wasn't any talking.

To learn from the driver's ed kids that much of Rose's garden is potentially lethal concerns Tim on behalf of the Glassmans. Simultaneously, it's thrilling. Unloading the flowers from the car, Tim grinned at the Asian lilies, throbbing orange with black, erect stamens, and the pink cyclamen, tissue-soft, wondering how their gorgeousness was tied to their danger and whether it was a misstep to tell June his mom's (finally understandable) theory that Rose "offed her awful husband with one of her delicious medicinal teas."

Once the car was unloaded, Tim had tasked the teens with removing and replacing soil, spreading compost, et cetera, and returned to the fungicide. The irony isn't lost on him — applying poison to the only nonpoisonous thing in the yard. But Tim's got no choice. If he balks, who knows? Rose might whip out that gun.

Tim hauls the tank over to where Sue now lies on the grass, letting Sage and Ed line her tattooed arm with cherries.

"Um, hi," Tim says, carefully setting down the fungicide. To occupy his empty hands, he picks off a withered blossom fixed to a twig by a gummy mass. "Rose asked me to get this." Tim bends over to read the label's minuscule print. "'Azoystro-bin.' Dan and Sy both gave the okay."

"Spray! Go!" Rose rallies from the audience. "Why the big

production?" Just sassing them. Rose knows full well you don't use pesticides with everyone standing around. "So do something else, then," Rose says, flapping her mottled hands. "Fertilize my lily of the valley. Or should I call it lily-of-the-help-me-Timmy-never-gave-me-any-water!"

Tim ignores her, watching June saunter over with a cardboard box for Sage's treasure. He can't spray the tree until the kid and her loot have been safely relocated.

"Are we going home?" Sage asks but June just puts the box on the ground and keeps walking.

Tim makes the girls uncomfortable. Anyone would notice. June never, ever makes eye contact with him. And Sage all-out winces when he kneels down beside her. It's the sight of his missing nostril so close up, Tim assumes. To the Glassman females (including Sue), it's totally repulsive. Unless what offends them is his red chin, his copious sweat, bad breath? From the treasure pile, Tim picks out a piece of light green sea glass (ancient Fresca?) and chucks it into the empty box.

Sage fishes it right out again, holds it to her naked chest. Her own nose is so tiny, it's more like two holes poked into her face. But she's smiling. So Tim tries again, throws a water pistol into the box. Sage removes it.

"What's that?" Tim says. "Can you talk a little louder, Ed?"

Sage giggles. "He's not talking."

Tim leans in confidentially. "No, he's whispering. A secret."

"Secret what?"

"Better treasure. Over there." Tim points down the lawn

to where the beach and street walls meet. In that corner June and Kenny are digging a hole for some climbing hydrangea. "That's the lucky plant," Tim continues. "How you can tell is, its leaves are shaped like hearts."

Sage's eyes gleam at the word *hearts*. She slowly places a piece of sea glass back in the box. Tim adds a doll's arm, a seaweed pod, a busted FDNY key chain that must once have belonged to him. Sage follows with a broken pink plastic pail. It's working!

Sue pushes herself up onto her elbows. Braced for approval, Tim feels a dumb warmth spread through his chest. When Sue instead asks what he's so dressed up for, the sensation shoots up his neck, covers his face. "Ah, you're blushing; it's a woman, then."

For a second, Tim's actually tempted to confide in Sue. Maybe she'd like him more. She'd definitely offer her honest opinion about whatever it is he and Peg are doing. Nah, too chancy. Easier to turn back to the safety of children. "Sage, Ed, look here." Tim shows them the fungicide. "This is tree medicine for the cherry—she's sick. But it's bad for kids and pirates. Really bad, like *deadly*, so nothing goes in your mouth. Stay away."

"Sage?" Sue asks. "Did you hear that?" The girl is following the progress of a huge ant across her hand. Tim knows everything there is to know about ants, which exist on every continent except Antarctica. But this is not the time, not with Sue getting to her knees, the homemade bandage around her thigh unraveling. "Say you understand what Tim said, baby."

Sage squashes the insect under her thumb experimentally. Her face twists as the creature stops moving and falls to the ground.

Sue lifts her small chin. "C'mon, baby, say it."

"We are not a baby!" As proof, Sage and Ed gobble down a handful of grass apiece.

"Spit that out! Now!" Sue shouts.

Bibi's flowing purple fabrics ripple in amusement. "Scolding a ghost! That's a new one."

"Ed's not a ghost." Sage glares.

But Bibi is still fixated on Sue, struggling to stand. "Oooh, look at you, puffy Mommy. Easy now. You don't want to wind up like Cheryl."

"Who?"

"That's my sister. The doctor had to dislocate her baby's shoulder to deliver. Of course, you're a lot older than Cheryl, so the risk is even great—"

"Bibi," Rose says, "shut the hell up!" Then she thrusts her hand into the white pocketbook.

Tim dives for Rose, yells, "Duck!" In his head (from the beach?) he hears one short toot—the lifeguard whistle for *freeze*. Then Dan explodes out the back door. That is, the back door is exploding, finally off its rusty hinges and onto the brick patio in a spectacular clatter of metal and wood. "What happened?" Dan yelps, jumping nimbly around the debris. "Everyone all right?"

June and Kenny crack up.

But Tim has laser focus. He hovers above the wheelchair. "Show me what you've got in there, Rose!" Tim's palms clamp on the wrinkly fingers, damp and frigid despite the heat.

"You're hurting her!" Sue shouts. "Let go!" Tim obeys, reluctantly. Rose pulls a cigar out of her bag, to taunt Tim, he's sure of it. She's got a gun in there! He has to do something. But Sue's berating him. "You should be ashamed, Tim."

"Yeah." Bibi piles on. "Calling yourself a hero. I still can't get over that."

*What?*

Bibi pushes Tim aside, lights the smoke, unzips Rose's sweatshirt. Tim's extra-rattled to see the old lady's got one of her late husband's cowboy shirts on underneath. Some of the snaps are missing.

"Oh my God, can't everyone just leave her be?" Sue asks.

Tim quickly backs away.

"Wait!" Dan calls, kicking aside a piece of door in his path. "You can't go. The garden! The party. You guys! Don't fight!"

Next it's Sy in his boxers and black leather vest. "Woohoo! Mets won!" He appears oblivious to the fact that he's standing where the door was (now a rectangular hole in the back of the house). Estes failed to hit Clemens with a pitch, Sy reports, but he did homer off him and "they won! Just came to say. Happy day!" Then the stick figure is reabsorbed into the house.

Dan plasters on a beaming mouth. "Who here would love a piña colada? On a beautiful afternoon like this."

Sage raises her hand. Bibi too. "Yes, please."

"Drinks?" Sue mutters. "Really?"

"Never mind! We're leaving!" Bibi shoves the wheelchair so forcefully, she loses her balance. The entire top layer of her braid starts to slide past her left ear, her shoulder...

"Hey! Your hair's coming off!" Sage shrieks.

Bibi rights herself, catching the extension. She tosses it onto Rose's lap. "Time to go."

"No!" Rose flings the braid back at her.

"Say good-bye, Rosie."

"Stop! I'm not ready."

And when Bibi won't listen, when she keeps pushing the chair, the old woman turns and touches her lit cigar to the aide's slender middle finger.

Bibi leaps back. Her mouth opens, closes, opens. Daintily, she raises the injured hand and regards the small burn there. "You're a sick woman," she says quietly. "Tell Maureen I quit." And, unable to resist a last jab at Sue: "Good luck birthing that big girl, Mommy."

"Oh no," Dan says, sensing some peril at last. "You can't leave without Rose." Looking back at Sue, he mouths, *Girl?*

"Bye-bye," Sage calls. Bibi's purple tunic balloons in the breeze like a jellyfish.

At a loss, Dan Glassman once again turns to Tim.

◦⌒

"And how could I say no to him, to Dan Glassman?" Tim asks Peg not an hour later, pacing her porch. After Bibi left, Tim's always-together neighbor began to crack. His linen shorts were covered in bread crumbs. A tiny splinter of door glinted in his eyebrow. Thirty people were due at his party tomorrow and he had no back door and four trays of possibly poisoned clams. Finally, he'd come around to his wife's view that Rose might pose a threat. And Sue had decided that in fact the old woman was instead a victim who needed them. So who is right? And who is Rose?

"Don't know," Tim says truthfully. Then he revealed to Dan (and now Peg) how much he actually feared the old lady—Scary Impoliteri. It felt great to unburden himself even of this, the smallest fragment of his story. But when Dan heard it, his broad chest caved. Turns out, the dude is not nearly as sturdy as he seems. None of the Glassmans, it turns out, are as sturdy. While Tim sprang into action, trying to herd Rose into his car, even Sue (the old lady's new defender) just stood there, stunned and aging. In the end, Tim had no choice but to lure Rose with Sambuca, or the promise of it. Point is, he can't stay long. Rose is outside in his car, anxious to hit the liquor store.

Peg sits on a case of tuna and listens. At least she gives the impression she's listening—head bent to reveal the gray under strands of her long, unwashed blond ponytail, chewed-up fingernails tracing a line down the thigh of her brown park ranger pants. Soon as Tim stops talking, Peg once again asks about her respirator masks. Don't tell her he forgot to bring them a third time. And what's he so dressed up for?

"Trying to impress you," Tim says, as if joking. He assures her the masks are in his trunk and gets up from the couch.

Around the batteries, over the blankets, to the side of five-gallon water jugs, Tim forges a path across Peg's living room, detouring only to kick at a pile of wetsuits by the TV. Peg's wetsuit hasn't been worn since 9/11, when, like many, like Tim, she had risen early to call in sick and take advantage of the hurricane-grade surf. Now she vows never again to take another fake sick day. Now she stalls and stalls on the date for the memorial paddle-out. Tim would like to tickle and tickle her until she changes her mind. "Did it work?"

"We'll see."

By the door, three full backpacks sit, ready to roll. No, Peg's not going camping. "Off the grid, then? I'll miss you guys."

Peg laughs, follows Tim out to the car. All her emergency preparedness has, she insists, actually made the kids feel safer. And who is Tim to argue? How many other eight- and six-year-olds know how to use a desalinator and tie three commendable knots apiece? But the older child, Bridget, has developed a habit of compulsively smoothing her right eyebrow. And whenever aircraft fly overhead (several times a day), little Ryan still pinches his face and asks if it's a good plane or a bad plane.

Not wanting to introduce Peg to Rose, Tim steers her around the back of the embarrassing yellow Steer-Rite Auto School vehicle. She's the one friend who hasn't ever razzed him about his ride. Yet he's amazed to hear her call the mess in his trunk "brilliant!"—wads of clothes, dog bones, fishing gear? Why didn't *she* think of having supplies in the car, at the ready. "So clutch!" When the next thing happens and she needs to get gone—

"*I'll* come get you," Tim says, touching her cheek with

an open palm. "This is the first place I'd come." Strategically, he should probably help the Glassmans first, but Peg comes before everyone. He's just realized. (Better grab a mask to take home and use while spraying the tree, though.) "The flak they gave me at the firehouse for requesting these...you wouldn't believe. We didn't even use them at Ground Zero."

Peg grabs Tim's hand and squeezes. "Hey, skip the liquor store? For *me?*" Her words might sound basic but they come at him like storm-surge waves made in deep water, intensifying as they head to shore, his ear. "Take the masks. I don't care. Only *don't* drink!" The kind of waves you both fear and fantasize riding. "This is important." No one, not even his mother, ever talked to Tim in this way, so specifically.

"Peg—"

"Okay, we'll do the paddle-out. Tonight. Let's just do it. From your house...eight? I'll call around." Peg moves in closer. "Just stop looking so sad."

Tim is so sad but also elated, feeling Peg press herself against him and say, "Stick with me...you and me." Over her shoulder, in the trunk's sandy, dank recesses, he spies the lilacs he bought for her at the garden center and retrieves them, presents them.

Years ago Peg took the firefighter test along with Chowder and Tim. And failed. But it couldn't have been fair. There is nothing weak about her. And nothing about her Tim doesn't desire—stale coffee breath, chapped lips, traumatized kids included. Two decades ago, on a cruise to nowhere, the two of them embarked on a brief, charged affair that healed Tim's first broken heart. One decade ago, at the Irish Circle, they confessed to each other (knees pressed together playfully, drunkenly, under the bar) that they weren't in love with their fiancés. Only ready to be in love, ya know? Ready to get going. Tim's mate, Alicia, was, unbeknownst to him, pregnant (and soon to abort, without his consent). Peg's fiancé, Chowder, was her best pal (and Tim's too). Now, their romance feels as wrong and right as an icy Vodka Grapefruit. Tim longs to knock it back, hard and fast. Peg's small braless breasts push against him under the pockets of her work shirt.

Then Peg's kids race up with their chocolate faces. You can hear the ice cream truck jingle recrank as the truck heads away, "Pop Goes the Weasel" fading. Chocolate also dots the part in Bridget's nearly white hair, the inside of one elbow, and a thin wrist. But even as Tim cheerfully notes this, little Ryan's cone is slipping from his chubby hands. "Uncle Tim, Uncle Tim!" the kid's shrieking. "There's a dead lady in your car!"


When Tim makes a play for the pocketbook, Rose hawks up a glob of saliva. It misses Tim's right eye, trickles down the bad side of his face. Talk about... "Nasty. Were you, like, *pretending* to be asleep?"

"Trying not to embarrass you in front of your girlfriend." Rose smirks and offers him a used tissue from her sweatshirt sleeve. Tim just wipes his face on his jacket and backs up the car, one last look at Peg before leaving. She is *fixing* the drips on little Ryan's cone, the way his own mother used to do, circling around it with her tongue. A ruse to eat some, he sees only now after all these years. Ha!

"Paddle-out. Eight. Your house!" Peg calls when she sees Tim watching. She waves the wilting bouquet and the ice cream cone, both. "Don't forget what I said..."

It seems as if Tim, not Peg, is the one receding from view. Not even down the block, he already, unreasonably, misses her. As Tim drives on, he tells himself she's right. He should skip the liquor store. And wrong: Just a task. No reason to attach any meaning to it. The key is that Peg cares what he does or doesn't do. Once he buys Rose Sambuca and gets her the hell home, the gun will no longer matter. Only then can they honor Chowder and move on.

"Jesus Christ, ghost!" bawls the sole Licker Store employee, Flounder. So called because of his flat face and eyes disconcertingly far apart. Flounder holds a hand over his heart as if he's about to say the Pledge of Allegiance. "Where've you been?"

Tim shrugs.

"I thought you were dead, man!"

Was he kidding? How could this be? Of all people, Flounder had to have heard about Tim's 9/11 alcohol-fueled disgrace. So did he hear and forget? Louie's never been the sharpest knife in the drawer, not even before his jet-ski accident. But still...

The man has tears in his eyes. Flounder turns away, to collect himself, or so Tim thinks, until the multi-tattooed arm reaches for the Stoli. Well, he remembers *that*.

"Hold up, I'm not—I quit drinking," Tim tells the thick neck. Eight months, three weeks, six days. "I'll just take some Sambuca."

If Flounder notices the contradiction in the sentence, he's kind enough not to mention it. His fingertips slide over to the shelf of liqueurs.

"Um, the travel size?" Tim specifies. "Like a dozen?"

Flounder squeezes his own biceps over his biggest tattoo. A skull encircled by anchors, some kind of Coast Guard symbol.

"It's not for me," Tim adds, only making himself sound more pathetic. Mercifully, the mini-bottles are already bagged. Flounder says they're on him, "for old times' sake."

Tim knows he should insist on paying, but he needs to get out of this store. The guy is gaping at him like he's some kind of apparition.

"Great to see ya, Chowder," Flounder calls over the door jingle. "God bless."

⌒

The seagulls know best how to open a clamshell: drop it from a height. "I could have saved myself a lot of trouble," Dan observes, swerving to avoid one of the many snacks raining from the sky. "This shit is dangerous." Sue and Dan stroll slowly down the shore, swinging Sage, still in her pink underwear, between them. Forced to join this "family time," June alternates between marching ahead and lagging behind.

"When I was a kid, we used clams as bait," Dan goes on. "Sy and I, fishing for stripers. My mother loved cleaning my catch."

"She did not." Sue laughs, admiring the way a cruise ship slides along the horizon.

"She did."

"Not."

"Well, she said so."

"No one likes cleaning fish!"

Dan stops, drops Sage's hand. Parenthetical wrinkles enclose his bright eyes. Of course that's right. Of course his mother just said that to make him feel good. Dan just never thought about it.

June groans. "You two should write an encyclopedia of all the most boring things to talk about."

"It's not boring to us," Sue says, but it is, kind of. Fish. If only Sue could think of a subject to interest her daughter, now making devil horns behind an oiled, wrinkled woman walking past in a string bikini.

"Remember your play about the porcupine? The porcupine that couldn't get comfortable?" June had won some contest for it. Fifty dollars and a plaque!

June sighs. "I was eleven." And: "You shouldn't have let me blow all that money at the arcade."

Strike one. Sue joins Sage, who's combing for treasure (there's never enough, is there?). Unfortunately, the long strands of washed-up debris consist mostly of broken shells strangled in putrid black seaweed with the occasional pink tampon applicator or beer-bottle neck.

"Your bottle with the message..." Sue thinks to try this on June. "It must be halfway to England by now. I mean, how storybook was that setting last night? Under the moon, the fire—"

"I don't want to talk about it," June mumbles, reddening.

"Ohh," Dan teases. "Junie sent a love note in a bottle."

"No!"

Sue imagines it was "probably more like a hate note. 'Help! Help! Save me from my dull parents!'" Sage guesses, "'Hello, mermaids.' Did you put that, Junie? Junie? Did you put 'Hello—'"

"No!" June explodes. "I just wrote 'Why?' plus my e-mail address, and some perv already found it, like, a mile down the beach." She motions vaguely eastward where blocks of housing projects seem to loom straight up from the sea. "'Suck my big dick!' they wrote back. That's it. Okay? 'Suck. My. Dick.'"

Dan's covering Sage's ears.

Sue's hands are balled into fists. These reactions make June laugh, despite or because of her obvious anguish.

"Vulgar boys," Dan says. "Why do I even want one?"

"How do you know it was a boy?" June scoffs.

"Well..."

June accepts an awkward hug from bulky Sue but her hands stay busy splitting her split ends.

Sunset pink sheens the sea, trims the clouds. The day's scorching temps have cooled and with them Sue's rage. She admires the waves, polished by the offshore winds. But a fire never ends abruptly. Sue pokes at the smoldering embers: Bibi's intense presence, Sy's entitlement, and the tense phone call with Maureen. Someone has to do right by Rose, but why does it have to be Sue? It's her house now, the only house in which she, a city kid, has ever lived. She can't be expected to just give it back. Gazing from the beach toward the house's ivied rear, viewing the blue pattern of tile and masses of greenery, you'd never imagine how badly the roof leaks, that the bricks need repointing, how hard it is for Sue to keep her piano tuned in so much salt and humidity. Solidity and refuge is all you see, a structure that appears somehow more real than the weathered wooden shacks, faux Mediterranean mini-villas, and dispassionate apartments lining the sand. Even the famous boardwalk, which starts two or three blocks east and continues for miles, might have been slapped together by the Mole-Kacy boys from two-by-fours.

Lost in thought, Sue nearly trips over a speckled-headed seagull she failed to see land in her way. The creature regards her with beady eyes, one foot protecting her clam dinner. Sue tries to apologize telepathically. And warn *Avoid the airport at all costs!* Her throat thickens.

"Are you tearing up about birds again?" June asks with undisguised disgust.

Sage tugs Sue's hand. "It's just a TV show, Mommy."

It's a trial trudging over the last bit of soft sand to the house. Sue's groin aches; all her calf muscles are popping. Stopping to rest, she starts at the sight of Rose's empty wheelchair like some kind of macabre lawn ornament. Tim must have forgotten it when he hoisted Rose into the car. "We have to get it back to her, Dan. And all her other stuff too. At the very least, after the party—"

"Let's drop it," Dan says, hooking Sue's arm with his.

"The party? Or Rose?"

"Both." Dan pulls Sue along—impatient? Devoted? People sit up from their towels, wondering. "Leave it! Sue. Please. Just be glad she's gone."

"Think again," June says, the first one through the beach door.

"Humdrum rhododendron," Sage adds, number two in line. Third is Sue. Sure enough, there's Rose, beyond the hedge. Tim's got her draped over his shoulder in the old fireman carry, only he's entering, not exiting, the house. His. The white pocketbook dangles incongruously from his muscular forearm.

"What's he doing to her?" Sue asks, then shouts, "What are you doing? You put her down!"

"Lemme guess," Sue says, remembering Bibi's bullshit. "He thinks Rose killed her son."

"What?" Dan's shocked.

June fans her thin arms around at the half-dug-up, half-planted garden. "She poisoned him?"

"That's ridiculous," Dan says, uncertainly. "Am I right?"

Sue thinks so. "If Rose was going to poison anyone, it would be Maureen." All the while, her eyes remain on Tim. Soon as his sliding door is cracked, Blacky squeezes himself out and barrels through the hedge toward Sage.

"So Rose is going to sleep there?" June asks, her voice full of yearning. She pulls off her pack, plops dejectedly into the vacant wheelchair.

"Get up!" Sue snaps, unable to bear the image of a handicapped June.

"Oh my God, chill." June takes her time rising. "I'll bring the chair back—"

"Over my dead body!" Dan says, startling even himself. The phrase was a favorite of his mother's. His mother, now a dead body. Dan looks fretfully from Tim's house to June and back again. "I don't like the way June looks at Tim. He's way too old."

"Exactly why I questioned driver's—"

"Stop talking about me like I'm not here!" June wails. "Forget it, keep talking. I'm going out!"

"You are out." Dan motions feebly at the air as June storms along the side of the house, her bright ponytail like a protest flag, waving behind her. Only then does Sue notice that Sage has climbed into the chair.

"Get up! Up! Get out of there!"

♌

"Heavenly Blue or Pearly Gates?" Kenny asks, holding up two mason jars of murky liquid. June stands warily at the door to his garage, which doubles as a bedroom, which triples as an R&D lab for an array of his current schemes, like nonmelting ice cream, biodegradable gum, and the "two flavors of Safe-n-Sound morning glory water" he sells, among other drugs, to help fund his "research." Kenny hawks Ritalin under the tag Test Boost; MDMA is Parent Coper, et cetera. Only Cipro goes by its real name. "No one has any sense of humor about that."

"Where's the egg?" June asks, intent on not looking at his king-size futon (a green bedspread strewn with AP test-prep books). Kenny had lured her here claiming he'd smashed his egg. That's not entirely true. As June walked down the driveway she'd known he'd pop his eager face out the window; she'd willed it. Now she's asking herself: Was this wise? What kind of sixteen-year-old owns a Bunsen burner and isn't embarrassed to say so? Are his ingredients alphabetized on purpose? Apple seeds, baby oil, cardamom. "What's that smell?" Seaweed meets corn? "Just curious."

"Could be my dirty laundry," Kenny says, "but it's more likely the Safe-n-Sound process." Bouding over to a large, messy worktable smack in the center of the room, he reaches across some seltzer cartridges ("for poppers") to grab a coffee grinder. "The morning glory seeds get crushed in here. Then the powders soaked in alcohol—I use gin mostly—before filtering...you're not listening." Kenny actually seems to care.

"Where's the egg?" June repeats, again not looking at the bed (Mutant Ninja Turtle pillow) but instead out the window, across her own driveway to the side of her house. There, right under the kitchen sill, is a brick patch that she's never noticed is pocked with BB holes.

"Target practice," Kenny admits. Of course, since the Glassmans moved in, he's been shooting the DEAD-END STREET sign instead. Aiming helps him concentrate. This he needs to do if he's going to win the Westinghouse science contest with his natural bug repellent made from sand-shark skin and essential oils. When that happens and he gets admitted to MIT early decision, he will "buy her a shirt."

"What?"

"A shirt, you know, that says MIT." He drags two fingers horizontally across the chest of his white wifebeater. Over that, he wears a plaid short-sleeved button-down and over that the ubiquitous gray windbreaker.

"So where's the egg?"

Kenny opens his jacket pocket to reveal the yolky goo inside. "You were walking by and I got excited."

"Oh God." June backs out of the doorway a bit, but not so far that he can't stop her. His direct, black-eyed gaze makes her feel, for better or worse, *seen.*

"Hey, June. Wait, I'm joking!" Kenny's real egg, with the blue number 9, has been in his other pocket all along.

"You're sick," June says, giving in and looking at the bed. Kenny sits on the edge filling two martini glasses from the sludgy jar marked *Heavenly Blue.* (*The guy's a drug dealer,* June wrote in her daily e-mail to Jake. *He shot me. He fucked me. But, I don't know, he's, like, safe.*)

Kenny holds up the glasses. "A toast! To the ghost of Gary Impoliteri."

❧

Tim places Rose on his couch. Oddly solid she is, for a ninety-year-old. Tim has lugged enough bodies to know.

Through water and flames, he's lugged them, out of cars, over collapsed ceilings, down fire escapes, away from swarms of jellyfish, floating used condoms, and strangulating wads of plastic six-pack holders. So maybe it's true: Rose is a witch. The freaky white pocketbook, the equivalent of a broomstick or wand. Rose has kept her hands on it the whole way from car to house, and now, seated, yanks it roughly off Tim's arm. Of course he could easily snatch it back, but with his luck he'd wind up dead on his own living-room carpet, a grimy orange shag left over from his childhood.

Then, too, a fair fight is only right. They've come this far.

After the liquor store, Rose refused to return to assisted living. Tim drove all the way out to Forest Hills before discovering she would not cough up the address, not a chance. When he demanded it, Rose used that second pair of brakes, making the car buck to a stop in the middle of a thankfully empty street.

It was the moment between day and dusk. The trees and houses were just starting to look lavender and stamped on. A single firefly winked on the windshield as Tim desperately dialed Dan (who had given him Maureen's number), then Maureen (who didn't answer), then Peg, who said, "Tennis? *Why?* Everyone's headed to your house for the paddle-out!"

Peg, like Tim, had only one association with Forest Hills — the U.S. Open. Back in the eighties, Tim had once spent a miserable afternoon there with his then-girlfriend, Alex, and her family. Should have backed out like Peg had begged him to do. Should have given Peg his ticket. On the way, Alex heckled her mom for wearing tennis whites even though they arrived to find loads of others wearing them. And Alex's mood kept blackening as Martina Navratilova beat the crap out of Chris Evert, her pick. Looking back, Tim saw that Alex had already decided to break up with him but had waited until after the tournament since she'd invited him months before. Peg had known this. Peg had tried to guard Tim's heart a little.

"Tell me what you want, Rose."

"To go home. I have things to do."

"What's the address?"

"I'm your next-door neighbor!"

Peg said Alex called after the Trade Center attacks to ask after their "old friends," but who exactly were her friends? And what exactly did Peg say?

Alex was too far away—in Botswana, with her Doctors Without Borders husband—to fly home for Chowder's bodiless funeral. But in a sense, she'd been there, just as she'd be haunting Chowder's paddle-out. You rack up enough real moments with people and they'll poke at your psyche forever.

In the car, in Forest Hills, Tim offered Rose a deal. "Hand over what's in your pocketbook and I'll take you back. No questions. No hassles." Without hesitating, Rose unzipped the bag.

Tim's pulse tripled. "Be careful!"

But all she pulled out was a decrepit-looking Ziploc bag filled with bills.

"No, Rose. The gun."

"The *gun?*" One wiry gray eyebrow curled up in surprise. "Is that what you think is in here?" Rose leaned in even closer than the too close she was, and Tim shivered from the smell of cigars and...clams, if that was possible. "No wonder you've been acting so crazy."

"Me? You're the one carrying around that...relic!"

Almost all of the Asians aboard the *Golden Venture* carried similar Ziplocs, buttoned, pinned, or sewn into their clothing. Inside would be a scrap of paper with a contact number on Mott Street or Avenue U and a wad of cash.

"There's three hundred dollars in here," Rose said, her tone weirdly tender. "It was Li's."

"Li? That's the guy you framed?"

"Saved! He would have died in my shower house." Then Rose couldn't resist the joke. "Died from the smell of Blacky's pee." Tim laughed involuntarily. "At least he died in my home," Rose added, "beside a friend."

Friend! That fucking word again. Through the windshield Tim watched two Indian kids in Boy Scout uniforms slog house to house with a big box. *Are there Boy Scout cookies now?* Tim still felt guilty for drunkenly chewing out the Mole-Kacy boys when they tried to sell him candy for their school on 9/11.

"*Vin's* gun?" Rose asked. "You know, I forgot. It really shouldn't be in that house."

"Just hand it over. I have to get home."

"Me too!" Rose shook the bag of cash. "If you take me, I'll give you this."

"I don't want your blood money," Tim said, sounding like a gangster. If anything, he was one of those losers in a Greek myth: mortal Tim, having angered Poseidon by losing a child in the sea, is sentenced to an underwater eternity. Any time he tries to surface, a murderous hag pops up to shove him down again.

Tim drove home. No choice. He had to pee bad. Badly? Had to get back before Peg and the others arrived for the paddle-out. No way was he bringing Rose to the Glassmans. Everyone (except him) was more secure with her here.

Rose puts on her bifocals to assess the living room. "Your mother's a lot messier than I expected."

"She hasn't been here for almost a year, Rose."

"So that explains the mushrooms." She lifts the couch cushions, reveals two fist-size clusters of fungus.

Even Tim jumps. Who knew? "It's the dampness? I guess."

"Or you're just foul."

Understandably, Rose demands her wheelchair to sit in.

"In a while... Take my arm, now. One, two, three." He helps her onto a nearby La-Z-Boy.

Rose peers under the chair cushions. Satisfied nothing's growing, she immediately gets to work arranging her tiny Sambucas on the end table. Circle? Triangle? Rose settles on an arrow pointing toward Li's plastic bag. Early on, she had called the 212 number on a scrap of paper inside, but whoever picked up spoke only Chinese. A second time she bribed the Wok 'n' Roll delivery boy to stand by and trans-late, but the phone just rang and rang. Any further attempts were squelched when Maureen "stole" the info.

"Why would she do that?" Tim asks.

"Why?" Rose leans back in the chair. Her cracked face is not that far off from the cracked tan leather. "She stole my son; why'd she do that? She stole my house. She stole my

Jewish friends and they stole from me too—my best knife. Don't even get me started on Bibi, who stole my lipstick, my bracelet..." Rose blinks at her bare wrist for a minute then curves it around the little bottles, no doubt shielding them from alkie Tim. "Because I'm the one everyone steals from."

The outburst cows Tim somehow. It's true he's been after Rose's purse for the past twenty-four plus hours, but...

He doesn't want to try and understand it. "What would you have said, anyhow? If you got through to Li's contact. What would you even say?"

"'My condolences,' dummy! You *are* slow."

Tim heads into the kitchen to get her a glass. If he can't learn her assisted-living address via pleading, the Yellow Pages, the Glassmans, or Maureen, maybe Sambuca will loosen her tongue.

"Knock-knock!" Rose calls after him.

Only one Fresca left. Even bleaker are the dinner options: more toast, Cheerios, frozen fish sticks. Returning, Tim's spooked to find those eerie doll eyes trained on him. "All right." He sighs, pouring Rose's drink. "Who's there?"

"Where?"

"*You* said, 'Knock-knock.'" The Sambuca is vodka clear, but the scent is all wrong, black licorice in place of that yummy rubbing-alcohol aroma. "*I* said, 'Who's there?'"

"Your friends." Rose scowls at the sliding doors. Sure enough, they're arriving. And it's not just his friends congregating in his yard but relatives of friends. Here's Bean and his wife, Patty. And Peg's cousin, that guy, and three out of Chowder's seven older brothers. The youngest of the older brothers, Billy, hauling—oh, wow! Chowder's first-ever surf-board, a lemon-yellow Plastic Fantastic with (now faded) red panels. But in case Tim feels too uplifted, here's also Mike Fucking Sloane, decked out in his police uniform.

"Knock-knock," Rose resumes. Here's Lefty and Ox. "Knock-knock."

"Who's there?"

Where's Peg?

"9/11," Rose says.

Tim knows he shouldn't take the bait. He already has goose bumps. "9/11 who?"

"You said you'd never forget."

It's like Rose stepped on that second pair of brakes again, only this time they are situated directly under Tim's ribs. He grabs the gardening clippers off the top of the TV and goes outside.

Right away Bean's wife, Patty, is up in Tim's face with her horsey jaw and chardonnay breath, "Look at yeeew!"

"You seen Peg?" Tim asks, heading for some beach roses. "Was there trouble about a sitter or—"

Patty follows, nodding her blow-dried bangs and repeating, "Look at yeeew! Ya nose is healin' sooo good."

Tim attacks the dark pink shrub with the clippers. "If you haven't heard, I'm retiring, Patty. So you can tell Bean this is a waste of time trying to sic you—"

"Whatcha talking about, Timmy? Timmy? You all right?"

Timmy. Timmy. Like a lot of guys on 9/11, Timmy switched shifts to enjoy the huge swells, whipped up by the fringes of Hurricane Erin. Unlike a lot of guys, he downed

three Vodka Grapefruits for breakfast then filled a thermos
for the bike ride down to Ninety-Second, the best surf break.
By the time Chris D. appeared on the shore, with his fire gear
half on, Tim could paddle better than he could walk. Chris
D. took one look and raced back to where his car idled by
the beach wall, key in the ignition.

"What?" Tim had dropped his surfboard to chase him.
"What?" Chris D. dove into the driver's seat, U-turning
without closing the door. His sister had called him from her
office on the sixty-fourth floor of the North Tower, Tim later
learned. Delusional Chris thought he could simply drive into
Manhattan and save her.

"Go turn on a TV!" he screamed as he sped off. "And sober
the fuck up, Timmy!"

Maybe it was after that that Rose spied him, in tears,
weaving into his house. Or maybe it was the next day, when,
massively hung over, he donned his gear to go help search
the wreckage. Other than pride, it doesn't even matter.

Tim puts Patty in charge of handing out an armful of
beach roses. Crinkled petals. Windy smell. They seem perfect
for the occasion. Like many locals who died or were "vapor-
ized" on 9/11, Chowder had been working out of a firehouse
close to the towers. The Rockaway companies, being farther out, weren't immediately called. As for Chris D., he
was forced to abandon his car at the mouth of the closed
Brooklyn-Battery Tunnel. After strapping on his sixty
pounds of gear, he ran the rest of the way.

"Don't wait on Chris D.," Tim says. "He's working."

"All those cats stuck in trees," says Chowder's brother

Billy. Ironically, the guy's fat ass occupies Chris D.'s usual Adirondack chair.

It's already after eight, past time to get going. This Tim knows from the thin streak of horizon glow, all that's left of the light.

But still no Peg.

Tim shakes Billy's hand, knocks his legs off the cooler. He's jonesing for that whoosh of cold air. If he can't drink, there's still this, like Christmas, the many cheerful green bottles nestled in their bed of snow. But all it takes is for one person (Patty) to complain about the ice melting, and the happy box morphs into a coffin, the bagpipes start up in Tim's head. He slams down the lid without even retrieving his Fresca.

"New York collects more trash than any city in the world," brags Billy, the lone sanitation worker in a huge family of firefighters. Clearly, he feels inferior to his dead-hero brother. *"In the world,"* he repeats.

Bean considers. "That's a lot of garbage. But the thing is, you guys just pick it up, right? You pick it up and put it somewhere else. You don't *get rid of it.*" To illustrate, he three-points his empty bottle into a bucket of sinkers on Tim's porch.

They all howl at this, even Chowder's bro, though he pulls his Mets cap way down over his eyes first. Tim asks a question about recycling to buoy Billy, but the answer is so long-winded, he ends up interrupting it himself, asking, "Who wants Chinese? For after?"

Of course, everyone wants Chinese. What Tim's really asking is, "Who's going to *chip in* for Chinese?" He knows these tightwads. Chowhounds, all. Never a big eater himself, Tim was routinely burned on their on-duty trips to Waldbaum's, where the cost was split equally because…it just was. Tim despised every last thing about those outings — clomping down the aisles in their big boots, listening to bird-brain arguments about oatmeal, and, most of all, having to face the public. Respect for the uniform was the norm, but invariably some jerk would come marching up to gripe, "That's where my taxpayer dollars are going? Chervil?" or some shit like that. Rose was in the mold of those self-appointed scolds, the ones who'd yell after them when they'd strand their carts to answer a call: "Not so fast, boys! You go put that milk back!"

Patty snatches the cap off Billy's head and begins collecting money in it. "Don't forget the General Tso's," she reminds Tim. "Chowder's fave."

Tim slinks back inside, ashamed. How could he complain, even silently, about shopping or money when he was supposed to be paying his respects to his dead buddy? True to his name, Chowder had been by far the best cook among them. This, coupled with the dwindling of post-9/11 casseroles, and, Tim guesses, the guys at work are eating a whole lot of Wok 'n' Roll lately. Reaching for the cordless to order the food, Tim vows that next time he'll get off his ass and barbecue. It's the least he can do for them, his friends. "Fuck Mark Heartless No Name," he tells confused Rose. "They *are* friends. They are *my* friends."

Across the hedge, Sue fingers her iPod. It's a samba kind of evening, or "Scarborough Fair"—balmy wind, steamy air. Over at Tim's party in the yard, there's no music at all. But Sue's vowed not to plug in until she sees the three stars in the sky that signify the end of Shabbat. Sy insisted they'd be on the conversion quiz.

Dan flaps a Hefty bag at her. "What's a conversion quiz?" He's cleaning up the debris from the broken door. Distractedly. More energy is spent trying to act like he's not in some default competition with those surf dudes next door. Sue can see by his puffed-up chest the lengths he'd go to hang out with these "heroes." Were they to beckon Dan over, he'd easily abandon her to go assume the Posture—beer in hand, face to the sea, eschewing all but the most crucial eye contact. They remind her of toddlers in parallel play or middle-aged Lost Boys. She even spots their outer-borough Wendy—a frosted blonde in skintight designer jeans and pumps. She stalks around with a wine bottle (for herself), offering chips, ruffling what hair remains, picking bottle caps out of Tim's flower beds.

Sue would like to blame Estelle and all her coddling for Dan's interest. Pretending she liked to clean his fish was the least of it. That woman deseeded his grapes; she peeled his celery, and always served him, her only child, first no matter who else was at the table. But if Estelle's at fault then so is Sue, or she will be when June joins the cult or the gang, the NRA or the FDNY. At least Estelle raised a gentleman. No small feat, that. Dan would not only thank Wendy for the chips, he'd whip up some tasy guacamole.

"Suzy," Dan says, cupping her shoulders with his big hands and turning her toward him. "Don't stare at the neighbors."

"You're the one—forget it." Sue had been thinking about her own friends. The older ones (ex-bandmates) off in far-flung, less expensive cities—Portland, Austin. The newer ones (Tribeca moms) now living full-time in their "safer" weekend houses—the Hamptons, the Berkshires, the Hudson Valley. She liked them all. A couple of them she even loved. But not one would Sue be glad to see sitting in her yard every single day.

Dan catches her off guard with his best blue wink. "You do understand there is no conversion quiz."

"I do?"

"C'mon." Dan reaches down under her dress. "After all these years, you can't tell when Sy's pulling your leg?" Dan gently pulls Sue's leg. She wants to stay angry with him on principle, but in practice, it's just too exhausting. So it is in a long marriage. Sometimes the need for comfort has to override the pride of being right. Sue lets Dan's arms surround her. They maneuver for his height and her swell and kiss. The garbage bag still in his hand grazes the back of her neck.

"I'm thinking we should go to Gettysburg," she tells him. "After the baby's born."

Dan nods, clearly perplexed. "Definitely Gettysburg or... Maui?"

"I'm thinking an *E* name, for your mother."

"Ed?"

"Edie?"

"The first star!" blinks on. "At three o'clock!"—above the

latest beach fire. Sue's surprised by her own speedy joy. That light took years to get here! And: "Look, over there, number two! Unless those are planes or planets, asteroids or UFOs."

"Stars," Dan assures her, returning to his cleanup. "Stars are fixed and they twinkle." His certainty is sexy. Not that Sue has the energy. Still, there's pleasure in how his large agile body moves around in the dark.

"Should I board this hole up?" Dan asks when he's done. "Or should we live dangerously?"

"You mean until Tim gets to it?"

Dan takes the excuse to gaze back next door and wonder aloud whether Tim has wood. He could go over there and ask. Sue thinks of June this afternoon, pining for the neighbor in the same (and different) way. They think he's so protective. But Sue knows the truth. Tim and his ilk are the people with the targets on them.

"Leave the hole," Sue says, putting her hand in Dan's back pocket, wanting to keep him now. "Who'd rob a haunted house anyway?"

"Bob Baum?"

Someone begins to strum a guitar, fast and raucously, out of tune. Still, it works in its way, accompanied by the steady inhale/exhale of the sea, the percussive crunch of cooler ice, the occasional unwitting lyric—"That your beer?" "Where *is* Peg?" Wendy stretches her arms up and dances like a wind sock. A chained-up Doberman tastes some moonflowers that twine around the porch rail and glow. "Chooooowder!" wails a silhouette crouched on his surfboard. "Chooowderhead!" A lonely, ecstatic song. Others join him, one by one throwing down their boards to ride the grass. "Chooowder!" "Where are youuu?" "You owe me forty dollars, man." "We love you, Chowder." "Adios!"

⌒

Tim has Wok 'n' Roll on speed-dial so the order's placed in no time. Meanwhile he eyes his friends outside, hoping they won't wreck his lawn. As for Rose, for some reason, she is trying to pour her glass of Sambuca back into its miniature bottle.

"You're making a mess. Aren't you going to have any?"

Rose wags her finger. "Not on an empty stomach, Timmy. You should know that. Drink with food, all is fine."

"Not for me it isn't."

Rose rubs her eyes as if awakening. "Yes, even for you. Even a drunk like you can do it...go on. Give it a try."

It's a trick, Tim thinks, to weaken me. Still, he can't help wondering, *Could I manage? Just one beer with my eggroll?* (Tim's also got Mark No Name on speed-dial.) "Well, I ordered Chinese, so you can lush it up then, Rose. You love Chinese, don't you? You and your Chinese friend?"

"Li was a Christian!" Rose hisses, as if that in any way applies. Then she quickly crosses herself, like she does, like a tic.

"Looks to me like God bailed on him, then."

"God doesn't pick who's born in China or Rockaway. It's Li's luck that went badly."

"*Bad.* His luck went *bad.*"

The correction seems to confuse Rose. She blinks, first slowly, then faster and faster, spastically, like she did yesterday in the Glassmans' yard. "Didn't expect a *grammar* lesson from a high-school dropout, didja?" Tim asks. And while he's at it: "What about your son? Were things supposed to go so bad*ly* with *him?*"

Tim can easily jack himself up with rage thinking back to that dirtbag Gary: Pushed his own cat out to sea on a boogie board. (Tim rescued her.) Cuffed his own mother just because she asked if his shirt might be too tight. (Tim hid.) Gary's shirts were always too tight and his hog face clenched like his fist, like Rose's.

Thing is, the old lady never let you pity her. As far back as Tim could remember, Rose regularly accused Tim's mousy mom of sleeping with her own player husband, ridiculed her comparatively deficient garden, and encouraged Vin to "have a word" with Tim when his flag-football game flowed onto Impoliteri property. ("If you micks keep this up," Vin would threaten, pointing his lit cigar real close to Tim's eye, "I have a gun and I'm not afraid to use it.") Tim's mother talked the Christian-compassion talk, but she planted that hedge early on. And the night Rose torched the leaves of her table, Mom did eventually stop laughing long enough to call the cops.

"Ever wonder why I never called the cops?" Tim asks Rose now. If he can't figure it out himself, maybe she can. "The night of the *Golden Venture?*"

"You hate them?"

"Just one." Mike Sloane. And it's not really hate so much as fear. Tim can hear the guy right now through the screen belittling Chowder's brother Billy ("Babble on, garbageman") for boasting that sanitation workers have twice the fatalities of police. "Yo, and seven times as many as fire-fighters."

"Babble, babble. Still, you'll have to face it. You'll never match your little bro. He's Saint fucking Chowder now."

As usual, Sloane has an audience for all the worst reasons. Even Rose listens, murmuring, "That loud one I know. How do I know him?"

"He's the guy I didn't call to arrest you," Tim snipes. "Hey, there's an idea." On this frustrated impulse, he goes and beckons the officer in.

"One sec," Sloane says, holding up two fingers. He's midway down the row of Adirondack chairs, head bent to allow each and every guest the chance to pet his new buzz cut.

Tim flicks on his Malibu garden lights and lets the oohs and aahs console him.

၁—

No wet wood, says this bossy girl Becky with a neck brace. That'll only make the beach fire smoky. She's appointed herself fuel supervisor. Any offering of paper or wood that won't smell toxic is acceptable so long as *she* gives the okay. The dearth of local trees coupled with the surges in séances (death) has forced the kids off the beach, into garbage cans and garages. This explains the Monopoly board in flames, the stacks of papers to shred, the pair of shutters on deck. While she officiates, Becky (or Necky, as June's silently tagged her) sits real, real close to Kenny. On his other side is June, poking paper into a flaming tent of driftwood and cardboard. She's not jealous of the girl. Why should she be? It's June for whom Kenny organized this séance. It's June's house that needs un-haunting, for the relief of June and June's family. Once Gary Impoliteri is summoned and set free, Kenny promised, the ghost of the murdered guy will move on.

Problem is, aside from the brace, which turns Becky/ Necky's movements robotic, the girl is completely stunning. Oddly, everyone at the gathering is—stunning and female. This includes a set of eighth-grade identical twins with identical glittery eyelids and a tan, leggy brunette still in her lifeguard orange. Where gawky June fits into this beauty pageant is a mystery. Feigning amusement, June tells Kenny she's on to him. "The supernatural as chick bait! It *is* novel, I'll give you that."

Kenny responds with a thumbs-up. "Don't discount the morning glory water."

After the burnt offerings are approved by Necky, the girls visit Kenny for their dose-in-a-baby-bottle, choice of pink or blue. The way they sit around and chew on the nipples long after the containers are empty makes June sorry she consumed any of the drug drink, even from a martini glass. Her stomach feels motorized, her inner thighs, achy. She peers down at the papers she's burning—Tufts, Brown, U. of Mich. She's setting fire to a whole pile of rejection letters!

"Torch 'em." Necky, their apparent owner, applauds. She doesn't need college. She's already designed a line of disaster-proof clothing and sold it to ten stores on Long Island. June wonders if this is related in some way to her brace, but she will not give the interloper the satisfaction of asking.

It's surprising how glad June feels when Regina finally shows up. "Late, I know, sorry." There's a broken banjo wedged in her armpit. It looks like a cartoon banjo after it's been smashed over someone's head, birds circling around it, chirping.

"Hold up." Necky blocks the newcomer. "Bring that instrument here."

Regina hands the banjo to Necky but she sure isn't waiting for the girl's permission. She reaches into Kenny's insulated bag, chooses a blue bottle of Safe-n-Sound, unscrews the cap, downs the contents in one go, winces, and falls onto the sand next to June. "Whoa, hey. You already tripping?"

"I don't think so. Just my stomach." June imagines a living creature moving around in there. So surreal. How does her mother stand it?

"All in attendance now," Kenny says, growing serious.

Regina grabs June's hand. "Don't worry. When the ghost of Jake appears, I'll be right here."

"Jake?" Necky asks. "Who's that? It's Gary Imp we're calling."

"Oh, really?" Regina's bummed. "I just assumed it was Jake. I mean, isn't he more deserving?" For those unfamiliar with "June's tragedy," Regina now tells the "devastating" tale, chock-full of twists that keep everyone, even June, enthralled. How she and Jake were "*the* power couple" at Stuy. How Jake saved up all his money working at the skating rink to buy her a special bracelet, "twenty-four-karat gold." And all about their last phone call, on the morning of 9/11...

The twins have tears running down their high cheekbones

by the time Regina's through. It's mortifying. June busies herself ripping up a *New York Post*.

"Well," Kenny says. "It's June's call. If she'd rather we try and contact Jake—"

But Necky pouts. She didn't miss *American Idol* to chat with some random ghost boyfriend. She's had personal experiences with the Impoliteri house. Two Halloweens in a row, the phantom Gary felt up her costume and shoved her back down the stoop.

"Maybe you're just a klutz," Regina says. "Or too old to be trick-or-treating."

The girls glower at each other. June just goes on ripping up newspaper.

Becky Necky is "truly sorry" for June's loss but urges her to "be realistic. The main conduit to the deceased is through his or her possessions and—"

"Yeah, yeah." June knows all about it. She points to her backpack with her foot. Inside is the "authentic object belonging to Gary" that Kenny tasked her with bringing. "Though I don't really get it. Isn't that the beauty of being dead? Not having to carry your crap around?" She thinks about the burden of the egg in there too.

"Let's use June's bracelet to call Jake," Regina suggests. The girl is obsessed with it. "It had to have meant a lot to the guy."

June unclasps the gold bangle, hands it to Regina. She'd gladly give it to her but June's too trapped in her fiction. As the bracelet is passed around, the girls deem it "dreamy" and "perf." Necky has no choice but to give in.

"June?" Regina asks for the go-ahead. How can she deny her? How far her little lie has traveled.

Kenny takes the bracelet, then instructs them to put down their bottles, hold hands, and "listen hard, harder than you have ever listened before." The eighth-graders giggle at his deep voice—half put on, but mesmerizing. "Jacob Leibowitz, we are calling you. Are you there, Jacob Leibowitz? Jacob? Jacob?"

"He prefers Jake," Regina says.

⌒

Mike Sloane had always had it in for Tim. Maybe he'd just been bored during the four consecutive summers they'd spent side by side on a lifeguard chair or jealous of his pretty girlfriend or actually steamed that Tim didn't share his worldview. (In brief: Don't trust anyone but your dog.) Whatever the reason, Sloane loved inventing creative tortures for his partner, replacing Tim's sunscreen with sour cream, leaving dead fish in his locker. Ha-ha. Once, Mike even pretended he'd seen a swimmer go under, reveling in Tim's anguished search. Of course, Sloane was also *the* guy in a crisis—Hercules-strong, coolheaded, super-skilled at CPR, super-charming to the lost kid or pet. Tim hated him almost as much as he hated Gary Impoliteri.

And here he was, a New York City cop, bouncing through Tim's sliding door, shiny badge held high.

"Him!" Rose points excitedly. "I know him!"

"Officer Mike Sloane, ma'am." He grabs the accusatory finger, brings it to his lips. "You Tim's grandma?"

Rose's hand jerks back. "No!"

"This is Rose," Tim says.

"Rose Camille Joan Russo Impoliteri."

"Impoliteri?" The cop's slitty eyes slide in the direction of the Glassmans'. "You mean, *that* house? Oh, jeez." He clutches the huge St. Christopher medal nestled in his chest hair. "You must be Gary Imp's mom? I am sorry…belatedly."

Tim can't hold it in any longer. "She killed him! Her own son! She shot—why the fuck are you smiling?"

Sloane's yellow grin has a freshly missing eyetooth. He flicks his chin at the dozen little bottles of Sambuca. "You slip off the wagon there, Butterfingers?"

Rose snorts.

"I was there that night, Mike. I was in the room."

"You witnessed a crime?"

"Well, technically, no, but—it is the reason I asked you in."

Sloane plops down onto the couch, no doubt trying to disguise his loud fart. Fail. "Haven't been here in a while. What happened to all the saint statues and all that? Crucifixes."

Tim's too wound up to explain that the religious decor went to Ohio with his mother. What was left, Tim threw into the garage. "I need you to listen, Mike."

"But I'm starving," Sloane whines. "You got pretzels?"

Rose informs him Tim ordered Chinese.

"Mike—"

"Ease up, would ya. I'm beat. This paranoid city. There's still soldiers in the subway. Today—" He lifts his shirt to reveal a multicolored bruise over his nipple. "From a stiletto! Don't even ask."

"But this is real, Mike. She's got a gun in there. In that white bag—"

Rose claps. "That's it! The gun! That's how I know you!" Evidently, Sloane was the officer who returned Vin's gun when the investigation ended.

Sloane scratches his fuzzy head. "What gun is this again?"

"The one she killed her son with! Pay attention! Mike!"

"He was trying to steal my house!" Rose shouts. "What was I supposed to do?"

To Tim's astonishment, Sloane chooses this moment to get up and check on his dog. "What the fuck?" Tim trails after him. "She just confessed!"

Sloane makes kissy sounds at Jill, his Doberman. Tied to the porch, she's straining on her leash toward him, drooling. For the first time, Tim's relieved to know that Blacky's on the far side of the hedge. "C'mon, man," Tim persists, grabbing Sloane's Popeye biceps. "Do something."

What Sloane does is slam Tim back into the end table. Tim and all twelve little Sambuca bottles wind up on the orange shag.

"Shit." Tim rubs the place where his head hit. "Why'd you do that?"

Tim recognizes Mike's disappointed headshake from their long days sharing a lifeguard chair. Fucking X-ray, Fucking Butterfingers, always bringing him dooooown. "Number one is, whatever happened next door is ancient history. And, B, I'm off duty. Mind if I use your john to change into my wetsuit?"

The door slides open and Bean's bald spot pops in. "What's wrong with *him?*" he asks Sloane of Tim, on the floor.

Sloane shrugs.

"Peg's a no-show so we're gonna hit the dart tournament at Tubridy's. Who's in?"

Sloane promises to meet them there later. First he's "planning to escort this fine lady home." He's sick of police officers getting crapped on while firefighters "are the shit." Turning to Rose: "Where to, honey?"

"Castle Senior Living," Rose says, just like that. "On Horace—"

Tim charges, rips the white pocketbook from her grip, and, once and for all, upends it.

"I don't see any gun," Sloane says. "Where's the gun?"

There is none. Amid the dirty, clattering shower of candies and wrappers, cigars, pens, crumbs, and tissues thuds a different heavy object, a canister wrapped in brown paper and stamped with the name GARY PAUL VINCENT IMPOLITERI.

"Ashes."

Rose sighs impatiently. "Now will you spray the damn tree so I can finally sprinkle him?"

A coughing fit descends on Bean. He withdraws his balding head.

Sloane returns Rose's things to the pocketbook. "Now that that's cleared up, let's get going."

"Nothing's cleared up!" Tim shouts. "She still killed him!"

"Oh, leave it alone already, man. If you're so concerned about murder, come to the dart tournament. It's a memorial."

"Every fucking thing around here is a memorial," Tim says, slumping onto the mushroom-infested couch. After nine years, his deepest, darkest secret has been revealed and, swiftly, dismissed. Done. It's worse than any prank or pain Sloane has previously inflicted. Even Rose is sympathetic.

"It's not your fault, Timmy," she tells him. "The detective didn't believe me either."

"What detective?"

"With a *V*? Voly something? The one who gave me his card. You know, in case I saw something suspicious." Rose laughs at this. "I called him right away to confess. I told him everything. Volystaga? Volystinya?"

"Volistaya," Sloane says. "I know the guy. Diabetic." He holds out his loglike forearm to help her up and she not only stands but also walks, *walks*, with Sloane across Tim's living room.

"Father Dunne, Maureen, Bibi," Rose adds. "None of them believed me either. Call your mother; I'm sure she'll tell you the same. *Nobody listens to old people.*"


But Tim's mother isn't home. If she were, she'd answer. Her generation can't seem to screen a call without guilt, always leaping up from tables and toilets to catch the phone before the machine. Dread is their default mode. This was so even before she and her nun sister fled back to the Midwest "to die where He first put us." Tim was raised on tales of car wrecks and crop blight. Several times a year, she tells the story of the tornado that made his infant ears bleed like she's proud of Tim for it, the closest her son would ever come to true hero-ism or stigmata.

Tim realizes he's been scratching his face with the buttons

on the cordless. He flings the phone to the ground. That's it; he's giving up trying to grow a beard. Wetting a razor, he thinks of the countless times he stood shaving beside Chowder at the firehouse. How his friend was always singing but getting lyrics wrong. Instead of "Life in the fast lane," he sang, "Life in the vast plain." Also "like a virgin touched for *the thirty-first time*." It occurs to Tim that Chowder might have been purposely messing up lyrics to amuse his friends all along. Another swell of grief to surf. Here goes. And since Tim would rather not see his reflection while he shaves, he's bleeding when the Chinese food finally arrives. It's the delivery guy who alerts him, pointing at Tim and frantically pulling out napkins from the warm greasy bags. The boy, maybe fifteen, has one of those ultra-tight-skinned faces that allow you to see the exact shape of his skull. And its horrified expression says just how bad Tim looks. Probably the kid thinks he shaved off a nostril.

At a loss, Tim offers the guy a spring roll. Declined! Duh. The last thing a Chinese food delivery dude wants is Chinese food. Tim notes the kid's perfect English, then feels racist for doing so. A drink? He gestures to the mini-Sambucas on the floor. Rose probably left them on purpose, to torture him.

"Thanks, but I can't. I'm working."

"Never stopped *me*," Tim jokes, trying to be friendly. But the kid keeps turning to look back at the door. He thrusts out the credit card slip from a full arm's length away. This may be the only human in history who has ever been frightened of Tim. It's a weird feeling.

He signs for the food—$200.48. The Mets cap full of cash

has gone to the bar with its owner, Billy. Tim's no longer hungry but a spare rib comes in handy for luring Blacky back through the hedge, into the house.

Then Tim dons a raincoat, a respirator mask, and a pair of rubber gloves.

ᲒᲔ

Regina's the only one to "feel" Jake's presence. She insists that the ghost whispered in her ear—something incomprehensible that made her feel "really nice."

"'You look hot'?" June guesses, and the two girls fall onto each other, a fit of rolling hysterics that would have gone on forever only Regina got sand in her eye. Now that June's stopped worrying that she's jinxing Jake, she's delighted to have this story to tell her old friend when she sees him, to have old friends to tell stories to and new friends to put in them. The curly tips of the flames are also delightful, also her lips, which feel soft, taste smoky. Even the word *delightful* is delightful when you say it aloud: "Delightful." Try it. Your mouth has to stretch in three different directions. So the drugs must be working. If all of the above weren't proof, there's the moon. All the females worship it because it's paying attention to them or looking "delicious like a crepe, the thinnest, most delicate—"

"No one needs any more descriptions of the moon," Kenny says, impatient to move on and conjure "June's Gary."

"He's not mine," June says. "I just sleep in his room." At least, June assumes it's his room (left untouched for decades)—*Miami Vice* posters, porno mags, more footwear than any one person should own. Kenny returns the gold bracelet to June, then reaches into her backpack and pulls out the red cowboy boot with white stitching he believes is Gary's "authentic" object. June waits for him to look inside—"What the hell?" He sees the real item, a snub-nosed wooden-handled gun. Finding the old-fashioned weapon at the back of the closet instantly changed the genre of June's pretend film. And now Kenny understands this too. Very carefully, he places the firearm down on the sand.

"Are you out of your mind?" Necky shrieks, attacking June's newfound delight. "What were you thinking?"

"We might need to shoot someone annoying," Regina says.

"I'm sorry." June's panicking. She knew she should have brought Gary's pinewood-derby car. Necky's right. Guns ruin everything. "Look, I'll bury it." June grabs a clamshell and starts to dig.

*Plink, plink.* It's like pressing a toy piano key. Every time the shell meets sand, *plink!* Scooping further down, June can get a real piano sound—right hand, treble clef. With another shell in her left hand? Yes, it's there, the bass register. A long, even stroke makes a lush, major chord. A circular movement turns it minor. She has figured out how to *play the beach!* It's incredible. Wait till her mom sees this! Her face aches from smiling.

Kenny slides the gun back into the boot for burial and waits while June gets the deed done. Then he has everyone stare up at the house. "Gary Impoliteri," he bellows. "It's safe to come out now, Gary..."

Tim kneels before the tree with the can of fungicide, trying to read the instructions in what's left of the moonlight. Inside his mask, his breath sounds monstrous. When a gust of wind pushes the empty wheelchair into his back, he yelps in fright, then looks around in embarrassment. Pulling the trigger to get the chemical flowing through the thin hose, he silently apologizes to any insects or dead souls swirling around in the poison mist.

"Where are you, Gary? Come to us," Kenny persists. Then both eighth-graders start screaming.

"He's there! He's there!" They point. "The ghost! Up there!" Up on June's lawn, a tall bigheaded figure rises from the ground in a kind of vapor. "Aaah, he's coming!"

Mayhem sets in. A mini-stampede of frenzied girls abandon their sweatshirts and shoes. June suppresses an urge to do a cartwheel while Kenny's all business, collecting and hiding his baby bottles.

When Tim runs up and pulls off his mask, Necky gasps. "Your nose!"

"Your neck!"

Regina laughs. "Good comeback!"

"Your eye!" Tim says.

"I got sand in it."

"What's all this screaming?"

"Your nose!" Necky rudely repeats.

"Skin cancer."

"What?" That can't be, June decides. He's lying. Hero Tim's just too humble to tell this stranger what really happened. "What really happened?" June gets the courage to whisper.

"Skin cancer." Tim kicks sand on the fire. "Sixteen years of lifeguarding...you know."

June can feel the last of the delight draining out of her.

"And your neck?" Tim asks Necky again.

"Driver's ed...kidding!" The horrible girl wraps her legs around Kenny's but she's still all about Tim. "You really do look like a ghost man. But stop pretending you're Gary because I know you're that driver's ed teacher."

"Yeah," Tim says distantly. His eyes scan the waves. They rewind, replay, rewind, replay in an infinite loop. Maybe that comforts him, but not June. She feels trapped on film, dizzy and hot, cold, shivery, going to vomit. Regina holds her hair.

"Party's over," Tim says, taking the scrap of moon back home on his left shoulder. Kenny said it. No one needs any more descriptions of the moon. No one needs any more descriptions of anything.

❧

Asleep in the dining-room chair, Sue is startled awake by June's willowy shape draped all around her. Even stranger than the hug is the milky face, eyes molten and shiny. "You look, you look...transcendent." But saying it causes the girl to vanish so fast, Sue has to question whether it even happened. Real June or apparition, Sue counts the vision as the third star she's given up waiting to see (clouds massing). Mostly, it's the excuse she needs to nix the prayers and reach for her iPod. "'I've got the blues, I feel so lonely,'" Bessie Smith sings, and Sue too. "'I'll give the world if I could only...'" She doesn't care if she wakes up the whole house. "'Baby won't you please come home...'"

~

"Hello. Hey. Did I wake you?" Tim breathes into the phone. He'd been just about done cleaning his yard of empties when he spied the lone Heineken, sitting in the moonlit grass — green glowing glass in the green grass, otherworldly. The beer was open but full, sweating but cold. Tim rushed to call his sponsor, Mark No Name.

"No, no. I wasn't sleeping," Mark lies. "Hold on."

Tim pictures the goateed malpractice attorney (fourteen years sober) as he puts his hand over the receiver and mouths, *It's him,* to his irritated wife before walking out of the bedroom. "How you doing, man?"

"Do you know if beer is bad for plants? I have to dump this out."

"Did you get into some booze, Tim? What's going on?"

Booze? "No." The baby Sambucas weren't so tempting in the end. It's this Heineken that draws him. The familiar heaviness in Tim's palm relaxes his shoulders like nothing else.

"Okay, Tim, talk to me." The alarm in Mark's voice is off-set by the sucking sound of the fridge opening.

"Any brewskies in there, Marky?"

A square of light appears on an upper Glassman floor, the corner bedroom. "'Baby won't you please come home,'" June's bluesy voice sings but all Tim sees of her is a white hand holding a pair of scissors. June must have been cutting away at the ivy, bit by bit, since she moved in, but Tim's only just now noticing. The thick plant that used to cover the window has been thinned to a lacy screen. It reminds Tim of his promise to replace the Glassman back door. He got wood from Bean and everything.

"Bean? Is that one of your *friends?*" Mark asks through a wad of food.

"What's that in your mouth?"

"Who's Bean?"

"A guy with wood." Bean works two days a week in construction. "Once he bit off part of a guy's nose in a fight, so that's the new joke. You know, that Bean got me too."

"Hilarious."

"I think it's pretty funny."

"And why are you hanging out with him?"

"Answer my question first. In your mouth is..."

"Turkey roll. Happy? Now talk to me. You miss being a fireman, is that it?"

Booze? Fireman? The dude's like fifty but he uses the same vocab as Sy Glassman.

"Tell me exactly what you miss about it, Tim. Go ahead. Unload."

"Hmmm. Knocking down walls. Women." Isn't that what Mark's dying to hear? "They throw themselves at you. It's fucking obscene."

"Really!" Mark loves it. "Sooo, did you, uh, do you—take advantage?"

More of June appears through the plant now. An arm. A freckly profile. "'I have tried in vain nevermore to call your name...'" He knows that song. It's not on the jukeboxes in any of the local bars—the Wharf, the Raintower, Connolly's, Tubridy's—but he's sure he knows it. "'When you left you broke my heart. That will never make us part...'"

Bringing the bottle to his lips, Tim tries to picture Mrs. No Name asleep in the other room. Mark said she's a nurse, so even though it's absurd, that's all Tim can summon—a fully dressed nurse, down to the white stockings and clogs, in bed. There was one hot nurse during his time in the hospital but she was Puerto Rican, which Mrs. No Name is not. And, then as now, the white uniform is, to Tim, a turnoff. Not like a park ranger uniform. Not like Peg in bed in her park ranger uniform. Tim rolls the bottle back and forth on his lips, sticks his tongue in the hole. No way could aluminum ever be this erotic.

"I'm in love with my best friend's wife," Tim admits experimentally.

"Howser?"

"Chowder."

"What's his real name, Tim?"

"Mark No Name."

"C'mon, man. Talk to me. This is—your friend who died?"

"No remains have been found." Whatever was left of him

was likely carted to Fresh Kills with the rest of the wreckage, but they don't know for sure. They might never know. Tim likes to imagine his friend simply has amnesia and has made his way to somewhere beautiful, one of those spots they used to drool over in *Surfer* magazine—Bondi Beach, Sydney; Taghazout, Morocco. Even California would be nice. Santa Monica, where Chowder and Tim had raised the money to send their homeless friend Seaver, or Santa Cruz.

"What's Chowder's real name?" Mark asks. "Tim? For God's sake, show the guy the respect—"

"Chowderhead."

"Tim."

"Have you ever done this before, Mark? 'Cause you suck at it."

"I see."

"Nothing to see here." Tim gazes at the cherry tree. "Just that same old imaginary pirate."

"You alone?"

"Do you want to know what I'm wearing?"

Tim runs his thumb and pointer finger over the long, silky bottleneck.

"Are you drinking?"

"I told you. I'm looking for a place to dump it out."

"Anywhere! Just do it. That's venom you're holding."

"I'm not pouring venom on my flowers—"

"Then pour it in the toilet, Tim. Tim?"

"Can you quit saying my name with a question mark, Mark?"

"Tim?"

"I said stop it!"

Abruptly, June's singing halts. The song plays on in Tim's head. "Baby won't you please come home, I need money. Baby won't you please come home." But even that ends.

"Hey, I didn't mean you!" Tim calls up to where June's standing now, almost all visible through the ivy lace. Backlit like that, June's ears look pink, translucent. Her orange hair, like a tropical plant. "I really like your singing."

"Who are you talking to?" Mark growls. "Are those friends still there?"

Frowning, June unbuttons her shirt.

"Stop that!" Tim says, not looking away.

"Easy does it," Mark warns.

A glimpse of June's large, white, buoyant tits is eclipsed by the egg, also white, falling from the window, falling, glowing.

"What are you doing?"

June's laughing. She just failed Health. But apparently it's the funniest thing ever.

"What are *you* doing?" Mark asks. "Tim? Are you humming?"

The bagpipes have started up again in Tim's head. "Going Home," the funeral song, replacing the one June was singing. To banish it, he imagines hanging around the Glassman kitchen, casual-like, one of the family. But "Going Home" just drones on. Tim squeezes the Heineken and tells himself, *Flowers will help*. He stares hard at a stalk of purple columbine brushing against his bathroom window.

"Tim? Tim?" Mark keeps on.

"Tim? Tim?" says a woman's voice too. Peg! She's coming around the side of the house and then, once she sees Tim, running to grab the bottle. She dumps it out on his head.

Hanging up on Mark, Tim bows to her higher power.

"Let's get this over with," Peg says, ignoring Tim's beer-soaked hair, the beer-soaked phone, her late arrival. She paces the yard, blond ponytail swishing. Washed, her hair looks two shades lighter and polished by Malibu light. Under one arm, instead of her own battered shorty board, she's hauling the pink foamie that Tim recently gave Bridget for her eighth birthday.

*"Now?"*

"Unless you're too busy." Peg looks up at June's darkened window, exposing her long, brown, incredible neck. A big waterproof flashlight hangs on a cord around it. So she's been spying awhile. Tim's not sure if he's more embarrassed or flattered.

"But everyone left hours ago," he reports. "There's that darts thing. Memorial."

"So?" With her free hand, she unzips his raincoat. She's only a couple inches shorter than him so they match up just right. "Take this off."

"Are you going to explain where you've been?"

"No."

Tim strokes her full bottom lip with his thumb. "Move in with me."

Peg's surfboard slips; she catches it, turns away, and

dashes toward the beach. She's so quick, she's already at the foot of the hedge when Tim grabs her and spins her toward him. Her round face is shiny with tears.

"Just get your wetsuit," she whispers.

"Answer first."

"What if Chowder comes back?"

Tim takes a deep breath, then presses his hands in what looks like prayer but that, moved up and down, is actually the lifeguard signal for "shark." When the water got too crowded, he and Sloane liked to use the gesture to clear people out. In an hour, they'd let them back in up to their ankles, *if they dared*. In two hours, they could go back in entirely. But by then the beach would be pretty well emptied. "Chowder's gone," Tim says finally.

Peg nods and touches the damaged place on Tim's face.

It's hard to stay still. "I'll get a new couch. Without mushrooms."

"You're disgusting."

"Yeah, yeah. But tell me you don't want a beach house. Everyone wants a beach house. The kids —"

"I do," Peg admits. "Yeah. I do. Of course, but...the hurricane."

"What?"

"The hurricane. It's inevitable."

Tim brings his mouth up close to Peg's ear and assures her that together they will "be really, really, really prepared."

All June wants to do is imagine she's the blonde in Tim's arms below her ivy-veiled bedroom window. The hedge at her back. His scarred face in her cleavage. The neoprene wetsuit can barely hold in her heartbeat. She's—

"Junie!" Sage interrupts from the other side of the room. Shit. Sage *would* choose this moment to wake up. After sleeping through all that singing.

It's a big corner space. Twin beds flank a nonworking fireplace. Three windows, two of which are side by side facing the beach and the third, the most important, overlooking Tim. Only after she's through clearing this one of ivy will she start on the others.

"Go back to sleep," June tells her sister, eager to return to her vicarious pleasures. But how will she ever reinhabit that blonde's body with Sage yammering?

"Those are *my* scissors."

"Yes, but this plant needs a haircut. So we can see out."

"See what?"

The blonde's surfboard is on the ground now and she's on top of it. Tim on top of her.

"Can Ed go in your bed...Junie?"

"What?"

"Can Ed sleep with you?"

"He's scared?"

"No. Annoying."

Sage has her own room down the hall. But, on June's insistence, they've been "temporarily" sharing this one since they moved in. "Fine. Send Ed over."

"I hear Blacky."

Down below, the dog has come home to discover his owner needs protecting. But as soon as the blonde reaches out to pet him, the barking stops. They're buddies. Tim leaps up and runs to his porch to retrieve his own surfboard, heaped with roses. One more kiss. Then they're on their way down to the beach. June snips frantically, uselessly, at the ivy, trying to keep them in the frame.

"Is it midnight?" Sage wonders.

"After."

"Do toys have bones?"

"Oh, c'mon!" The happy pair plus mutt glide totally out of view. "These preschool scissors are worthless."

"Can I cut plants too?"

"No!" June flops back onto her bed.

"Watch out!" Sage shrieks. "Ed!"

With a sigh, June rolls over to make room for the pirate. "Did he have a bad dream or what?"

"What." Sage throws her ketchup bottle and catches it, throws and catches. After a while, she asks, "Why do you got no shirt on, Junie?"

"I'm hot."

"Can I not wear that?" Sage points at the dress someone's left hanging on the mantel for the party tomorrow. Pink. Fluffy.

"It's cute," June lies. "Try it." As if in response, the dress seems to coo. June can't even blame morning glory because Sage also heard it.

"What's it talking, Junie?"

June laughs. "Did you just ask me what the dress said?" Being four is like tripping all the time.

"No," Sage says. "The wall, silly!"

Of course. The dress is innocent. The cooing, like all the other sounds, are coming from somewhere inside or around the fireplace wall. So much for Kenny "de-haunting" their house. It occurs to June that "maybe it's God in the wall. I've seen weirder." First to come to mind is the Upper West Side to which she and Jake fled on 9/11. There, it looked like nothing had happened. People eating in cafés. Children on playgrounds.

"Is God a ghost?" Sage asks.

"I guess."

"Then God's dead?"

"Oh! No! I didn't mean...no one knows, is the thing. It's a mystery."

Unbelievably, this lame answer satisfies Sage. She curls up, conks out. Why should she sweat about creepy God cooing in their walls? Or anything. You think you understand your too-familiar sister and she you, but that's just another way to fool yourself that you're safe. At Sage's age, June was already fearful of everything. An oft-told family story has her "utterly inconsolable" after hearing the sun would burn out in a few *billion* years.

Wide awake now too, June stares at nothing. In the movie, Ed would choose this moment to materialize, lying beside June, keeping her company. They would harmonize on "Baby Won't You Please Come Home" the way she and her mom used to do when she (always) had trouble sleeping. Nice touch. Then, just as June has soothed herself at last, her eyes land on it. The discovery shot. A sinister sprig of ivy has crawled its way up through the heating vent.

THREE

# SWELL

*Sunday, June 16, 2002*

MOM'S EVEN BIGGER now that she's a Jew. It's not rational, maybe, but it's true. As the designated surprise-party lookout, June is the first to see her approach. And it's a shock, that massive belly, turning the corner onto the block. It strains the buttons of Dad's big and tall man's cardigan and even doubles as a bookshelf for a load of ominous new hardcovers. Could be June's still high on morning glory (she did wake up laughing with shells in her bed) or it could be some trick of the smudgy hall window. But the baby bulge seems to have tripled in size since it left to get converted this morning. And still it's growing and what with the imminent—*Surprise!*—Mom will most likely just *pop*, a human space launcher left bleeding on the blacktop while the creature births herself up through the ozone into limbo.

Of course, the pope outlawed limbo years ago. And with the fetus now a Hebe, its afterlife options are vague to none. Best-case scenario: The newborn shoots straight up into live satellite orbit to be accessed at some convenient time slot. The Discovery Channel, say, Sunday, seven to seven fifteen?

So June must still be tripping. Realistically, the only thing that could save her from a summer of diaper changing is death (hers or someone else's). June's already practically raising her sister. Even now, Sage is whining for June to pick her up so she can see Mommy, pick her up so she can see Mommy, pick her up.

For distraction, June sounds the alert—Sage's empty ketchup bottle, which squeaks when squeezed.

Mayhem! The guests whirl in all directions.

Grandpa directs the flow from his command center on the frayed gold living-room couch. "Behind there, Bob, not there, *there*. Fran, you too, vamoose. Take cover!" A stampede rushes past June and Sage and on up the stairs. Another faction flows down the hall to the kitchen, where Dad's already (always) hiding. Tim wedges himself and a bottle of Fresca under the piano. Mole and Kacy, Kenny's divorced parents, disappear into the bathroom *together!* Even mom's mom, Grandma Louise, who keeps insisting that this is a baby shower, manages to blend her androgynous torso (shirt and tie!) into the drapes.

Adults love a surprise, that's why. Adults love any excuse to be passive-aggressive. If it's ritualistic, better still. All these adults are just rooting for a boy child so they can slice off his penis tip and celebrate with cold cuts. Even Mom's cousin Pastor Dale (who'd prefer an icy baptismal dunk) would happily cheer on a bris-in-progress. Adults love a good jolt, while preschoolers crave the same-old.

"Pick me up." Sage won't stop. "I wanna see. Pick me up!" It's that itchy pink dress Dad paid her five dollars to wear. It makes her squirmy. "Pick me up! I wanna see." As if there's anything worth viewing. The row of chalk-drawn princesses

Dad also commissioned from Sage, for party decor. (Earrings for hair and legs growing out of their necks.) Some Mole-Kacy boys dragging their miserable cat on a leash. Yet another car-service driver who screwed up and needs to make a U-turn on the dead-end street. The belly dragging Mom incrementally home.

Back in Tribeca, their Franklin Street window was, for a time, its own activity. The constant parade of hairdos and accessories, the shapes of dogs. These helped June think. A marimba used to roll past every Tuesday at four. She saw a blind boy being led by a miniature seeing-eye horse and other thrilling turn-of-the-century sights as the neighborhood gentrified. She does love looking out at the ocean too. But instead of thoughts, this vista gives June feelings, the feeling of being lost but calm about it, content to be insignificant. June assumes that's how it is for all of them: Dad watching it from the bedroom. Sage and Ed, looking up from their treasure pile. Grandpa, en suite, through his widower tears. Tim, checking the waves. These days, even unpredictable Mom is mostly found in the dining room with her eyes on the blurry horizon.

June should crack open the window and warn Mom to run, run, the relatives have come! But did Mom warn June about her new address, religion, school, sibling? She should rush out and help Mom carry those books. But when's the last time Mom helped June? She should forgive Mom (or at least blame Dad too). But will Mom forgive June when she finds out she flung the egg out her window last night? Why?

"Up!" Sage continues to beat on June's thighs. "Pick me up! Please!"

June blows the frizz out of her eyes and pulls her sister onto the sill. Not to be nice. Not to reward Sage for remembering the magic word. Not even to shut the pest up. But for something besides a ketchup bottle to hold while June watches Mom's approach and wonders aloud, "What's with that ugly brown scarf she's wearing?"

"A *kepela?*" Grandpa rejoices, twisting to see out the window from his seat.

"A *kepela?*"

"You know, a *tichel,* to hide your skull from God." Sy pulls the little cover off the couch arm and plops it on his head. "A schmatta like my mother, may she rest in peace, used to wear out to haggle with the butcher on Avenue M."

Somehow June's the only one embarrassed by this outburst, by her grandpa entirely. The way he rakes his hands through a bowl of nuts—vile. Nut skins fleck his face and his leather vest. But everyone else seems charmed. Laughter streams from all the hiding spots.

Even Tim, under the piano, is entertained. "I get it," he calls out. "Like a bandanna?" No doubt envisioning Blacky, who frequently sports a similar look. "She's got to wear that all the time now?"

"No. No way." June refuses to be the new Jew in town with a mom who wears a rag on her·head. "Suzanne Ainsley Gibson Glassman, the Jew? It's too sick."

"Oh, she went to the liberry!" Sage says, noticing the books Mom's hauling. June can't see their titles yet but—

"Don't expect *Curious George and the Puppies*." Those are hard hardcovers, about to slam down on them. From on high. Between Grandma Estelle, Jake Leibowitz, and a well-earned A minus in Honors World Religion, June knows the whole scoop, from Auschwitz to *zayde*. What those real titles are hardly matters. It's what they signify that June questions.

No more Christmas trees?

No more BLTs?

No more forgiveness?

The bell! "For He's a Jolly Good"—

Grandpa springs up. Nuts fly. "Why doesn't she have a key?"

The wind is ripping the door from June's hand. There stands Rose in a red-and-white-checkered dress, a knife in her fist! Within seconds, the dandruff-y driver has unloaded the old woman and her big pocketbook onto June. Maybe he's heard the haunted-house rumors, because he literally gallops back down the stoop to his idling Lincoln. Behind him, June glimpses Mom's brown scarf. Rebel! Mom's hurrying past the house toward the beach.

"Hey!" Sage shrieks, seeing her too. "Hey, it's Mommy," inciting the bomb—"*Surprise!*"

The loud eruption literally knocks Rose off her feet and forward onto June. She catches her biceps, sliding down to...a forearm. The knife drops. Then the woman's on top of her—bizarre, for sure, but no biggie. She's soft in her largeness. June's egg is already smashed. There's a rug. They lie there on the foyer floor, motionless. June wonders if it's the drugs still in her system that cause Rose to look this much like a shar-pei—pleated face, huge eyes pulled down by purply pouches. With the checkered dress thrown in, Rose looks like a puppy tangled up in a tablecloth.

"Mommy, Mommy," Sage continues at the door while somewhere behind the mass of shins and shoes, Grandpa's uselessly shouting, "False alarm. Go back! Hide! Go!"

June wishes for Tim's flip-flops to appear. But it's a pair of tasseled loafers that stop at her face.

"Everyone in one piece?" says a Queens accent attached to Bob Baum. June can feel Rose's body tense against her. When Bob leans down to help Rose up, she reaches for the blade.

"Uh, Rosie! Don't!"

"Oh, for Christ's sake. It's my best knife, Bob. I finally found it out there in a planter. You think I'd dull it stabbing someone like you?" With difficulty, she wedges the knife most of the way into her pocketbook.

To June, Bob is the bow-tied geezer who biannually pulls pennies from her nose and is husband to Fran of the dowdy homemade sweaters. That Bob is also part of Rose's world is slow to compute. "Come, now, let me help you up. We're old friends, Rosie."

*"Friends?"* Rose pinches Bob's arm, hard. "You stole my house!"

"That's ridiculous!" Nonetheless, Bob leaves the rescue to...Kenny? June didn't even know he was here. Sand spills from his pockets as he bends over them wearing last night's clothing.

"God in heaven!" Rose mutters as Kenny hauls her upright. "God in heaven." She crosses herself, glaring at the ceiling.

"Isn't that redundant?" Kenny asks. "I mean, where else would God be?"

June can tell he's still a little drugged too. One look at his big, glittery pupils makes her want to run to a mirror. Instead, June retrieves Rose's purse from the floor. Not only is that knife kind of sticking out, it's "heav-y!"

"Where's your wheelchair? I'll go get it," Bob says as though everything's normal. "That was some fall you took! A real doozy."

"Get away from me," Rose says.

Bob sways over her, pleading. "Please, Rose, please. I didn't know what to do. We were all so worried, what with you here alone and refusing to move. Maureen was desperate." He turns to appeal to the confused spectators. "How could she take care of this big house all by herself?" He turns back. "Rose, please, talk to Fran. We were scared for your safety."

"You should be scared for *your* safety," Kenny says, reaching down into his sock and pulling out his air rifle.

A woman screams.

"Put that away!" June demands. Kenny sheepishly obeys. "It's just a BB gun," June tells the dispersing crowd. Only Sage remains fixed at the open door, in her itchy pink dress, pining for Mommy.

June shoves Kenny's shoulder with all her strength. "You think you're in some fucking movie? Why would you bring a gun to my house?"

"The place creeps me out."

"Then leave."

But Rose insists he stay, her "knight in shining, *grazie*." Kenny's reminded Rose of something she needs to do up in Gary's old room. If June and Kenny would assist? "Careful, Red, my elbow."

Five minutes later they've gotten only as far as the foot of the stairs. Sage is still behind them, wailing, her plea shortened to "Mom, Mom, Mom." On about stair three, she's switched to "Sue." By six, she's on to "Sue Ainsley," soon to morph into "Sue Ainsley Gibson." Then "Sue Ainsley Gibson Glassman, Sue Ainsley Gibson Glassman... Mommy."

"Humdrum rhododendron," Rose says.

⌒

Sue has kept walking, over Sage's chalk-drawn princesses, past the DEAD-END STREET sign, toward the beach. As if the morning weren't strange enough, Sue has come home to find Rose, in a checkered dress, *standing* atop her stoop. It's the first Sue has seen of the woman's boxy back and pancake butt, and, frankly, it's jarring. She hurries on till her shoes hit sand. Then she drops the books the rabbi has given her and just stands there, unsure what to do next.

Umbrellas flap and ripple against the newly greenish sky. The beachgoers labor to tame them and flee. Too bad Sue's iPod is out of power. Some ragtime would accompany this jerky slapstick nicely. She likes watching the wind flip the book pages to suggest an invisible reader. Ed? The small muscles near her armpits still twinge from the weight of them.

An object, a flip-flop, grazes the top of Sue's head scarf. Here's Tim again, apologizing. Blacky bounds after the shoe.

"Why are *you* here?" Sue asks but thinks, *Why am* I *here?* She plucks her soggy handkerchief from the pocket of Dan's sweater and spits and spits.

"Um, I got bored waiting for you under the piano so… checking the waves."

"Still there?"

Tim nods. "Erratically."

Blacky's already back with the flip-flop. He drops it at Tim's feet. One's bare. On the other, Tim wears the second sandal. Sue can't control a smile.

"Something wrong with a tennis ball?"

"Lost at sea." Tim looks different. The blustery air lifts his fluffy hair up and sideways into a little halo.


"So much weather out there," said Mindy, the rabbi's Russian wife, chasing Sue out the door with the scarf. The sweet woman even tied it on over Sue's earbuds. Zeppelin, "What Is and What Should Never Be." It went perfectly with the hot, gray day and the baby's heavy-metal kick.

The ritual (the *transaction*) had been set to take place in the rabbi's home office/gym with smiley Mindy and a plump Filipino housekeeper attending. Fresh from the shower, Rabbi Larry glistened.

"Do you believe Jesus Christ is the Son of God?" he asked Sue.

"Have we started, then?"

"You tell me."

"Do I believe Jesus Christ is the Son of God?" Sue repeated, a stalling technique she'd learned from Dan. Incredibly useful, that. Also the phrase *I'll look into it.* "You want to know, do I believe Jesus Christ is the Son of God?"

Behind the rabbi, the dimpled housekeeper slowly nodded her head yes. Sue thought of how Estelle's nurse had, right at the end, called out, "Tell my daddy I love him!" and of her own cryptic father, now off teaching North American studies in South America. "Show me ten righteous people!" was all he said to the news that Sue was both converting and pregnant.

"I believe Jesus Christ was...a great human being."

"A great Jew," Mindy amended.

"Yes, yes."

Manischewitz was poured, blessed. A contract put before the convert, the *ger,* for Sue/Sarah to "autograph." Then the rabbi rose from the exercise ball he used as a desk chair and handed Sue a pen. He squeezed her shoulder with a pumping motion while she bent, sweating, over the paper. The too-sweet wine (the first alcohol she'd had in months) made her gag.

"Now for the summer reading!" the rabbi said. And the housekeeper hustled over. In her arms were the books currently at Sue's feet in the sand—the Bible; *Exodus; The Aleph, Bet, Gimmel of Jewish Cookery.* He did not appear to notice that

Sue hadn't signed the contract, that she couldn't bring herself to sign, that she had, in fact, *succumbed to confusion.*


"So, are you going? In?" Tim interrupts her thoughts.

"In?" There's an idea. Immersion *is* a conversion ritual, one of several the rabbi took it upon himself to edit out. Of course, this usually happens in a pool, not the ocean. There are rules. But... "Why not? Yeah. I like that! DIY Jew?"

Tim's flustered. "Going *in* to your party, I meant. The house."

"This first," Sue says, propelling herself toward the ruffled, frigid waves.

Tim's hand leaps to his throat for a phantom whistle. Old lifeguard instinct, he explains. Very pregnant woman, bad weather, riptide. "If I were you, I'd think twice."

ᴁ


One step, long rest, another step, long rest, is how it goes with Rose. They're on number eight when Sy appears below them demanding to know "where you think *you're* going?"

"Straight to hell!" Rose calls down. "Wanna come?"

Kenny says they'd make a good couple.

"Me and the cripple?" The old lady's amused. She mimics Sy's distinctive hobble.

June reminds her to watch where she's walking. The green carpet is loose and torn in places. "You could trip."

"No more tripping!" Kenny laughs softly, wildly.

"Wait!" Rose says, grabbing June's wrist. "You little thief! That's my bracelet!"

"I—I found it in the bathroom." After her weekend of lies, the truth feels awkward in June's mouth.

She waits for Kenny to cross-examine her about Jake Leibowitz but he starts to sing instead. "'I'mmm coming up...so we better get this party started.'" Happy! And when June offers the bracelet back, Rose snorts and waves her off. "It's a handcuff. But if you happen to see my good knife—"

"This?" June asks, holding up the pocketbook. "You already found it."

Rose smiles blankly, blinking.

Forty-five minutes later, the old woman is finally lying in bed, hugging that giant white purse. Does she want a nap? No. But June does. Some water? No. But June does. Drinking from the bathroom tap, June overhears Rose tell Kenny to do her a favor and check the back of Gary's closet for some red boots with white stitching.

June's head slams on the faucet. She recalls burying the red boot (and the gun) last night but had forgotten the score she'd composed out of sand. Heavenly Blue. Magnificent.

Naturally, Kenny will say that he can't find the red boots. He knows as well as June that the one with the gun is under the sand and the other is still in the closet, empty. June left it there herself yesterday by that creepy boot box marked *Gary's Box of Pain*. Inside—two pulled teeth, some dental headgear, parts of an arm cast, a lice comb, and the saddest middle-school note ever penned: *I'd rather die than go out with an ugly ginger like you.*

"I don't know, Rose. I'm just not seeing any red boots," Kenny says. Coming from inside that closet, all the way in the next room, the half-truth sounds muffled and far off.

"Well, they can't walk off by themselves, can they?"

"What if they can?" Kenny's tone is serious, hilarious.

In the bathroom mirror, June works to arrange her face into an acceptable expression. One eyelid twitches in a one-one, two-one, one-two rhythm. Her skin looks like salami.

"Keep hunting!" Rose urges. "We've got to find that gun."

Kenny gasps. *"Gun?"* June can tell he's stepped out of the closet to give depth to his performance.

"It's my husband's gun," Rose says. "I know, that's no excuse. I'm a dummy! How could I be such a careless dummy?"

"Don't worry, Mrs. Impoliteri," Kenny says kindly. He tells her he won't stop until he finds it. (Not.)

"It's inside the right boot." Rose frets on. "I think...I'm not sure. Oh God. What if it's not there? What if I left it somewhere else? A loaded gun should not be in a house with children."

❧

Tim shows Sue the line of foam traveling out to sea. This riptide is slow-moving, but that could change quickly. It's baptism Sue's after. Tim gets it; he likes it. "But when those currents surge, it's like a bathtub unplugged. You'll be sucked right out to meet your Maker."

"Meet your Maker!" Sue hasn't heard that in a while. She rubs her crystal-ball belly. Soon she'll be meeting her new child face to face. Not that she's equating herself with God, but...

"Why not?" Tim says, distracted by the sight of Blacky digging by the remnants of last night's fire. What's that red thing he's got in his mouth? Looks like leather.

"My heart is whacking," Sue confesses, still moving toward the water despite Tim's warnings. "I feel like I'm forgetting something... but something I knew."

"Do you really need to go in *now?* It might get hairy..." Tim glances over at the lifeguard chair. The red (No Swimming) flag should already be raised but there's no sign of it happening. Guard one swings his whistle around and around. Guard two is hunched inside his orange windbreaker, napping. Tim understands. He's been there, but... it's insane when you consider it. A pair of woodenheaded teenagers put in charge of people's lives? Kid people, old people, the unborn? Tim points to Sue's midsection. "What about the —" For some reason, he can't get his mouth to say *baby*.

"Oh, you'll save us, worst case," Sue says.

However misguided, her trust in him is thrilling, an unexpected triumph on top of his other spectacular news. Peg said yes! He's bursting to tell a Glassman. Peg and the kids are moving in! And it's not a dream. He triple-checked this morning. But Sue began liking him only ten minutes ago, so Tim's cautious. For sure, she's still no fan of Blacky.

"What *is* with your dog?"

Over the years, Blacky has dug up some truly offbeat footwear, but this is his first cowboy boot. Tim yells for the dog to "drop it!" No chance. Tim pulls off his flip-flop and nails the dog square on the snout. Blacky goes on gnawing. The red boot looks familiar, too, rodeo-style, white stitching...

"Don't let me overthink this," Sue says, having made it to the shore. Tiny perforations in the wet sand glitter beneath her feet. If she asked, Tim would tell her that's how sand crabs give themselves air. But she doesn't ask, so he reminds her about the party instead. "Everyone's up there expecting you. Your mom, your cousin. Dan made you a mountain of food."

"I'm starving!" Sue says, as if just now remembering. Along with giving her the head scarf, the rabbi's wife had chased her down with a batch of homemade Russian tea-cakes. Sue pulls the container from her bag. The buttery cookies are buried under a hill of powdered sugar that swirls up in the wind when the lid's removed. With his eyes still on the churning ocean, Tim right away inhales three, then exclaims, "Powdered sugar, the poor man's cocaine!"

Sue removes her sweater—well, Dan's sweater. None of hers fit at this point. The wind plasters her dress to her various bulges. Stalling, chewing, she tells Tim the rest.

Six, maybe seven, blocks from the rabbi's house, while eating these very cookies, Sue was struck with remorse. Her iPod had mysteriously jumped from Coltrane to Mahler but that couldn't explain it. Something just felt...wrong.

"Something's wrong." Sue panted when the rabbi's door opened a second time. There stood Larry himself, fisting a clarinet. He thought Sue was in labor.

"Mindy! Mindy! My car keys!"

Once that drama was shut down, Sue finally confessed that she'd never signed her contract. Wasn't sure. Didn't like the way her father-in-law operated. (In exchange for Sue's express conversion, Sy had whipped out his Star of David checkbook to fund the temple's new handicapped bathroom.)

Here she hesitates, holding Tim's gray gaze. "Maybe I shouldn't be telling you this."

"What?" He plays along. "I can't hear you. The wind." It *has* intensified. Even Blacky walks around the boot to turn his back to it.

"Come in, please, breathe," the rabbi urged. "I can't understand a word you're saying." He slid the clarinet under his arm to relieve Sue of the books.

"No. I got them." The burden seemed necessary, a sort of first trial. "If I could just do this the right way, a real way," Sue tried to explain. But she was struggling to breathe, to believe.

"This problem, I have also during my pregnancy with Noah," the rabbi's wife, Mindy, commiserated over black tea too bitter to drink. "Some jerk in the movie once told me if I was breathing too loudly."

"*That* you were breathing," the rabbi corrected.

"I gave the point. Why pick?"

"Because you've been in this country for too long not to speak properly."

"Pick, pick."

The rabbi's wife was a mail-order bride from Sochi circa 1968, or so Sy had told Sue. She could easily imagine how her father-in-law had, in turn, described *her*. The stubborn shiksa who wouldn't convert even after getting knocked up. The red-haired vixen who'd given his wife a heart attack. ("You finally broke her heart" was a sentence Sy actually uttered to Sue at Estelle's funeral.)

"Pick, pick."

It was plain to see that Larry and Mindy had been having this same argument over and over for decades, just as Sue and Dan fought about Sy. Like endlessly burping up the taste of the same lunch. Arguing about Rose had, at least, given them some diversion. But even that argument involved Sy. One way or another, it was time for it to stop.

Petite and bejeweled, Mindy had ushered Sue into her mint-green living room, insisting she put up her swollen feet, eat. Teacakes were Mindy's specialty but she had also baked babka and a honey cake to rival Estelle's. Sue braced herself for another maternity horror story—how bad Mindy tore birthing Noah or the botched epidural that paralyzed a friend. But effusive congratulations followed. Apparently Sue had passed some kind of test. The rabbi burst into the room, contract in hand.

Tradition dictated that he had to make three attempts to dissuade her from converting. To this end, he pretended not to have met her, gave her no guidance on preparing to convert, and performed a half-assed ceremony from which any sane person would flee. That she could not bring herself to sign the contract only spoke to her integrity. And, more important, she had come back! "For the sake of heaven!" His dark eyes glittered out from his hairy face. "Finally, you are ready." He sat down.

"I doubt that," Sue said through a mouthful of spit.

"Doubt's the way," Mindy gushed, nodding at her husband. "He's the fraud who gets a little too cozy with knowing."

"Don't look at me," the rabbi protested. "I'm not cozy!" He pulled the lumbar pillow from behind his back and threw it playfully at her head.

"Sure, Larry!" Mindy laughed and threw it back at him. "You reflect plenty. On your golf swing!"

They flung the pillow, and soon more pillows, back and forth between them. They got up and ran around, throwing and ducking, working themselves up into a kind of zany jubilation that made Sue miss Dan. Mindy and Larry were all right. Individually and, after all, as a couple. They tried. They were good people. But they hadn't gotten Sue any closer to spirituality than had the pretty cross on the church or the sounds in her bedroom walls. Letting herself out, Sue caught the housekeeper with the clarinet in her mouth, trying, failing, to make a sound, and she paused to give her a few pointers.

Now, on the overcast beach, a loud, low-flying jet skywrites an illegible message. As signs go, a rainbow would have been preferable, but this'll have to do. Sue kicks the books, hands Tim her bag, stares down the army-green waves. She is only feigning bravery. Worse, she can't shake the sense that she's missing something.

"A bathing suit?" Tim asks.

"I know! Witnesses! I'm supposed to have three. Would you mind? I mean, do you have any friends?"

᠔

Sy has Dan in a headlock. "This is not the celebration we planned." Who told Sue's mother, Louise, she was coming to a baby shower? What's with those pink balloons, the chair with ribbons, those gifts! "You want to know why Rabbi Larry and Mindy aren't here? Because your wife balked! Balked or tricked him. After all that, Sue didn't even convert! At the very least, someone owes them an apology." Sy twists Dan's head to face the picture window and have a look-see who.

With Tim at her side, Sue stands on the empty beach, her black dress and head scarf puffy with wind. Dan frees his neck from his father's foul armpit. The zigzaggy border that portends his migraine has begun to shimmer at the edges of his vision. This is Dan's biggest fear, and yet here it is outstripped by an intense admiration for his wife. He should never have asked her to convert. Apology daisies are overdue! Sy too should be ashamed, Dan tells him.

"Baloney. Your wife is out of control. Now go get her."

"No."

"I said *go*."

Dan smells baked clams on Sy's breath, the baked clams he didn't serve lest they were poisoned.

"She'll come when she's ready."

Sy's white eyebrows meet. "Either you go get her or—"

"*Or?*" The red dot in Dan's vision grows spokes. "Whatcha gonna do to me, *Daddy?*"

Sy shakes his fist. "I—I have a mind to—"

"Kick us out? Kick my butt? Take back the business?"

"I should."

"Too late."

"You little ingrate! After all I've done—"

"Which is what exactly, Dad? Stole me a house. I know more than you think. If—"

"Shhh." Sy claws Dan's biceps. "I have it all under control. I'm paying back the company in small—"

"You billed the house to the company?"

"You shut up if you want to talk to me! It was just a little contracting—"

The spokes have turned a throbbing yellow. Here Dan was asking if Sy had been aware he had bilked Rose, and he goes and admits to another crime altogether. "Is that why you gave me the business? To avoid indictment?"

"Shhh," Sy hisses. "Everyone's listening!"

"No one's listening, Dad!" They really aren't. Through the entire flare-up, the guests have remained huddled around the table, fully absorbed in Dr. Mole's account of "the night of the *Golden Venture*," right here, *right in this very room*. Mole whispers for effect or in case Rose returns from upstairs unannounced. He lives right next door, mind you. He heard *everything.*

Dan turns back to the window just in time to see two ripped-looking dudes join Tim and Sue. One wears Ray-Bans and a zinc oxide–whitened nose despite the lack of sun. The other, a Hawaiian shirt, unbuttoned.

*If there's enough blue in the sky to make a pair of pants, it's not going to rain,* his mother's voice says in his head. Luckily there's enough blue.

Dan's pretty sure that's his new cashmere sweater out there, balled up on the sand.

☙

"Hoo-ah!" Ox runs up on his thick bowlegs, yowling. "Do I get to wear a yammy?" But Sue's poker face straightens him up fast. He whips off his mirrored sunglasses and dips his patchwork head; there are fuzzy spots where his burned-off hair is still regrowing. As for Chris D., he's already buttoned up his flowered shirt and shoved the ends into his sweats. This is a rite, not a lark. Altar boys, lifeguards, firefighter — their entire lives have been bound and magnified by such rituals. By now they've long repented for believing Jews killed Jesus, for using the word *Yid*, for riding their bikes up and down the boardwalk tipping the hats off Orthodox Jews. Clear-eyed, heads up, arms by their sides, at the ready, they are more present than Tim can ever be, honestly doing their best not to check out Sue's gigantic tits.

Sue's smile — all the way up to her gums — is contagious.

Tim just once let his friends goad him into tipping, and immediately he was flooded with regret. Only twelve years old, he'd circled back on his Stingray. Retrieving the big black hat, he had the expectation that his victim would thank him. What an idiot he'd been! The man just flashed Tim a pitying look and put the hat back on his head.

"Who will say a prayer?" Sue asks, passing around the last of Mindy's teacakes.

"In all dual respect," Ox admits, "we don't know Jewish."

Chris D. cuffs him. "In all *due* respect, bonehead. And you mean Hebrew."

"I heard Butter rattle off some good Scripture," Ox says. "In the hospital, I —"

"Uh-uh." Tim stops that idea cold. He only did that to placate his mom on the phone.

The wind whips Sue's hair across her mouth as she tries to slow her breathing. "Someone make something up before I back out, please."

Whereupon Chris D. just holds up his hand, bows his head, and appeals to "Mary, Mother of God. Bless this woman coming in."

They all razz him. But Sue's satisfied; grateful, even. So what she's not in a regulation mikvah, the witnesses aren't women, the prayer is ad hoc *and* Christian. Marching into the lacy backwash, she listens for the major, mounting chords always played at the climax of the climax. Ah, but her feet are cramping; all the nerve endings on her lower body fire. At the rise of the first, veiny-bellied wave, she holds her gut and turns sideways, eyes closed. But she's determined to go on, deeper. When her feet lift, she imagines she is the baby floating inside a body that is floating inside a body...of water. The actual baby is quiet. Stunned, maybe. Sue forces her head under—Holy God, brain freeze—and emerges in time for a second wave to leap up and slap her in the face. Wake up! Naturally, she thinks of Dan, ever conscious of what he can't see, of what's coming. Dan would never have let that wave surprise him. And had she invited him, he'd have thought to bring Sue a towel. Hot drinks. His best self. In Dan's honor, she invents a fantasy. She is Marilyn Monroe converting for Arthur Miller. Seagulls are her paparazzi. Along the shore, hunky men line up, watching her, wanting her. At last, she is one of the Chosen People.

ᐰ

"...right *here*, right where you're sitting," Mole says, still milking the tale, to Dan's dismay. "Almost nine years ago to this day. Blam!" His palm slams the table to simulate a gunshot. Group wince. Sy stumbles. Bob Baum leaps up and slides a chair under him. But Sy's eyes stay fixed on the neighbor's lips forming the words "Murder...her son...right in front of her! And *me* next door the whole time."

Sue's mom, Louise, fidgets with the ribbon on a baby gift. Sue's cousin Pastor Dale wordlessly consults the imprint of the cross on the wallpaper.

"I'm *still* shocked by it," Mole says, peeling his bald head.

"It *is* shocking." "Completely shocking!" is the consensus.

Only Sy objects—a gurgle from deep in his chest like a pigeon makes. "You have a boat jammed with Orientals trying to get a free pass into—"

"Dad—"

"What? There's bound to be chaos with the Chinks on the run, dart—"

*"Dad!"*

"—darting and hiding like roaches!"

It occurs to Dan that his father is truly a terrible person, that this can be so even though the man stayed married to a good woman for forty-two years *and* paid Rabbi Larry to quit smoking *and* gave his workers profit sharing *and* donated half his fortune to Save Our Shores. Dan can love him *and* he can still be a . . . total, fucking jerk! "You can't talk like that, Dad. Not in *my* house!"

Sy rubs his dyed hairline. Now everyone *is* listening. (Although the Baums do so nervously, Bob rolling crumbs around the tablecloth, Fran hauling out her knitting.) A shudder travels through Dan as he watches Sy's pale, wet eyes calculate. *Got the stage.* Pausing for . . . *What's my move? Hmm.* It's almost a letdown when he reverts to his default mode. "Do you hear that, everybody? Do you hear the way a son talks to his dying father?" Woe is me. Woe is Sy.

"You're not dying," they recite. "Dying? Sy, don't be silly." "You're healthy as a horse. You look swell. Terrific!" And blah-blah until Dan can no longer stand another second.

"That's right, you're dying, Dad! You're on the way out. Any day now!" There's a bleat in Dan's ears. He's giddy with rage. *And as soon as you're gone, I'm gonna burn that pimpy leather vest,* he is desperate to add. But Dan knows what's required of him is a lot more adult, a lot grimmer. After taking his father aside, out of earshot of the others, he sits him down and quietly fires him.

The message ripples across the old man's saggy face. It flows down his long, bony body. When it reaches his loafers, they plant themselves. Without looking at Dan, without arguing, the despot slowly rises, lurches across the scratched tile, and exits through the hole inside which the back door once hung. *Before and after the back door,* Dan thinks mystically.

"Where ya going, Glassman?" All the busybodies commence. "Be careful, it's gusty!" "Sy, honey. Come back! Eat!" When ignored, they turn on Dan. "What did you say to him, Danny? Tell him to come back! What's wrong with you? That's your father. What's gotten into you today?"

The spokes in Dan's vision begin to vibrate, then rotate. The pattern, now complete, is exquisite. Save for the birth of his girls, it's the closest Dan's ever come to a religious experience. That is, real terror. Any time now it will come, the sensation of being stabbed with an ice pick above his left eye for the next forty-eight hours. Dr. Mole told him they actually once used this method to treat mental illness, only the ice pick was plunged *through* the eye. This to cheer him up.

Dan hustles for the door. Misreading his actions, Sue's mom starts chirping, "Cleanup! Cleanup time," whereupon a saucer-size chunk of ceiling suddenly drops, ricochets off the gift pile, and skids onto the floor.

"Okay, Gary, we hear you!" Mole jokes, eyes skyward. But if there's cosmic intervention, Dan credits his mom. The plaster tore a hole in the wrapping of Pastor Dale's present, a life-size, arguably Christian, stuffed lamb. After the startled have a chance to recover and the piece of ceiling is thoroughly examined, Dan's mother-in-law starts in again, now demanding tape.

"Tape?"

"To fix Dale's wrapping! And while you're at it, also a paper plate? For the baby-shower hat we make with the bows. It's tradition." Other than the fact that Louise wears a suit and tie, you'd never guess she was a linguistics professor with a PhD in semantics and seventeen academic publications.

"I'm sorry, I have no clue where to find either of those things," Dan says, anxious for meds and bed.

"Don't you live here?" Louise is surveying the room. Falling ceiling. Cobwebs on the light fixture. Sand collecting between the tiles. On the huge marble sideboard, Dan's offering—the antipasti and the pasta, the two meats, the vegetable side—has been utterly pillaged, smeared, scattered, mashed. Tomato sauce stains the stone, the floor. Strings of cheese connect serving utensils; the carcasses are shaggy with meat. "Why isn't my daughter nesting?" Louise demands. "At this stage, she's supposed to nest, not...roam the beach? Is that what she's doing? Did something happen between you two, Dan? I sensed something—"

Dan keeps on toward the kitchen but he can't outrun the fierce Louise. "Oh, listen to me. Like *I* ever nested! I'm sorry, Dan! It's just...this house. I keep imagining that poor woman having to watch her son get shot. But I can't even really imagine. Can *you*? Imagine?"

Dan can. He does imagine. You could say he obsesses.

Just how bloody? Splattered brains? A bullet to the heart? And where *exactly* in the room did Gary go down? Table? Window? There had to have been rising hostility, panic, misery, a void. And where do those energies go? He thinks of all the little faces crowding the World Trade Center windows.

"Sorry, my head is about to explode," Dan apologizes before retreating upstairs. "It's nothing personal."

∽

Elated by her plunge, Sue insists the guys come to her party. Her husband's the best cook. And if the salt air hasn't already knocked the piano out of tune again, she will play requests. But Chris D. promised to drive his mother to Kings Plaza Mall. And Ox's shift starts at six. So she'll have to owe them.

"Just convince our friend Butter he's FDNY," Chris D. says before literally racing his pal to the car. Blacky keeps his focus on the red boot he dug up. But as the men pass, he begins to nose the treasure home. He wants to show his find to Sage and Ed. Sweet. Some dogs, you wouldn't be surprised if they started talking.

Talking, talking. Sue braces herself for the onslaught. Where's she been? What's the matter? Friends and relatives drove down from Westchester, over from New Haven, across from Amagansett. They paid sitters or put up with kids on the drive. They made rugelach or bought her trees in Israel. Surely they have a right to know. Sue's mother will use her rude absence as an excuse never to come "all the way out" to Rockaway again. Sy will be livid, seeking revenge. And yet, Sue tells Tim, it's facing Rose that freaks her out most. Earlier, when she saw the old lady *standing* on the stoop, it seemed as if a spell held her upright. "That sounds absurd. A driver was helping, but...probably I just feel guilty."

Tim describes how disturbing it was to see Rose simply get up and walk across his living room last night. He imitates her arms and legs, "like a marionette's," but distractedly. Blacky has momentarily abandoned the boot to bark and bark and keep barking.

"Maybe you feel guilty too," Sue offers, too late. Tim's flying. On the lawn, Sy pinwheels his arms.

"Help!'"


It's the cherries, Tim knows without knowing; Sage ate from the sprayed tree. From beach to house, he's wasting precious time establishing there's no cell phone signal to call 911 or Poison Control. *"Help! Help!"* Swallowed up in the wind, Sy's shouts sound like birds. He's standing over the empty pink dress smeared —*not* with blood, thank God, just cherry. Sweat sprouts from Tim's scalp, mingles with sunscreen, blinds him. When he peels open his burning eyes, Sue's at his side, a half-eaten fruit in her open palm.

"Sage!" she's thundering. "Where are you, Sage? Come out here this instant!"

The girl emerges headfirst and naked from the hole Blacky made in the hedge. "I was scared, so I hid. Did you go swimming, Mommy?"

Tim scoops up the kid before Blacky can lick off the chemical. Her tiny mouth is red and ringed with rash. Tim tilts her head back to confirm her breathing's right, spits on his shirt, wipes her lips, all this as he's running for the car, yelling, "ER! ER! We're going!" He is supposed to have retired from this, first-responding. And yet here he is in another Technicolor emergency—Sage's pumpkin curls barbed with twigs, blazing pink limbs scored with white scratches. "Tim!" Sue pants, somehow keeping up. "What about Dr. Mole? Can't we—"

But by then they're shearing off the side mirror as they jam out of his driveway in a crooked screech because Tim is pulling a Fresca from the glove compartment for Sue to give Sage in lieu of water. "Give it to her, hurry now. Hurry up!"

Shouting at Sue helps Tim keep it together, keep it together. He can do that until somewhere on Beach Channel Drive when he hears Sage say, "Do my seat belt!" punctuated by a fountain of vomit. Then Tim loses it. A flood of relief and sorrow so complete he cannot stop his shoulders from heaving. Sue can't possibly know that he's sobbing for another little girl, the one he lost in a riptide sixteen years, eleven months, how many days ago. (Butterfingers.) Or that when he bawls, "It wasn't my fault," he means *that* tragedy. But when she leans in, lightly touching Tim's arm, and assures him, "No. No. It's *not* your fault, *not* your fault at all," he feels, for the first time, absolved.

Calming, Tim tells Sue what she ought to know. Mole isn't really a doctor, just a pharmacist in love with his white coat.

The red boots are gone. June and Kenny emptied the whole closet and all of the drawers pretending to look. They slid under the beds, came out sneezing, their eyelashes coated in dust. Black boots, yes; brown, even silver. But no red boots (at least plural) and, thus, no gun.

Rose has decided that Maureen took it all. "That bitch!" Enraged, thrashing around, she accidentally overturns her pocketbook, spilling its contents all over the bed. Given the chance, Maureen would steal her soul!

"Who's Maureen again?" Kenny whispers under a stream of fresh Italian curses.

Like June has a clue.

The tirade crescendos until Dan, nursing a migraine in the next room, moans for Rose to "have mercy."

The old noises in the wall fill the new quiet. Scratching, rustling. Whatever is in there is getting closer.

"Did you hear that?" Kenny asks, pulling out his BB rifle.

"You found it, hurray!" Rose cheers, confused. She thinks it's her husband's gun and demands to have it back.

But Kenny's weapon remains steadily pointed at the fireplace. The sounds are definitely coming from in there now.

"Who are you?" Kenny whispers, probably to scare June. No need. She's already hiding behind him, wielding Sage's preschool scissors. They both jerk as a cloud of soot shoots out from the fireplace. A bird! It flutters in a panicked path once, twice, around the room, then abruptly lands on Rose's thigh.

June marvels at the tiny starling, eight inches if that, with black iridescent feathers, sturdy pink legs, and a sharp yellow beak.

"Get it offa me!" Rose croaks. "Get it off!" She shakes her leg but the bird, oddly, hangs on.

Kenny lunges toward the bed with the gun still in his hand.

"Don't!" June shouts.

Dan whimpers in the next room.

Thankfully, Kenny's only rushing to open a window. June watches him register that two are woven shut with ivy before he opens the third, overlooking Tim's house. Maybe this was the reason she's been hacking the plant off the glass all week. Maybe an unforeseen entity tricked her into believing she was spying on her hero neighbor when actually she had a bird to free. *Nah. That's stupid.*

The bird's stupid or not interested in the window. Over and over Kenny whooshes the gun through the air to show it the way out but it just sits there, staring at Rose.

"What does it want?" The old woman is practically hyperventilating, clutching and unclutching her checkered dress. "Make it go!"

But it takes Dan pleading, "For God's sake, my head," for the starling to lift into the air and flap out the door. Chasing Kenny chasing the bird, June again admires the wily creature. It knew its way out all along.

◦—

Dan lies diagonally across the bed in his American-flag boxers, needing, praying for, relief. All this yelling isn't helping. Nor is the radio, which Dan doesn't remember having left on. But to turn it off would require moving his head, and that's definitely not happening. So he tries not to let the sound of broadcasted threat levels get to him. Since the code system's inception, the level has been stalled at yellow, the third-most-dangerous tier. To remain that alert for that long, you'd have to be a meerkat or part of the Secret Service. Even Tim, with his two decades of lifesaving training, has opted out of that pressure. And what could Citizen Dan even do? Scan the horizon for warships? Hire bomb-sniffing dogs to guard Glassman Locks & Keys? Pray?

Dan flips the pillow to cover his eyes lest light bullets shoot through the blinds. It's not even sunny out. The cool of the unused side of the pillowcase is better than compassion...though fleeting. If an asteroid can almost obliterate a city without warning, then more space junk (and other plagues) await. Dan can see only two options. Allow anxiety to shred him or cultivate denial.

Denial, then. The new pill, still partially lodged in Dan's throat, is fuchsia and big as a nickel. He wills himself to believe in it as he has believed in all the previous remedies and remedy hawkers, as he believes in Dr. Mole. That is, fully, desperately, and even though Sue just informed him that the guy isn't a doctor after all, just a pharmacist who gets off on pretending. Only then did Sue let on she was calling from the ER to report another narrowly avoided nightmare. Sage ate a poison cherry. "But she's fine now, all is well. You just rest." All this Sue said in the mildest possible murmur so as not to aggravate Dan's head. Because she loves him. There can be no other reason. Above Dan's left eye, the ice pick twists, yet he's determined to again reach for the phone and call the florist.

# Swell

Once Sage is released from the hospital, Sue lets loose on her. "Never, never, never, never do that again!" Sue's wedged sideways in the front seat, the kid across her knees, her feet in the parking-lot gravel. All four car doors are open for air. But no breeze can help the humidity and stench. Like being trapped inside a plastic bag of puke, Tim thinks. He would like to add NO PUKING to the list of rules taped to his dashboard. No puking unless your name is Bridget or Ryan. The idea of Peg's kids being his makes the Glassman family so much less glamorous. Or maybe it's the reality of mopping up the contents of Sage's gut with an insufficient supply of paper towels and bottled water. Despite being thrown in a shower and thoroughly worked up, the girl refuses to admit to eating a single bite of cherry. Only Ed ate it.

"Don't give me that!" Sue yells. "I saw Tim wipe it off your mouth! Tell her, Tim. Tell her you wiped it!"

Like Sue, Tim would like to unload on someone. He'll never get the half-digested fruit, bacon, and milk out of the car carpeting. Like Sage, he's afraid he's in big, big trouble. He's the one who originally suggested spraying the tree. So he figures it's best to remain silent. Sue resumes her harangue—"Never, never"—until poor Sage is way too afraid ever to admit to it.

"Ed ate it, not me," Sage lies, to save herself, "Ed ate the cherry and he died."

Returning home, they find Sy still outside, though slumped in Rose's wheelchair, facing the house. Lingering guests hunker down in the new but already distressed lawn furniture, also turned backward, away from the view. It's the wind. It menaces hairdos and flower heads, ripping at the red flags down on the sand. They've finally been hoisted to warn no one from the frothing current. The only remaining beach patron is Blacky, with the boot now in his jaws. He pulls a bit, rests a bit, pulls. Is he sick? Did he eat something bad again? In the hour or so Tim's been gone, the mutt has hardly moved his treasure, as if the shoe were quadruple its normal weight. Then again, Blacky's an old dog. Tim forgets.

"Bring her here," Sy orders, spotting Sage in Tim's arms. He pats his lap for his granddaughter to come sit. "She's all right, then? She looks pale. Is she pale or just naked? Get the kid some damn clothes! Why all the squirming?"

The old man makes a show of not looking at Sue. Unsure what to do, Tim brings the girl over, reporting to Sy that Sage is fine, great. "Just a little smelly." Tim nods at the others. Evidently, all the out-of-towners have fled. All present are local and are eating cake.

"If we don't eat cake," Mole says, slicing more, "we'll be letting the terrorists win."

But Sage doesn't want cake. She wants Ed. ("Where's Ed? I don't see him!") And Tim doesn't want cake. He wants the girl to go sit on Grandpa. (Each time he tries to lower Sage onto Sy's lap, she resists, scratching, kicking, calling, "Ed!") Sue says she wants cake, but after accepting the plate of devil's food, she just lets the fork hover, not eating any.

"C'mon, Sagey, come sit with me?" Sy keeps on, an edge creeping into his singsong.

Sage whips her curly head back and forth defiantly.

"My own granddaughter will no longer sit on my lap. How about that?"

"She's preoccupied," Tim says, only partly to help the old man save face. Underneath his arm, he can feel Sage's small heart hammering. If Ed isn't here, in his usual spot, then what? Did her lie come true? "Ed ate the cherry," she said, "and he died." Sticks and stones, Tim's ass! Sage has inadvertently killed her own imaginary friend.

He lets her wriggle down his legs, watches as she walks, trancelike, past the cherry tree and out the door onto the beach. Blacky's tail blurs at the sight of her but quickly slows as he comprehends his friend's distress. Tim wonders if the dog can actually notice Ed's absence. Whatever it is, depression or exhaustion, the mutt whines and lies down on top of the boot.

Meanwhile, Sy, in parallel despair, wails, "I lost my own grandkid. After losing my Estelle and Abe, my little brother. Just last year was Abie's stroke. I lost my daughter-in-law—"

"I'm right here," Sue says. "Take it easy." But Sy's pity party has just begun. "*Both* my kitties, I lost last winter. Sophie hit by a car, Strumpet—"

"You still have your hair," Mole, the baldie, cheerleads.

Sage has doubled back onto the lawn. Tim watches Sue's forehead wrinkle as she takes in the girl's sluggish march along the hedge toward the house.

"I lost my job." Sy's chin sinks to his chest. "I lost my business."

Bob chokes on his cake. His wife, Fran, puts aside her knitting to whack his back, loosen his corduroy bow tie. "Our livelihood depends on Glassman Locks & Keys," Fran reminds Sy. "Clarify 'lost my business,' *now.*"

But Sy chants on, from the top. "I lost Estelle, my one love! I lost my little brother, Abie—"

"You have food. You have a beach house," Mole tries.

"Only if Rose declines to buy it back," Sue reveals. She's decided that the old woman *will* have that option. "It's only right."

"I'm losing my house!" Sy howls afresh. Slumped over the burn-hole-pocked arm of the wheelchair, he raises his frightened eyes to Sue. For the first time since the Glassmans moved in, Tim can't wait to get the hell away from them.

"Why?" Sy's demanding Sue tell him. "Why? Why do I lose everything? What's wrong with me?"

"You're a bully," Sue says simply. Flickers of compassion compete with her stern expression. And win. She puts down her plate and bends over to hug him. In turn, Sy lifts the hem of Sue's dress to his face. Wiping a nose full of snot off on it, he tells her to go fuck herself.

Tim rushes over with a napkin. Saint Tim. If Sue tries to thank him again, she might crack. So she jokes, offering a piece of her dress in which he too can blow his half a nose. They slap backs. Then Sue goes off to find Sage. The girl is by the side of the house, naked, in tears, holding, of all things, June's health-class egg. A large crack runs across the shell, right through the pink number 3. But it's intact. Seeing Sue, Sage takes off into the house as if spooked.

Here she goes again. It seems to Sue she's been chasing people all weekend. She follows Sage past the dining-room table (on which sits a piece of ceiling and a stuffed animal, a lamb), down the hall (where the obscure wallpaper forms finally reveal themselves — ah! Cherries!), and up the stairs, where Rose lies on Sage's pirate sheets, her pocketbook gaping, the checkered dress all bunched up on one side.

Sage shrieks, flees.

"The egg," Sue calls after her. "Be careful!" She can hear Dan in the next room, shushing Sage's sobs. But they won't end until Sage confesses. What she told wasn't right. Really, *she* ate the cherry. Not Ed. But she lied that he did, so he died. She didn't know words had that power or she'd have said it right. Really, *she* ate the cherry. Not Ed.

"Shhh, shhh," Dan says. "It's okay... there'll be another."

But Sue knows better. Kicking through a jumble of boxes and shoes to reach Rose in bed, she's sorry but sure. Ed's the last. Dan and, on some level, even Sage must also know this. Nearly five, starting real school in the fall, Sage would have had to off Ed soon enough. Yes, others had preceded him, notably an imaginary older brother, Brother, and Pipi and Lou-Lou, twin polka dots born in Sage's sock drawer. But there would be no more.

"Why the long face, Red?" Rose says, opening her eyes to find Sue sitting on her bed. The comforter is strewn with the contents of the white pocketbook, which Sue begins to re-fill. *Wallet, tissues.* "You wish we went away with the Indians, don'tcha, Red?" *Sewing kit, parking ticket.* "When the Indians came to Rockaway with the feathers and drums?"

"Native Americans?" Sue asks. "Weren't they here first?"

"Not *those* Indians. The ones from Arizona. St. Camillus auditorium, you remember? When they came to entertain?"

"Sorry, but—I'm Sue." *Bifocals, coffee candies...knife?* "Do you need help?" Rose is clutching her stomach and wheezing.

"At the end some of 'em sang Irish songs and a whole gang of us walked them back to O'Reilly's. The young one said he sang for *me*. He thought *I* was Irish."

It's not that hard to picture, the Queens stop on the Tribal Exploitation Tour. Young, fiery-haired Rose dazzled by the "primitive" show. More difficult is the idea of her own mass of bright hair shrunken to a see-through tuft like the one now in front of her.

Sue shifts her weight—the baby's pressing—and a canister rolls out from under the sheet. Rose's breath starts to rattle as it thuds on the floor. Label says GARY PAUL VINCENT—"Oh my God. Rose! Is this—Rose!"

The old lady's mouth is open. Her teeth, as white as bone. But she can't talk back anymore.

Sue will see to Gary, Rose knows. Sue's no dummy. Anyway, it was too hard to explain. Such a bellyache Rose hasn't felt since the old Sunday-dinner days from eating that massive

meal too fast while jumping up to clear and serve — the antipasti *and* the pasta, two meats . . . Except Rose hadn't eaten
anything when the little squeezes started, rising from her
stomach, into her spine, picking up speed to her shoulder,
throat, jaw. At the top of her head, she simply went with
them, through the space made by a thick tendril of ivy forc-
ing open the once-sealed window. Out here, an indifferent
wind whips around her. No sand in it. No sound. Far below,
on the shore, are her grandkids, waving hello. They've come!
Only Rose's arm won't work to wave back. That's how light
it is, too light even to cross herself, so light she has no choice
but to let the white pocketbook go.

# ACKNOWLEDGMENTS

Special thanks to my wise and generous readers: Debra Eisenstadt, Ajay Sahgal, Darcey Steinke, Zeke Farrow, Connie Rosenblum, Beth Greenberg, Kevin Boyle, Michael Redpath; inspiring people: Carmela LaGamba, Jessica Morris, Ed Pilkington, Beth Harpaz, Robert Knightly, Leslie Daley, Kate Fincke, Marian Fontana, all The Eisenstadts; and those who literally made this book happen: Cynthia Cannell, Terry Adams, Lee Boudreaux, Reagan Arthur, Tracy Roe, Michael Noon, and the *indispensable* National Endowment for the Arts.

Most of all, I am grateful to Mike, Jane, Lena, and Coco Drinkard.


Sections of the novel have appeared in other versions in *Queens Noir* (Akashic Books) and *BOMB*.

Some of Rose's recollections were inspired by *The Wave* 100th Anniversary Collector's Edition, in particular

"Memories of Rockaway Long Ago," by Mary Hennessy Trotta.

Sage and June's discussion of God on page 220 was inspired by an anecdote told by Stephanie Wilder-Taylor on the "For Crying Out Loud" podcast.

Related recommended nonfiction reading:
  *A Widow's Walk* by Marian Fontana
  *Braving the Waves* by Kevin Boyle

# ABOUT THE AUTHOR

Jill Eisenstadt is the author of the novels *From Rockaway* and *Kiss Out*. Her writing has appeared in the *New York Times*, *Vogue*, *Elle*, *Boston Review*, *New York* magazine, and *BOMB*, among other places. She lives in Brooklyn.